JUST FOR NOW

VICTORIA R. BENSON

Just for Now

Visit:
BLACKDRESSBOOKS.COM
to preview other books authored by Victoria R. Benson.
Daughters of Boersen Series:
Captured / Claimed / Concealed
Diamond Cliffs
Indie Songs
Perfect Timing
Reversed Roles
Someone Else

ISBN: 978-1-7325443-3-8

Black Dress Books

Dedication:

This book is dedicated to every young woman in the dating world... Don't ever be afraid to choose the one person you know is right for you, or simply be courageous enough to wait, and choose yourself. If you have faith, God will make sure your decisions always work out best for you.

Chapter 1

"Who is that in the middle? I see Brody and of course Kieron, but who is that sleeping between them?" Ethan whispered curiously.

I had my head completely buried under a pillow.

"Oh, that's just Evi," his mother Sonja replied.

"Evi Jordan?" he asked with a shocked and raised voice.

"Shhh! Ethan, they're sleeping. Don't wake them up yet. I'll have to feed them. I'd like to enjoy my quiet house for a little while longer. And, of course it's Evi Jordan. Don't be silly."

Sonja turned to walk back upstairs.

Still whispering, Ethan called to her, "Mom? How long has she been spending the night over here?"

"I guess since November. I'm not exactly sure. She and Kieron are just always here. Well, except when they sleep over at her house or at Kieron's. We moms sort of share the cooking duties. Each of us had one child leave for college, and we magically adopted two in your places."

Ethan's curiosity continued intensifying. "Who all knows about this?"

"I guess everyone apart from you, but now you know too." Sonja laughed at his shock and took a step up.

"Mom, wait. Is she dating one of them?" Ethan asked trying to hide his concern.

"Oh lord no Ethan! We'd never let them stay together if any of them were dating. Besides, you know Evi. If she's not on the mountain or in front of a camera, she's at church. She is the one girl I trust more than any other in the world."

"Wait, mom? Does Jarren know she does this?"

"Ethan, for heaven's sake, ask him yourself!" Sonja, finally done answering questions, turned and went to have her coffee.

Ethan stood in the doorway staring at us for quite a while. He was completely unable to pull himself away from the scene.

The clanging of pots and pans caught my attention first. Then, the smell of coffee and bacon sealed the deal. I was awake! Kieron and Brody were still sleeping on either side of me. I desperately wanted to mess with them, but I knew their paybacks would be far worse than any devious plans I could ever imagine. Therefore, I gently crawled on my elbows to Brody first.

"Brody. Brooooodeeeee..." I extended his name in a singing tone. "Wake upeeeee." I snickered because I thought I was so funny and clever. When he didn't move, I rested my head on his pillow for a moment. I really wanted him awake because I wanted to eat and I wanted my coffee!

Seeing that Brody wasn't budging. I lifted my head and pretended like I was army crawling on my elbows over to Kieron this time.

"Kieron," I whispered quickly. Then, "Kierrrooooon..." in the same singing tone. I dropped my face to his pillow and giggled this time because I couldn't think of anything that I could make rhyme with Kieron.

Still on my stomach, braced up on my elbows, I looked back and forth at the two of them trying to figure out who was going to be easiest to wake up. I kicked my sleeping bag, that I had been dragging with me on the floor, off of my lower body. I sat up and leaned over on all fours. Then, after crawling back to Brody, I turned over, rested my head on the center of his back, and stared at the ceiling.

"That's not how you wake him up Evi," a deep voice calmly mentioned.

"Agh!" I screamed. As my body instinctively jumped up, I dug my elbows hard into Brody's back.

"Ugh!" Brody grouched. "What the hell Evi! Get off of me!"

Ethan covered his mouth laughing and confirmed, "*That's* how you wake him up!"

I rolled over burying my face into Brody's back. I was also laughing so hard I curled my knees to my chest as I pounded my fists into Brody's back with each gasp for air.

"Evi! Stop! What the heck is wrong with you? Are you having a nightmare or something?" Brody was not amused and made no attempt to change his comfortable position.

I hugged him because I know he truly did not care at all about me lying across him. I looked over at Kieron and he was still asleep. Finally, I looked up at Ethan who was sitting on the couch just above our heads. I saw the most beautiful smile and blue eyes I'd had ever seen in my entire life looking down at me.

Feeling humored about the first few minutes of my morning, with my mouth agape, I grinned at him and asked, "When did you get home, and how long have you been sitting there?"

"The answer to both questions is about an hour ago and for an hour." Ethan bulged his eyes at me. Then with a more serious expression he asked, "So how long have you been sleeping with my brother Evi?"

"Don't be gross Ethan, you should be ashamed of yourself for asking me that question." I rolled my eyes, and smirked at him. "I don't sleep *with* your brother. I sleep *beside* your brother!" Then I added defiantly, "And, all the time, for months. The three of us are hardly ever separated. When all of our brothers moved away last August, we just connected, and here we are."

Ethan's glare turned into half smile, half smirk. He didn't feel bad at all for the way he worded his question. He was trying to make a point, although I knew he wanted to assess my reaction. Perhaps he was judging my tone to see if there was any interest in Brody that he could detect.

"Evi, sweetie, come on. Let me fix you some coffee. I know you and I know you are dying to have some right now. Leave these two losers here. Come with me." Ethan offered me his hand and I took it.

With his face buried in his pillow, Brody mumbled, "We're not losers Ethan. We're winners. You're such a bully!" He then pretended to be crying under his blanket as he added, "And, take her. You can have her. She's a bully too."

We all laughed, including Kieron this time.

Leaving the basement, holding onto Ethan's hand, I stepped on Brody's back instead of over him.

"Omph!" Brody's air released. He yelled, "Evi! You *are* a bully! See Ethan, she is a bully!"

"What a perfect way to start my Spring Break," Ethan said, his amusement beaming.

My face was beginning to hurt from laughing and smiling so much this morning. As we walked up the stairs, I didn't immediately notice we were still holding hands. However, once our connection came to my attention, I wondered if he was noticing or not. Then, a slight squeeze and he complimented, "Nice commando crawl Evi. I'm very impressed."

"Commando?" I looked at him with a weird expression because my mind didn't jump to military jargon. I thought of something more inappropriate.

Reading my expression and my thoughts, Ethan yelled out another laugh. "Ha! Oh my gosh Evi! Not commando like you're thinking. Commando, as in a trained soldier."

I was very embarrassed by the fact that I momentarily needed clarification. I covered my face with my free hand and said, "I think I've been hanging out with those two knuckleheads for too long! I'm sorry Ethan."

"Oh no, don't apologize. I am seriously having so much fun today. I don't think I've laughed this much… ever!"

"Well, I'm glad I could be of service."

As we reached the top step and arrived in the kitchen, Ethan raised our hands in victory and said, "Captain Mom, we've made it.

I have rescued this young innocent from her evil captors. She needs sustenance."

We finally released our hands and took a seat at the breakfast bar.

"Oh, you're such a hero Ethan." Sonja sarcastically appeased his need for attention and we all scoffed. She then stepped from the room.

I looked to Ethan and feeling bossy I asked, "Hey, I thought *you* were going to fix my coffee for me?"

"Oh, yes. I did say that didn't I?" Ethan jumped from his barstool to prepare my coffee.

Once it was placed in front of me, I sipped. "Mmm, perfection. You should be a barista, not a soldier," I said sounding impressed with his skills.

Ethan winked at me, and I had to seriously concentrate on not dropping the hot mug in my hands. He wisely informed me, "I don't think so sweetie, I could never handle the pressure of thousands of women needing their coffee first thing in the morning. That takes a special kind of hero."

I simply nodded with my eyebrows raised, then changed the subject. "So why didn't you text me and tell me you were coming home?"

He shrugged his shoulders, "I don't know. I was going to call you later, but now I'm so glad I didn't warn you. Surprising you this way was much more entertaining."

I replied while attempting to flirt, "I'm glad your Spring Break is off to a good start, and I'm glad I get to be a part of it."

I was certain I could see a hint of interest from him, but being so young at the time, I looked away almost immediately. Ethan confidently turned our conversations casual and we continued our thorough enjoyment of the morning.

Not long after Ethan and I got settled in the kitchen, Kieron and Brody joined us. My two dearest friends and I made our plans for the day, which were pretty much always the same. We'd ski. We'd eat. We'd hang out. We'd sleep. Then, we'd repeat.

Chapter 2

A light dusty snow had fallen so Ethan's dad was out front clearing the driveway and sidewalks. The rest of us were all still in the kitchen enjoying our morning.

Ethan was kind enough to give up his seat for Brody. He then moved to my other side and stood next to me. I turned my seat so I was facing Ethan as he rested his elbows on the counter. We continued our chat about things we both had been doing since he left for West Point. Looking back, I'm sure my crush on him was beginning to show even though I was genuinely trying to hide it.

"Good morning babe!" a voice squealed from behind us.

Surprised, we all jerked our attention toward the front door. Hannah had arrived. Ethan jumped back, putting distance between us as his girlfriend ran into his arms. My body froze while my mind strained to endure their kiss.

I gaped and felt like I had just watched a train wreck. I turned my head in horror and locked eyes with Brody. Without a second's hesitation, he grabbed my hand and pulled me fiercely off of my barstool, which banged into the edge of the counter. He and I were the only people in this house who knew how I felt about Ethan, and he was determined to hide my face and my feelings from everyone in the room.

After pulling me off of the seat, Brody pressed my face into his chest and kissed me on top of my head. "Take a deep breath Evi. Be cool," he whispered so protectively.

With Hannah still in his arms, Ethan glanced quickly over at Brody embracing me. "You okay Ev?" he asked, leaning to the side looking around her back. "Brody, be careful," he commanded.

Brody released his hold on my head and intertwined our fingers. Without looking toward Ethan, I simply nodded a 'yes' response to him.

"Come on Evi, let's go back downstairs," Brody instructed. He then said, "Kieron, Evi and I will clean up the basement. I'll run her home to shower and get ready, and we'll meet you back here in a couple of hours."

We both knew Kieron wouldn't suspect anything because those instructions were pretty standard for us. Also, we were all in the process of winding down for the morning.

As Brody pulled me toward the stairwell, I tortured myself by looking over my shoulder at Ethan and Hannah. He was focused on her and didn't even notice I was still in the room. Brody tugged on my hand and when I looked at him, he said, "Don't."

The embarrassment I felt was all consuming. When we got to the basement, I frantically began folding blankets and rolling up our sleeping bags. I carried linens to the closet. I threw socks, shoes, magazines, and anything else that lay haphazardly on the floor, into Brody's room. I fluffed pillows on the couch. I scooted the coffee table back to its position. I placed the remote on the table where it belonged. Then, shaking, I looked for anything else that would keep me busy.

Brody finally stopped me after all this. In such a big brother way he said, "Evi. You have to let it go. There is nothing you can do about him, or *her*."

In frustration I said to him, "This is all your fault Brody. Ethan would have never, ever been someone I would have fallen for if you would have never told me what he said about me. You know I have never gotten over you telling me that last year."

"I'm sorry. I had no idea at the time that he would go running back to Hannah. I thought he liked you. He said he liked you. He said he knew beyond a doubt that he was going to marry *you* someday! How the heck was I supposed to know that he was going to go back to her eight months later?"

Brody stepped back from me and put his hands on his hips. "Evi, I was cheering for you for a long time. I even felt like this morning he still had feelings for you. Why else would he have sat down here staring at us for over an hour? I think he was really uncomfortable with you being here in between me and Kieron. But Evi, he and Hannah are going on over three years together. They don't seem to be having any problems. Maybe you should think about getting over him. There are a lot of guys at school you could go out with."

"Huh!" I interjected. "None of those guys are going to like me hanging out with you and Kieron. None of them are going to like that I'm not the kind of girl who likes to, shall we say, have fun. I don't think I want to date anyone."

I paused, took a deep breath, then added, "I like Ethan, but I really like me too. Oh, and I like you and Kieron. I can shut off my feelings for your brother. I had done that until this morning. I guess I'll do it again now." I was somber but trying to be convincing as well.

"Come on Ev. Let's get some fresh air. We're sixteen. Who cares about dating? Shredding cords is all that really matters. Right?"

My chin raised and I smiled. His warm, loving expression nudged me and I couldn't help but follow Brody to the door where our coats and boots were all piled. We layered up and stepped outside into his snow covered back yard to soak up the view.

My parents are both teachers, so we are just normal by financial standards. The Parker's, however, are pretty well off. Their house is enormous, and their property is professionally landscaped and designed. It's all like a scene from a movie. The back yard is sloped and there are tiers leading down to the edge of a wooded hillside. At the bottom of the hill is a boat dock and a beach that goes partially around a lake. The lake is crystal clear, and it is surrounded by the most beautiful blue, green and sometimes white mountains. I'm named after this lake. My name is Everclear Jordan, but everyone calls me Evi. The scenery here is picture perfect. This place is in our hometown of Ponderosa, Idaho.

"So, are you done staring at your lake? Do you feel better Everclear?" Brody asked sweetly.

"Yes, you can take me home now."

Chapter 3

That crazy morning happened during Spring Break in early March of 2010. I was a junior in high school at the time. By then though, I had already been in love with Ethan Parker for a year and a half. I was honest with Brody, and I did my very best to ignore my feelings for Ethan, but he had been burned into my brain and into my heart when I was just fifteen years old. Perhaps going all the way back to the very beginning will be helpful.

Most of the kids in Ponderosa had grown up together. My brother Jarren and I were late joining their circles, because we didn't move to this little, mountain town until I was fifteen and he was seventeen. I thought it would be tough having to uproot our lives in high school, but my brother Jarren and I stuck together and we handled the changes just fine. Jarren was outgoing, smart, athletic, and handsome. It was no surprise that even though he was a senior, he fit right in and became immediate friends with the popular Ethan Parker before school even started.

As for me, at fifteen, I didn't make much of an effort to get to know many people. At our other school, I had kept to myself because I stayed very busy with sports. I didn't plan on being any different at Ponderosa High. I did try out for the cheerleading squad and made the team. My parents strongly encouraged me to cheer so I would make friends faster. Having been a competitive gymnast most of my life, I didn't mind trying cheerleading for a year. Also, with all of my years of tumbling experience, I had no problem making the Varsity team. I didn't argue with my parents about cheering because I knew it would help me stay in shape and fill my schedule. I didn't suppose I'd have much else to do until ski season started.

Snow skiing is my truest love as far as sports are concerned. Our parents made sure Jarren and I were on the mountain before we could even walk. I've been a nationally ranked snow skier and have done a lot of modeling for big name ski gear companies.

As you can certainly imagine, here in Ponderosa, everyone skis or camps, hikes or bikes or boats. It's very outdoorsy; this is why my parents moved here. After all, remember, they loved it enough to name me after Lake Everclear. Our mom and dad both got teaching jobs in Ponderosa so we could live where we love to play. Basically, even though we didn't move to this town until I was fifteen, I still grew up here.

Although I didn't get much notice when I first came to this town, it didn't take long for the senior girls on the cheer team to pick up on the fact that I was the sister of the fascinating new guy they were always chirping about at practices. Not being the least bit interested in joining those conversations, I'd just sit to the side stretching, rolling my eyes, feeling grossed out, and laughing on the inside. However, once word spread that I was Jarren Jordan's sister, I wasn't as invisible anymore.

In addition to being the sister of the new popular guy who became best friends with the always popular guy, I began to get noticed as a strong competitor in sports. I didn't believe in half efforts in anything, and I didn't believe in being a part of high school drama. The only thing that got as much focus as sports in my life was church. I certainly was not your typical high school girl. For better or worse, like I said, people were taking notice.

However, everything that made me who I was at age fifteen, was about to change. Although my life changing moment may not seem like a very big deal to you, it affected everything about me. This moment made all the difference in which paths I would take and it altered me. I was about to change from an athletic, emotionally secure, independent, tomboy, into a teenage girl!

It was in September of our sophomore year that Brody thought it would be funny to fill me in on the bit of gossip he'd heard. "Hey Evi, someone said something to me about you."

"Oh really Brody, gossip about me? What did they say?" I may have been a sort of wallflower most days but I was certainly not insecure about who I was, so in reality, gossip didn't bother me. I braced myself for my brand new best friend to say something ridiculous.

Brody caught me off guard when he informed me, "My brother said he's going to *marry* you someday, and he said it like he really meant it!"

This was not what I expected to hear, but I thought, *Okay, I'll play along.* "Really Brody, this is your big piece of gossip? Your brother wants to marry me huh? So, who's your brother?" I was thinking he'd say some freshman.

"Ethan, Ethan Parker is my brother."

"Ethan Parker is your brother?" I repeated his full name as if he were a movie star. I was also shocked that I had somehow missed their connection.

"Yeah. I think he likes you. I hear he's told other people too."

I just smiled and tried to be casual, but I was completely embarrassed! Being only fifteen, I didn't have any idea how I was supposed to respond to this kind of information. I was speechless! Therefore, I escaped as quickly as possible while mumbling, "Uh, see you later Brody. I have to go."

I had to process this alone somewhere. For some reason, this wasn't a joke or just gossip to me. It branded my heart as I slowly walked away.

Walking away I thought, *What? Ethan Parker said what? He's going to marry me someday. I didn't even know that Ethan knew I existed. How was I even on his radar?*

Ethan was the superstar, the big wig at school, the guy that always, literally, had a crowd of girls around him after every sporting event. One time I tried to just wave at him after a game, and he couldn't even see around the gaggle of girls surrounding him. It was embarrassing. I couldn't even imagine how on earth he had noticed me.

Brody telling me this flipped a switch in my entire being. I wasn't thinking, *Wow, someone like Ethan noticed me.* No, I was thinking, *Oh my goodness, Ethan could be that one person for me!* In that moment, I fell in love, real love, with Ethan Parker.

After catching my breath and letting Brody's words sink in, I went straight to Jarren. My brother knew I preferred to fly under the radar in social circles. However, reading my facial expression, he sweetly reminded me, "Evi, you do cheer at all of the games and assemblies. You are new here so you stand out like a sore thumb. People always seem to be enamored by your blue eyes and long, blonde hair, so perhaps you are a lot less invisible than you like to think you are."

Shortly after receiving this life-altering piece of gossip, I began to hear other people at school saying the same thing. I was terrified to even look Ethan in the eyes. He was so nice though. I don't think he wanted me to be embarrassed or uncomfortable, so he asked for my phone number and started inviting me to all of his parties. I felt like this was his way of protecting me from the whispers and stares at school.

Soon, he was calling me and texting me almost every day. Talking with him was easy. I hung on every word. I absorbed the sound of his voice. I never wanted our conversations to end. He kept me close, but just as a friend. My entire sophomore year was spent waiting for Ethan Parker to decide he wanted us to be more than friends.

Each weekend, I anticipated an invite on an actual date. However, one was never received. During Christmas Break, I thought he'd ask me out, but no, he did not. Spring Break, nothing. When Prom was only a month away, Ethan was still calling me for casual chats, inviting me to Friday or Saturday night gatherings at his house, and he was still talking to me at school. He was not seeing any one, so I thought he would certainly ask me to be his prom date. Again, I was left disappointed.

I waited and waited, but I never received any word nor action from Ethan Parker that would indicate he was interested in me as anything more than a friend. My young sixteen year old self was hurt, and I wondered if being his friend forever was going to have to be enough for me.

Ultimately, my second year of high school ended with Ethan graduating. I received a sweet hug from him, and within a week he left Idaho for the east coast.

Before he boarded a plane, I received one more phone call from him.

"Evi, it's Ethan."

"I know. I thought you were gone and wouldn't be allowed to talk for eight weeks."

"I'm about to board the plane now."

"Oh. Are you excited?"

"Not anymore."

"I'm sorry, but you'll do great Ethan. You can't help it. You're stronger when others depend on you. I'll miss you, but I'm not worried about you."

"You'll miss me Ev?"

"Of course!" I raised my voice a bit.

"Okay. I have to go now. Thanks for being a great friend this past year."

My heart was crushed. I took a shallow breath so my voice wouldn't crack, and I replied, "Yeah Ethan, no problem. You're a great friend to me too. Be careful and call me when you can."

We both said "Goodbye."

Ethan flew to his new life, a life with a very distinct path that had been clearly mapped out. As for me, I felt lost. I knew I was very much in love with him. The world left me two choices, I could either cry or hope. Therefore, I decided to convince myself that we were going to be truly great together... when he was ready.

Chapter 4

As May 2011 arrived, almost three years had passed since Brody leaked Ethan's future plans to marry me. Two years had passed since he left for West Point. And, one year had passed since that Spring Break encounter when I thought he had returned home to confess his true feelings for me.

Memorial Day weekend arrived and Brody, Kieron and I were still best friends. We were all eighteen and had just graduated from Ponderosa High School. By that time, I had spent three years, which were *all* of my high school years, obsessed with Ethan. Even though Brody had tried many times now to convince me to move on, I just couldn't. I had to, unfortunately, continue learning the hard way that teenage boys are very fickle, and that Ethan Parker wasn't actually as committed to his initial proposal idea as I thought he was.

I awoke the morning of our graduation ready to close one door and open the next. A resolution was made that declared Ethan Parker officially erased from my heart, mind, and future diary entries. I took a deep breath, held it as long as I could, released it, and reset my thoughts... college... that's all I need to think about now... college!

Lying in my bed, hearing nothing, I figured it must be very early. Perhaps my anticipation of the day's events had caused me to stir before even my early bird parents. I reached for my phone to check the time, and the instant I had it in my hand, it buzzed.

"Call me when you wake up Ev. As you should know by now, my parents are hosting the 'End of Year' party this evening!"

I replied, "It's six a.m. Ethan, why are you awake?"

"It's eight a.m. for me, and I've been awake since three!"

"Of course you have!" I began, then trying to stick to my vow I casually added, "Thanks for the invite. I'll see you at graduation, and I'll be over after family stuff this afternoon."

Even though I hated it, I was instantly excited to hear from him. During my sophomore year, Ethan would call me or text me almost every week, but by the time I was a junior and then a senior, I only heard from him every few months when he was home from school.

"Not feeling too chatty this morning huh?" he replied.

"We can chat later. I need—"

Another message came before I sent my response.

"Obviously you haven't had your coffee yet."

I laughed. He was reeling me in. I typed, "For someone I only speak to once every few months when you're home for holidays, you sure seem to think you know me quite well."

I waited.

"I do. I'm in your driveway with a large latte macchiato laced with 4 very poisonous shots of espresso. And for fun, I had them add extra whipped cream that has been specially infused with thousands of calories."

He was in my driveway! I sat up. I gaped at the phone. I could not withhold an ear to ear grin. My room overlooks the backyard, so I ran to Jarren's room to look out his window. I lifted one of the blinds and peeked through the small opening. The most beautiful man in the world was leaning against his car door staring at his phone. A coffee was placed on top of his car. I wondered if I should make him wait for a reply or knock on the window.

I decided. "Look up goober!"

Ethan read, then looked up, but not toward our house. I laughed, again.

"Evi, what are you doing in here?" Jarren's groggy voice asked.

"Nothing. I'm leaving in a sec," I whispered, remaining focused on the outside world.

Ethan turned toward our house and smiled when he saw me. He lifted the coffee and held it up to me while raising his eyebrows in a teasing way. Hook, line and sinker. I took the bait. I smiled back. He had done it; he reeled me in. I had no idea I could fall even harder than I already had.

"Be right down delivery boy. Should I bring a tip?"

Ethan checked his phone; laughing, he put the coffee cup down again to type. He replied, "Nah! This one's on me, and the delivery charge is included in the price."

I ran down the stairs and stopped at the front door. With the line between desperation and excitement so easily blurred, I pulled myself together before exiting. I managed to act like I was being quiet so I didn't wake anyone. Then, I tiptoed quickly to him with a broad, open-mouthed smile on my face.

Ethan's arms went around my shoulders while mine went around his waist. He mumbled next to my ear, "I can't stay Ev, I just wanted to bring your first graduation day gift."

With my chin pressed to his shoulder, I said, "It's perfect. Just what I've always wanted!" I pulled back, took the coffee from him and sipped.

Although my hopes were high, I knew to let him lead. My instincts quickly proved right. Ethan truly did leave right away.

"I'll see you in a little while," he said sliding both of his hands in his pockets and looking at the ground.

"You sure will," I replied.

"Enjoy your poison." He looked at me once again and winked.

I had no idea what was going on in his mind, but in mine, I repeated, *college, college, college.* Then, 1 held the cup up and said, "Thanks for bringing this to me."

"Don't thank me Ev. It was a selfish act." He paused, then said, "We'll talk later."

My brow pinched in curiosity and I simply nodded. Two things were apparent: Ethan obviously had something to say, and he did not want to say it. I didn't see any point in trying to force him into a conversation, though I did wonder why he even bothered to come over if he was just going to leave so quickly. With one arm crossed over my stomach, I took another sip of the coffee and bid him farewell.

Before climbing into his car, he opened his mouth. Nothing came out, except, "Bye."

I watched him drive away. He never looked back to me.

When I went inside, my mom was sitting in our kitchen with her coffee. She asked about the cup in my hand and without adding emotion, I said, "Ethan brought it to me." She shrugged; I shrugged; we carried on with preparing for our day.

Family members were in town for the big event and chaos ensued. Between everyone getting ready in our normal sized home, schedules needing to be kept, and carpool arrangements being made, we all survived the rush out the door. The ceremony was standard, photos taken afterward screamed disorder, and the post graduation lunch was crowded due to minimal options in our small town.

Before we headed to a restaurant for lunch, my mom was sure to get pictures of Brody, Kieron and me being crazy, wild, and squished together. Tongues were hanging out, eyes were crossed, kisses were simulated, I may have been lifted off of the ground in several of them. Mrs. Parker stayed nearby and snapped a few of us as well, but she was careful to also include with one of Brody, Ethan, Jarren, and me.

Ethan and I didn't give each other any special attention, nor was his private coffee run mentioned at any point in time. Based on how we interacted, his visit that morning almost seemed like a dream. A casual hug and congratulations were offered by him, and I politely accepted. His girlfriend Hannah remained mostly attached to him as if she might actually get lost if their connection was broken, so I gave him a lot of space.

College! I thought to myself repetitively.

Post celebrations, my family returned to our house so everyone could collapse. I wanted to be with Brody and Kieron so I changed, dropped onto my bed for about thirty minutes, then headed out.

Driving to Brody's house, my spirit was unsettled, anxious. There was no reason for me to be nervous, but I was. My presence at their home was as normal as in my own, but I had an uneasy feeling that would not cease. Fate had plans for me that evening.

23

I arrived around seven o'clock and was one of the first people there. I parked my car on the street and walked through their gate to the backyard. A few people were already sitting around the fire laughing and talking. But, instead of making an effort to speak to any of them, I merely smiled and waved. As always, I was much more interested in the scenery, so I stood and soaked up the view for a few minutes. Then, I went into the house to search for Brody and Kieron.

Even though countless nights had been spent in that house over the previous three years, I immediately felt like an intruder because no one else was around. I decided I would sit in the kitchen at the breakfast bar and wait for someone else to arrive.

The silence was comforting and I think graduating had me feeling nostalgic, because I began daydreaming about all of the times I had been there. What surprised me most and kept my brain intrigued was that I could only think about the times I had been there and Ethan was home. I remembered our hilarious encounter when I was a junior. I remembered the Christmas and New Year's parties he had always invited me to. I remembered the few weeks he'd spend at home in the summers before having to return to school. I remembered all the times we had sat by the fire in the back yard until dawn talking. Each memory contained an encounter with Ethan, until a sound awakened me from my millionth daydream about that guy.

The clunk sound of a drawer closing came from his room. Although I did feel scared and thought about quietly running the other direction, I got up and moved forward giving myself a pep talk with each step. "You've been friends with him for three years. You've been here too many times to remember. You're eighteen years old. He stopped by your house this morning to see you. You don't need to be afraid to talk to him for a few minutes. You can do this."

I crept down the hallway and saw that his door was slightly opened so I tapped lightly on it. If he didn't hear me, I could walk away and this never happened. However, he opened the door almost instantly.

"Come on in Evi, I'm cleaning up a bit," he said casually looking around his room. "I'm trying to find something to wear tonight. Since I'm always in uniform at school, I leave almost all of my civilian clothes here at home. Now, I've made a mess trying to find a pair of jeans and shirt to wear!" He then looked at me with raised eyebrows, and his facial expression seemed to say, "Aren't you going to say something?"

I was just trying to think of something to say so I didn't look or sound like a complete idiot. Not being very eloquent with words in these types of situations, "Uh, why do you care?" was all I could come up with in that moment.

"What?" he replied, looking at me a bit confused.

"Why do you care? If we are all just going to be sitting in your yard, hanging out, playing games, doing whatever, and you have a girlfriend who you've been dating for years, why do you care exactly which pair of jeans and shirt you wear? You're *Ethan Parker*! You're going to look *perfect* no matter what you go out there wearing." My reply was a bit dramatic with a hint of sarcasm.

The whole time I was thinking, *I am such an idiot. I knew I'd make a complete fool of myself. This is why I should have just walked away.* Emotionally, I'm always stuck somewhere between this is the man I am going to marry someday, and I am so furious I can hardly stand the sight of this jerk who is *still* choosing his ex-girlfriend over me! Their constant relationship cycle is frustrating. They dated. They broke up. They dated.

Thoughts zoomed through my mind faster than I could track. I wondered if he was ever going to want me. He had hurt me and I was certain he didn't even know it. I had been in love with him for three years and had been heart-broken for the past two years because he went back to Hannah right before he left for college. That moment became the very first time I stood alone with him, in his room, and I had nothing to say to him. It was no wonder to me that he had decided Hannah was the better choice!

Thank heavens he broke my panicked thoughts and answered back, "I guess I care because I want to look nice since I only see all these people a couple of times a year. Besides, you're always beautiful, so you must care about how you look."

Did I hear him right? Did he just say I'm always beautiful?

"Well you do make an excellent point Ethan," again my reply contained sarcasm. "But you see, I have to care about how I look. I'm still single and I'm eighteen! No matter how hard I try, sometimes, to look good, as far as any guys around here are concerned, I don't exist!" I rolled my eyes and laughed before I continued saying, "I've still never had more than one date with a guy or even…" I stopped myself suddenly.

"Even what?" he asked.

"Nothing!"

"No, even what? I want to hear the rest."

"Nope. Nothing more to say on that topic," I responded, and my voice cracked because I had completely humiliated myself.

Ethan wasn't dropping it though. He prodded, "I want you to say anything to me. We've known each other a long time. Remember when I was leaving for basic training, and we were on the phone all night before I left?"

Remember? How could I forget! I thought he was calling me because he was ready to have a relationship with me, but the next day, after he had left, I found out he had gone back to Hannah. I had no idea. I was crushed. Right now I'm in disbelief that *he* remembers our conversation.

Ethan continued, "I wasn't afraid to tell you how nervous I was, or tell you I wasn't sure if I'd made the right decision. I spent the entire night on the phone with you knowing that beginning the next day, I wouldn't be in contact with anyone for weeks. You were the only person I felt comfortable enough to tell I was scared and I wasn't sure I'd made the right decision. And now, you can't finish one sentence?"

"That was two years ago Ethan. You don't really stay in touch with me anymore. You and Hannah have made quite a commitment since then. I'm not sure I should even be in here with you. If she saw me here, she'd probably lose her mind!" I was angry and of course very jealous.

"Well, I still see us as friends, so I'd like for you to be able to tell me anything. Finish your sentence. I won't judge. I promise."

How does he always keep such a level head? How could I argue, or stay angry with him? All I could think for a minute was about how I told myself over and over again, I don't care how many girlfriends he has, he's going to marry me... someday! Somehow, I still feel like he is meant for me, so, of course I gave in.

"Okay Ethan," I said smiling this time. "I was going to say, I've never even been kissed by a boy. That is what I was going to say. Happy now? Uh, I'm humiliated." I shyly pulled my hair over my nose and mouth, then buried my face in my hands.

Keeping a distance between us, Ethan sweetly pulled my hands away from my face. He softly tucked my hair back behind my ears and said, "Well, first you don't need to feel humiliated; second, I think that is great; and third... what?"

Looking directly at me he then seemed afraid to ask, but he did, "Not even Brody?"

My chin raised, my eyes widened, I gaped. "No! Not even Brody! Why would Brody kiss me Ethan?" I stammered, "I, I, can't believe you'd ask that!"

"I'm sorry. I had to. I just had to know. Forget it. Back to your statement." He tried erasing the thoughts for us both. "So why haven't you kissed anyone? You've been out with some great guys at school. They all seem to really like you. They move mountains just to ask you out. Doesn't anyone ever just call you to ask you out? They all have to make up big *theatrical* productions to ask you on one date!"

Although the image of Brody and I lingered momentarily, I maintained my sanity and stayed in the conversation. I replied, "Yes, *one* date, *one* time! They ask me out one time. Then, when they realize that I am truly, um..."

"Whaaaat!?" he asked in frustration.

Just for Now

This time, I turned away from him in embarrassment and whispered, "When they realize that I am saving myself for my husband, the guys don't ever want to go out with me again. Now, it's pretty well known at school that I am not a 'fun girl' to date, so no one even asks me out on first dates anymore. Well, except the guys I am friends with of course. I spend almost all of my time with Brody and Kieron. But, so you know, that's because I am one of the only girls around who is a wicked skier!"

"Yes, I'm very aware of you being here all the time. That is the only reason I brought my brother up a few minutes ago. And, I've heard him mention your skills a time or two over the years."

Ethan smirked then continued, "Let's get back to the topic."

I rolled my eyes in dread.

"You're saving yourself for your husband? That could be a long time. You're young. Are you ready for that?"

Without hesitation I said, "Uh yes! I've made it this far. You know my faith comes first. My faith certainly comes before a bunch of random guys who will be gone from my life within the next few months. I've never put much stock in high school relationships. They don't seem to have a point in my opinion unless two people are going to college together or staying here and getting married right after graduation.

"I plan on moving away, like my brother did, like you did. I plan on packing up and going to college in the south. I'm leaving, so why would I get involved in an intimate relationship with someone when I know that it will be temporary and therefore meaningless? I want all of my first moments to be with someone I plan on being with forever. Otherwise, I've wasted myself, my promises and my time."

29

I paused then said, "I want to be with the one person I love, and I want that person to want only me and love only me. I want to be the only one for someone. If that someone isn't willing to pursue me, perhaps they aren't the one for me."

And just like that, I had accidentally let this secret that I had held onto for three years slip out. I desperately hoped he didn't pick up on my reference.

"The one person you love? You said that in present tense. You're in love with someone, right now? Evi, do you already have someone in mind?"

Uh oh, he caught it. My mind panicked. I thought, *Oh my goodness. What do I do? What do I say?*

I responded calmly, "Maybe I do. Maybe, but you also need to pay attention to the second part of that statement. If someone isn't willing to pursue me, they aren't the one for me. I want to be the only one for someone. I don't think I'm being unrealistic or asking too much."

"So *maybe* you have someone in mind?" He responded quietly this time, turning his head slightly to the side as if he may have been trying to figure out who I was thinking about.

"Why do you keep going back to that?" I replied feeling irritated.

"Because it's important to me. I keep you close, so, I can keep you close. I always have Evi."

"That explains the coffee this morning," I said to him with one eyebrow raised.

A very subtle smile appeared, then disappeared from his face.

Ethan moved over to where I was standing until he was right in front of me. This was it. This was the first time I had ever stood, alone, that close to any guy. We had hugged a thousand times, but we had never just stood face to face before that moment. His eyes looked back and forth at mine. The warmth of his gentle breath brushed my lips.

I was terrified that he could see through my gaze that there had never and would never be anyone for me except him. It was so difficult to look at him. My heart was yearning for him with every beat.

He took both of my hands and held them in his. He moved even closer to me. He leaned so close to my face and said, "I've watched you grow up for the past three years. I want you over here every time I'm home. I feel a connection to you, and I always want you near me. I want to know what you're doing. I want to know who you are with. I want to know everything about you all the time. I don't know why, but you are very important to me, and you have been since the very first time I saw you."

I stood completely petrified. I couldn't move. I couldn't think.

He continued, "But, I need you to know, for now, I've been in love with Hannah since I was fifteen. I am not a person who will ever be unfaithful. She's good to me. We've grown up together. If your 'someone' is committed to someone else, I want you move on. You are amazing. You are everything that a guy wants and needs. You are beautiful, too beautiful actually. You're funny, you're kind and caring, you're talented. I could go on and on. But Evi, you need to find someone as wonderful as you who will pursue you like you want. You're right, if a guy isn't willing to pursue you, he isn't worthy of having you."

I was frozen. First of all, I could have sworn Brody had said very similar words to me over the years. And second, I was in complete disbelief that he was crushing me, again. How on earth did I get myself into this? He is reminding me how much he loves someone else! I was so embarrassed and very hurt. All I could think was, *just don't cry, just don't cry.* I'm pretty sure he said something after that, but I didn't hear anything else, because I was busy talking myself out of crying.

Just as I got the clarity to jerk my hands away from his, there was a knock on his door, and we both snapped out of our thoughts.

I gaped, then pleaded, "Please don't tell anyone I'm in here. I would die if anyone knew I was alone with *Ethan Parker* in his room, or alone in any guy's room for that matter."

"Of course not," he whispered before asking, "Evi, are you okay?"

Even though I had broken his grip, he gently rubbed his hand down my arm, then he kissed me on my forehead. He now knew I was in love with him, and he was letting me know that he didn't feel the same way. I looked down. My anger returned, but I didn't respond.

The person knocked again and yelled, "Ethan! Open the door! What you are doing in there?"

"Geez!" I said with a quiet chuckle. "It's Kieron. Open the door."

Ethan opened the door about half way so not to look suspicious but also making sure I couldn't be seen standing behind him against the wall.

"Come downstairs!" Kieron barked.

"I'm on my way. I'm changing my clothes. Give me a minute," Ethan replied.

"Where's Evi?" Kieron asked loudly. "Her car's out front, but I can't find her anywhere."

"I don't know Kieron! Maybe she's down on the beach."

"No Ethan! Evi wouldn't be down there. She hates climbing down through those trees to your beach. She thinks there are snakes in the brush." Kieron looked at Ethan like he was crazy.

"Well, why are you looking for her anyway? What do you want with her? I thought you had a serious girlfriend? And isn't your girlfriend one of Evi's best friends?"

"Geez! What's wrong with you? Why so many questions Ethan? Maddie and I decided to break up a few weeks ago after almost three years together! It's all cool though. There are no hard feelings. I think she's already seeing someone else."

"So again, why are you looking for Evi?" Ethan asked as he looked a bit sideways at me.

I could not believe Ethan was asking Kieron that. I rolled my eyes at him and gave him a glare as if to say, "It's none of your business after what you just said to me."

"Ummm... because she's my best friend and I plan on hanging out with her tonight. Besides, I think I want to see where things could go with her. Maybe it's time for us to be more serious about our relationship. Evi was the first girl I ever asked out on a real date you know?"

"Yeah, I know. Then, you put her in the friend zone, and within a few days you were going out with her best friend."

I could not believe Ethan was sounding so protective of me.

"Dude, stop with the lecture! Have you seen Evi or not?" Kieron asked in a frustrated tone.

"She's around somewhere. Go find her. I'll be out in a minute. Tell everyone, I'll be downstairs soon."

Ethan closed the door and looked at me standing there.

I spoke first. I was mad and upset that he embarrassed me with his speech about how much he *loves* his girlfriend. "We better go. *Hannah* will probably be here any minute. Oh, and for the record Ethan, you're not my brother, my dad or my boyfriend so you really didn't need to be so nosey with Kieron about me!"

Once more, Ethan leaned toward me. Standing a few inches from my face, he looked me directly in the eyes, and softly said, "I couldn't help myself. I really don't know why, but I have to keep you close Evi. I came to your house this morning because I wanted to be the first person to see you."

I cocked my head at him speechless.

He backed away and opened the door just a crack to make sure there was no one around. He smiled and motioned for me leave.

I wondered if he was playing some sort of head games with me.

Still smiling, Ethan positioned himself in the doorway so I would have walk under his arm and very close to him in order to exit. I felt like a switch had been suddenly flipped inside of me. I became someone else, but only for a matter of seconds. As I exited, confidently and boldly, with full intention, I brushed my body against his. Once we were pressed gently to one another, I paused and used a light grip on his waist to lean close to his face. With my mouth slightly open, I exhaled very slowly. Then, pulling back, lowering my eyes to his buckle and biting my bottom lip, I raked my fingertips across his shirt just above his belt.

Before I walked away, looking up one more time, feeling strong, I focused on his eyes. This time I was hoping he could read my mind. I was sad and hurt. I said to him without actually using any words, "I am the one being cheated on here. You are supposed to be with me."

Ethan smiled at my courage. His instincts forced him to slowly attempt a kiss, but he stopped himself.

I made no reaction. I simply turned and left him standing there.

Chapter 5

Walking down the hallway from Ethan's room I had to give myself a pep talk. I needed a distraction. It went something like this: "I cannot believe I have graduated from high school and I'll be moving to South Carolina in two months! I have a whole new life ahead of me. There are so many beginnings in life. High school is over; that part of my life has ended. Going to college, this is my next beginning. I have one summer before saying goodbye for four years to my home. Ethan will be back in New York soon, so life will be more bearable for me while I get ready to leave. Now, in the meantime, I'll find out what Kieron meant by 'see where things could go with her'."

I went to the backyard to see who all had arrived. Several of my friends were there. Brody had appeared from wherever he was when I arrived, and there were people there from at least three different grade levels from our school. Music was playing, games were set up, a fire was blazing, and the sun was setting. I stopped and said hello to some friends, and it wasn't long before I was literally swept off my feet.

Kieron ran up to me, scooped me up in his arms, and spun us around a few times.

"Do you have any plans for the night Evi?" he asked still holding me.

"Um, well, I was planning on being here for a while. Why do you ask?" I said to him laughing as I squirmed out of his arms and onto the ground.

"I plan on considering this our *second* date! Is that okay with you?"

"Are you asking me to be your date for tonight Kieron?"

"Yep."

"Really? Are you sure?" I asked.

"Yes Evi. I'm sure. Let's try it."

"Okay. We can try it. What are we going to do first on this *second date*?" I was trying to flirt, but I was not sure if I was succeeding.

"Well usually on dates, people eat, so we'll get something to eat. Then, we will team up and beat some people at ping-pong and pool, maybe horseshoes too. After all that, we can sit by the fire. And finally, we can conclude our evening with a long walk on the beach. Can you think of a better date? We've got it all right here at the Parkers' house!"

I thought to myself, *Wow, he's right, we can actually have a date right here, tonight.*

"Kieron, it all sounds great! Let's do this."

To be honest, at first, I was nervous about shifting our friendship into a possible dating situation, but I figured we'd probably never make it to a third date. Therefore, I decided to enjoy the evening.

Kieron and I ate, then played games. After a few rounds of pool and horseshoes, we decided to sit by the fire and chat for a while. I was having a really good time with him. He was a perfect distraction from how the evening had begun for me. It seemed like a week had passed since my private talk with Ethan. I knew I would think more about it the next day, and the next, and for probably many more days. I knew I would feel the pain again soon, but in that moment, Kieron was keeping me laughing and busy.

Kieron took my hand and walked me over to a place on the ground near the fire. He of course chose a spot beside Ethan and Hannah. They were settled on a blanket and had their arms around each other. As we sat down next to them, I tried desperately not to make eye contact with Ethan. I was still embarrassed, and I didn't want to give any sign of how I felt about him. I'd gotten very used to just going on with my life as far as Ethan was concerned because I had had to be around him and his girlfriend too many times.

"Hi Evi. Having a good time tonight?" Ethan asked.

I smiled politely and softly answered, "Yes, Kieron is keeping me very busy. He had big plans for us tonight. Thanks for hosting the party again Ethan." My heart was pounding.

Hannah didn't say anything to either of us. She really preferred her own crowd, and since Kieron and I were two years younger than her, we never got much notice. Her complacency never bothered us.

I was more concerned and angry with myself that I could not turn off my feelings for Ethan. I was having a great time with Kieron, but just sitting so close to Ethan had my heart racing. Kieron and Ethan talked as I stared into the fire. I listened to the constant hum of their voices without actually listening to any words. I don't think Kieron sensed how I was feeling. I'm sure he thought I was just getting tired. However, since Ethan was the cause of how I was feeling, I was confident that he was noticing. As he spoke with Kieron, he would glance at me every few seconds and smile like he knew a secret and felt sorry for me.

Kieron was still holding my hand and I hadn't really noticed it. I was comfortable with him. Once it came to my attention that we were still connected, I gave him a gentle nudge and asked, "Isn't there one more thing we have to do on our second date before the night is over?"

"So this is officially a date huh?" Ethan asked.

Kieron replied, "Yep! I decided this would be a great second date to follow up on our awesome first date from three years ago. I swept her off her feet, asked her to be my date for the entire evening, and am now making sure every moment is perfect for her!"

"Oh! Sounds fun! Very theatrical Kieron!" Ethan said.

My thoughts in that moment: "Theatrical, he said "theatrical." Now I *know* he is just trying to remind me of our talk in his room earlier. Why was he trying to embarrass me?"

I changed the subject quickly, "Of course not many people wait three years in between their first and second dates Kieron. You're lucky I agreed to this. How high can you count? Maybe we should go for that walk so you can count your lucky stars! Then, we can talk about whether or not there will be a three-peat in our future."

Thankfully, everyone laughed.

I needed to think about something else, and I needed to keep moving. I stood, offering a clear message that it was time to leave the conversation. Kieron grasped my hand again and as we turned to walk away, Brody ran up to us. A natural reflex within me caused a squeeze to Kieron and a clasp to his wrist with my other hand.

He sweetly smiled, obviously enjoying that he was my only support in the moment.

"Why the heck are you two holding hands?" Brody asked with urgency while looking like he was witnessing a joke.

"We're on a date Brody," Kieron replied confidently.

"A date? Evi? Are you aware that you're on a *date* with Kieron?"

"Yes Brody. I figured maybe it was time for me to get over, um, my fear of dating. Why not start by going on a date with one of my best friends?"

Kieron spoke up again, "Brody, this is important to me."

Brody wasn't mad. He made deep eye contact with me and I knew what he was thinking. He actually didn't want *me* to hurt Kieron. Brody was the only one who knew how I felt about Ethan.

"Fine, but uh, Evi, can I speak with you alone for a minute?"

Without looking at Kieron, I bowed my head like a child being scolded. I peaked behind me and saw that Ethan was fully engaged in the interactions between me and his brother. Returning my eyes to Brody's, he stood expectant. I followed him to the edge of their wooded hillside.

Brody just stared at me at first with his arms crossed in front of him. He didn't say anything. It was very unnerving, but I was not going to speak first. Standing there, eyebrows raised, waiting for him to speak, for the first time I noticed his resemblance to Ethan. I immediately shook that observance from my mind.

"Evi, don't mess with Kieron just because you've been hung up on Ethan for three years." He moved his hands to his hips.

That comment offended me! "I'm not messing with him! Maybe I like him, or maybe I want to see if I will like him long-term. I can't very well date you. I might as well date someone I do sincerely care about, someone I know better than almost anyone else in my life. He and I are curious to see if we could be good for each other Brody."

The part of my statement that Brody heard triggered his only question. "What do you mean you 'can't' date me?"

"I just mean…" I paused because I wasn't entirely sure what I *did* mean by that. "I just mean that you truly are my best friend. You know everything about me, and I could never date you because you will always be a part of Ethan's life. I can't be in a relationship with the closest person to him!" He continued staring at me as I justified our decision. Trying to ease his concerns, I concluded, "Brody, Kieron and I are curious."

In a lowered tone he said, "Don't mess with him Evi."

I was mad. In a silenced yell, I asked, "Who do you think I am? Why would you even say such a thing to me?"

"I didn't mean anything by it Everclear. I think you standing between the three of us for so many years just has me confused. I care about you, and Ethan, and Kieron."

"Brody, you know me. You are the only person on this earth who truly knows me. Kieron and I are just spending time together tonight." I shrugged. I didn't know what else to say.

He and I both knew we weren't going to be able to go sit and work out whatever issue he had in that moment. Therefore, he replied, "Fine! Enjoy your date!" He held his hand out as if escorting me back to the group.

I didn't prod any further. We both walked back toward the fire while Brody stayed about five steps behind me. He then disappeared into a crowd.

I took Kieron's hand without saying anything. Together, we waved at Ethan and Hannah. My heart hurt. It was hard to breathe.

"Everything okay Ev?" Ethan asked.

I looked into Kieron's eyes. He was so happy, so sweet, so fun to be around. His expression told me we could make our own decisions. I got this, I thought. I can move on… again. "Yup. Everything is fine Ethan." We turned together.

After parting the group, Kieron was ready to move us to a more isolated place. He nodded his head toward the lake and we headed that direction.

The walk down to the beach was tricky in the dark. The Parker's never built steps because they like the natural path through the trees. Between the fallen pine needles, decomposing leaves, and the hidden roots, the terrain was a bit challenging. Kieron held onto me and would catch me each time I slipped. I felt like an idiot, but I also didn't want to knock myself out by falling face first into a rock or tree limb.

Kieron chuckled at me and said, "Maybe this would be easier for you Evi if you had your skis."

I loved his distraction. "Oh my gosh, Kieron! You are so right. I'm not meant to walk, I'm meant to ski!"

We laughed as I noticed that being with Kieron was so natural. I kept forcing myself to think about it on purpose. I know he had been dating my friend for the past two and a half years, but it seemed like that had never even happened.

Would any relationship have been this natural, no matter who I was dating? How was it that I had been so in love with Ethan since I was fifteen that I had never let any other guy close to me? I was enjoying my night, my date, with that amazing and fun person.

Once we reached the beach, since Kieron and I both lived for skiing, hiking, biking, camping, and always being outdoors, we both stopped and stood in awe of the shimmering moonlight on the lake. Again, the only word I can use to describe the view is majestic.

The mountains were black with the tops shining white from the remaining snow. The sky was a navy blue with millions of stars glimmering. The moon was bright. The lake water was dancing. The anchored sailboats were swaying, and their ropes and hooks were clanging against the aluminum masts. There were no streetlights down by the lake so the view was pure. Since Kieron stood silently too, I was sure he was as much at peace in this moment as I was.

Within a few minutes, we realized we were still holding hands; we looked at each other and smiled. We didn't need to say anything. The night air was chilled and we were bundled in our jackets and hats, but we both wanted to feel the sand on our bare feet. So, without saying a word, we slipped off our shoes and started walking.

As we walked, our conversation centered on high school, things we had done, and people we had dated over the past few years. I didn't have much to say at first. I wanted him to be able to share his feelings about Maddie. I wanted to know if he was really over her, or if he was still working on facing the break up. Kieron told me they were going to different colleges and wanted different paths in life.

Once I was satisfied that he seemed truly ready to move on, I opened up more about my past three years. In no way was I ever going to reveal to him my true feelings for a particular someone else though. I figured that perhaps my feelings were just a school-girl crush. I had been in love with Ethan for three years, but I was realizing after being a part of just one evening with Kieron, perhaps I'd been wrong, or just immature.

I told Kieron, reluctantly, how I'd only been out with each guy who asked me out, one time. I informed him, "No boy, including *you* has ever asked me out on a second date. Well until tonight! And that took you three years. Maybe some of the other guys are just waiting another three years to ask me out again." We laughed about it.

Then I asked, "Kieron, we live in a small town. You know pretty much every boy at our school. What do people say about me?" I knew this was a dangerous question, and he probably wouldn't answer it, but I couldn't resist.

"I guess everyone, including the girls, know that you spend a *lot* of time at church, and that you don't show much interest in any of the guys at our school. No one says anything bad about you. They just all seem to figure that dating you is pointless. You are either a really 'good girl' or you are hung up on some mystery guy that no one knows about."

That wasn't so bad I thought to myself. They were actually both true, and I sort of giggled inside thinking about it for a minute. Then I responded, "So why did you come looking for me tonight? Do you think like apparently all the others? You know me better than almost anyone on the planet, other than Brody. Weren't you concerned that I might be 'hung up' on some mystery guy?"

"I just wanted to spend an evening with you and I wanted to see where it lead. You're beautiful. You're sweet. You're hilarious. We like to do a lot of the same things. We've been friends for years. You didn't hate me when I dated your best friend for the past few years."

I interrupted, "Not that you know of!!" We laughed more.

Then I asked, "So how do you feel about the 'good girl' part of the opinions Kieron? What if instead of being hung up on someone else, my problem is, I'm the good girl everyone accuses me of being? Do you still want to see where this goes?"

He didn't hesitate. "Absolutely," he said in almost a whisper.

My heart pounded again! "Okay. I guess we can talk specifics on that later. Let's just keep walking," I said softly looking down at the sand.

We walked holding hands and didn't really talk much after that. I let him know when I was starting to get tired and we turned to walk back up the beach. We put our shoes on and climbed back up the hill to the Parkers' yard. There were only a few people still there, and they were all sitting by the fire.

Ethan and Hannah were still sitting in the same spot. Ethan looked startled and puzzled as we walked up the hill from the trees. I think he had forgotten we were there and maybe he was a bit curious about what we were doing. It didn't matter. We waved and said good night as we walked by everyone. I looked at Ethan and smiled. I had had to recover every summer from seeing him with Hannah. Perhaps this summer I'd recover quicker than usual. I was ready for whatever the next two months were going to bring… with Kieron.

Chapter 6

The entire month of June was close to perfect. Kieron and I spent as much time together as we could. We were both working in town because we had to save money for the upcoming school year. Brody had gotten a job with a rafting company. He was driving vans, running rafts, and sometimes on weeklong trips cooking, so we didn't see him very often.

Kieron and I always found time during the weekends to swim, boat, hike, or bike ride. I was glad to only have him with me on weekends. I knew that spending everyday together would have been difficult because we still had done nothing more intimate than sit with our arms around each other or hold hands.

Ethan had gone back to school in mid-June, so I could once again try to forget about him. Kieron made that very easy for me that summer, but I could tell he was noticing how I always kept him at a slight distance.

As Fourth of July approached, Kieron told me he wanted to go camping, just the two of us. Although I was eighteen, I discussed it with my parents, and they assured me that they trusted my decisions and knew I would never do anything that I would regret. They were such hippies. They said they knew how strong my faith was and they knew I'd be safe with Kieron. We were both skilled and knew how to handle ourselves in the outdoors.

I called Kieron and told him I was excited to go camping. The planning began.

Deep down inside, I knew what that time alone with him would mean. It would either leave us still together, or it would be the end of our few short weeks as a couple. I was so nervous. I knew, during that trip, I was going to have to tell Kieron that I had never kissed any guy. I was going to have to tell him that that was the reason I never let things go too far with him. He was either going to want me the way I was, or he was going to end our relationship.

The one thing I was certain of was that I was holding onto my commitment to kiss, and be intimate, with only the man I planned on marrying. I loved Kieron, but I was pretty confident that he was not the man I planned on marrying. We had a lot of fun together. He was crazy, affectionate, exciting, and entertaining. I just didn't believe he was the one for me. Kieron was the perfect guy for the girl who only wanted to chase winter around the globe.

Could that girl be me? I often wondered.

Before packing, we went shopping for everything we'd need for our weekend in the woods. As we strolled down an aisle of the town's outdoor gear store, I asked him, trying to be casual, "Where will we be sleeping?"

"In a tent!" he replied loudly and sarcastically.

"Oh, a tent… one tent?" I asked.

"Yes, one tent." He looked at me like I was crazy.

"Um, okay. One tent." I paused.

He was looking at me with his head cocked and his eyebrows raised, waiting for me to ask another dumb question.

I obliged with, "You *do* plan on us sleeping in *two* sleeping bags though, right?"

He laughed out loud hilariously and said, "YES EVI! We can sleep in *two* sleeping bags. I'm not bringing you on a camping trip to steal your virtue. I just want to go camping and since you *are* my girlfriend, I figured you'd probably be the best person to take with me." He laughed some more.

I started laughing too, then I hooked my hand under his arm, touched my forehead to his shoulder and held onto him.

I'm his girlfriend? His girlfriend? How'd that happen? Pounding heart again all of a sudden. I was holding myself back from throwing my arms around him and never letting him go. I probably should have, but I restrained. I knew why I wasn't letting myself get attached to him. A three year addiction was still clogging part of my brain.

Friday morning arrived and Kieron's truck was loaded. We were off.

The town we live in is pretty far from any cities, so we didn't have to drive too far to get to remote hiking trails and camping areas. The entire drive we listened to his music. Kieron loved alternative rock bands from the nineties. I loved his taste in music. It matched his personality and his look.

Kieron had a very stereotypical look. If we lived in California, people would assume he's a surfer. His tan skin, blue eyes, and shoulder length, blonde, curly hair made him a stand out. He was always shaggy and I loved it. Kieron dressed like a surfer and sometimes talked like a surfer, except he was not a surfer. Those traits in the northwest are clear marks of a kid who has grown up on the slopes.

We were a perfect match in so many ways, but our outer appearances and similar traits connected us. You see, on most days, I was pretty shaggy too. Kieron and I both liked our tie-dyed, baggy shirts, our ripped up, cutoff jeans, our hiking boots, and our grungy bandanas tied around our heads. I loved that I never had to be "girly" around him.

We arrived at the trailhead that lead to several campsites and together we unloaded the car. Both of us grew up hiking and camping around here so we knew the way to some great sites by the river. I was having so much fun as it occurred to me that this was my first camping weekend without my parents, and my first trip as the *adult*, or should I say one of the adults.

After an hour, we found a spot to set up. The sounds were mesmerizing: the birds, the breeze, the chirps, and the flowing river rolling over boulders not far south of our site. I often wondered if I was going to miss that life when I moved away in a few weeks. I tried not to linger on those thoughts for too long.

We set up our tent first and got everything we needed inside neatly. We got our food secured, then we grabbed our fishing rods and walked to the water. The part of the river where we were camping was only waist deep at its deepest point. The current wasn't very strong, so you could wade in without losing your balance. The water was so cold. I've honestly never been a big fan of the cold water, but I tough it out. You don't have much choice around here so you suck it up.

After fishing for a while and not catching anything, we returned to our site to make a fire and cook dinner. There was a large boulder near the fire pit. It was as if it had been placed there by nature as a recliner for us. We laid a blanket on the ground and together draped it up over the boulder. Kieron sat down first and without even thinking about it, I sat between his legs and leaned back on his chest. His arms slid around me and they felt so good, so relaxed, so safe. We sat together staring at the fire and listening to the sounds around us.

After a while, he asked "Are you happy about moving to South Carolina soon? Aren't you going to miss all of this?"

I couldn't even imagine moving away in that moment. How could I think about that? I was loving that minute of my life. I loved being right there.

I could not believe tears formed in my eyes. I tried to hide it from Kieron but when I blinked, they ran down my cheeks and dropped onto his arm.

To this point, I hadn't let myself spend any time thinking about what I was going to be leaving behind in Idaho. I hadn't thought about my parents, my brother, my friends, or my surroundings; and I hadn't thought about leaving Kieron. I hadn't thought about how that part of my life was about to be over forever. Until then, when I thought about going to school, I thought about what I was going to, not what I was leaving behind.

He softly said, "Why are you crying?" He shifted and pulled me around so I was facing him. "Why are you crying?" he asked again. I was crying a bit harder. "Tell me," he insisted, but I couldn't speak.

Kieron kissed me on the cheek and I pressed my face against his lips. Then, I turned back around and settled back into his arms. After a few minutes, while looking into the fire again, I was able to speak. I told him all of the things I had been thinking. I said, "Kieron, I don't think about leaving. I don't think about who and what I'm leaving behind. I only think about what I'm going to and what is ahead of me."

He let me relax for a little while before he asked me his next burning question.

"What's going to happen with us?"

I felt his grip tighten. I wasn't crying anymore. Before I answered though, I rolled to my side and buried my face in his chest so his shirt could absorb the tears that remained from his first question. With my face still pressing into his chest, I responded, "What do you see happening Kieron? Do you think we can stay together with three thousand miles between us?"

He was quiet.

I looked him right in the eyes. I turned my body more so I could straddle his lap, and he sat up closer to me. I had never been in that position with anyone! I wasn't even thinking. I grabbed his hands and held them against my chest. I was trying to form coherent words.

I said to him, "This feeling right here is the reason I have never dated anyone before you. I knew this moment would come. People think I'm a prude, or a snob, or too good for anyone. People who don't know me very well think I'm crazy and unrealistic because I don't even kiss guys I go out with. To me, a kiss will form a bond between me and someone that will hurt when it's broken. This is why I am the way I am. I have always been terrified that I would fall in love with someone who wasn't going to be with me forever. And now I have. I love every minute with you. I love playing with you. I love talking with you, sitting with you, and just having your arms around me. But reality is catching up with us fast. This will end soon. We can stay together as long as you want, but you have to make that decision knowing that I'm not changing, I'm not going to be *making out* with you, and I will be leaving in four weeks. I'll see you during holidays, Thanksgiving and Christmas, if you want, but this is all I have to offer."

My tears were gone. I was feeling strong, but very curious. I was still looking right into his eyes trying to figure out what he was going to say to me. I rested my forehead on his chest again. He pulled my face up gently by my chin. This time he was looking at me. He pulled the bandana off my head and fluffed my hair. His hands were placed on either side of my head. I could feel his breath on my face. He pulled me close and kissed me so softly on each cheek.

"Let's enjoy the next four weeks, then decide in November if we want to see each other over break. After that, let's decide in December if we want to see each other over Christmas break. Let's just be here now and forget about tomorrow or the next day. Let's put this fire out and go snuggle down in our TWO sleeping bags and play some cards." He wrapped his arms around me and hugged me so tightly I was sure he could feel my heart pounding. I could feel myself wanting this relationship.

I thanked God for him, and I thanked God that Kieron could make me laugh even in that scary moment. That was the first time I had to face a boyfriend with my beliefs. Kieron handled it, no, Kieron handled *me* perfectly.

Later as we were falling asleep, Kieron put his hand on my back just below my neck and he rubbed me very slowly. I looked at him and scooted as close to him as I could. I closed my eyes. I knew he was telling me he liked me just the way I was.

I thought, *he sure is going to make someone very happy someday.*

Chapter 7

The summer flew by too quickly. August and my time to leave snuck up on both of us. Kieron and I said our goodbyes a week before I left so when I went to the airport, I could look forward to my next adventure. He and I decided that trying to continue dating didn't make any sense. We were both sad, but agreed that we'd stay in touch and see how we felt at Thanksgiving Break. We both knew we'd just be friends by then, but neither of us needed to say that out loud.

I was leaving for school a few weeks before classes started. My family and I were going to make a vacation of the trip, then my parents would be returning home once I was moved into my dorm.

The night before I left, my phone rang around seven o'clock. It was Ethan. My hand started shaking. I was shocked. I took a deep breath and answered it casually.

"Hi Ethan, what's up?"

"You leave tomorrow?"

"Yes, tomorrow afternoon. How'd you know?"

"Kieron was over the other day and told me."

"You're in town? When did you come to town? Why didn't you call? You always call me when you come home."

Strangely, I felt like Ethan was mine and I was stunned he hadn't called me.

"I got home a few days ago, and I am calling now."

"Yeah, but you usually call me when you get home or when you are on your way home so I can see you," I said.

"Tonight is the first time I've been alone since I got to town. I wanted to wait to call you when I had time to spend with just you."

Instantly, I got so excited I was having a hard time breathing again. I was processing our conversation and what he just said to me. I calmed myself down. We're friends. We've been friends for several years. He's made that clear. I need to not read too much into what he says to me. I'll only set myself up to be hurt.

"So tonight is the first time you're alone. Well, I wish I had known you were home sooner, but I'm glad you called. When do you go back to New York? If you've been home for a few days, you must be leaving again soon."

"I leave the day after tomorrow, on Sunday. I've got to get back for training and then prep for classes to start."

"You don't spend much time here anymore do you? I guess this is your life for at least another six years though. Did you just call to say goodbye Ethan?" I was chattering nervously.

"No, I called to see if you wanted meet for coffee or something." His voice was smooth and relaxed.

"Sure, I'd love to." I was trying desperately to be cool.

We decided to meet at the locals' favorite coffee and ice cream shop in town. It was located near the marina on the waterfront. Neither of us had any reservations about meeting there. Our families are friends, and he and my brother have been best friends since we moved to Ponderosa, so no one would think anything was strange about him and me being together.

Ethan arrived first because he lives very close to town. Since his house is on the lake, he just has to follow the road that encircles it and he is in town. My family lives in a small cabin off the main highway up in the mountains. It took me a bit longer to get there.

I street parked a block away so I could walk and hopefully calm myself before arriving. When I rounded the corner, I saw Ethan standing outside waiting for me. We smiled, waved, and walked toward one another. The standard hug was exchanged and he placed his hand on my lower back to escort me into the cafe.

After surprising Ethan by ordering a water and a cup of ice cream, we chose a table on the lakeside of the shop so we could enjoy the evening breeze blowing off the water.

Our conversation was as if we were two high school friends catching up on each other's lives, which we were I guess. We chatted about his schedule each day at school. Then we talked about what my life might be like when I start school. I told him the things I was afraid of or worried about. We talked about roommates. We talked about where we saw ourselves in ten years. Two hours passed by quickly. Sitting and talking with him seemed like a normal part of my life.

The shop had closed and the only light that illuminated our surroundings was the glow from the docks of the marina.

"Let's go," he said.

I assumed the evening was over and although a bit disappointed, I was happy to have had time with him alone. The last time we were alone together, he was declaring his love for Hannah. However, this conversation was much more like the one we had the night before he left to go to the military academy two years prior. I liked that feeling much more, of course.

"Okay. It was great seeing you Ethan. Thanks for spending time with me without a crowd gathered around. It's so nice to just be able to relax and hear about your life. Now I don't have to wonder so much about what a normal day looks like for you. I can imagine the real thing. Maybe sometime you can come visit me in Charleston and see what it's like there. You'd love it. You know I'm going there because I grew up vacationing there with my family. I can show you around. Okay, I'll stop nervous talking now."

"Are you sure?" he said sarcastically with a breathy chuckle.

"Yes, I'm sure. Have a good trip back to school."

"Evi, when I said 'Let's go' I didn't mean the evening was over. I'm just tired of sitting here. Let's go to my house and hang out there a little bit longer."

"Oh! Sounds great," I replied feeling surprised. Then I added, "I'd love to. I'll meet you at your house."

"Where'd you park. I'll drive you to your car," he offered.

I thought to excuse him from such chivalry, but I didn't bother. I simply pointed and mentioned the street where I had left my car. Again, Ethan placed his hand on my back to point me in the direction of his car. I tried not to read too much into his touch as I proceeded.

Not much was said during the forty-five seconds we shared in route up the small hill to my parking spot. I got out, told him I'd see him in a few minutes, and I got in my car.

As I drove to his house, I couldn't help but wonder why he had all this time alone to be with me. Where was Hannah? Where were his parents and Brody? Then, reason took control. I said out loud, "We are just friends, don't think too much right now."

When we got to Ethan's house, I watched him jump out of his car and run inside. When I saw how fast he was moving, I slowed my pace. I assumed we were going to be sitting by the fire in the back. Sure enough, Ethan came back out the front door with a blanket.

Walking to me, he said, "Come on Evi."

He took me by the hand and pulled. We walked through his gate to the backyard. What shocked me was that he didn't stop us at the fire pit, instead, he led me to the edge of the yard to the trees. I wasn't thrilled to have to traverse that steep hillside, but I didn't complain. It was a perfect night to sit by the water. Ethan and I slipped our way down the hill to the beach.

"Are your parents ever going to build steps!? I am seriously going to fall down this mountainside one day!"

"My parents like the natural look."

"Doesn't your mom worry about coming down here?"

"She uses the neighbor's steps when she comes down to the dock or the beach," he replied casually smiling.

"Ah! Now that makes a lot more sense. Smart woman! I wish you would have told *me* about the neighbor's steps."

"Nah, it's way more fun watching you fall on your butt every few seconds. You do know you are the *only* person who can't seem to navigate this path without falling right?"

"Well first, there is no path! And second, thank you for that information. I was certainly not aware of that, but also not surprised. Please do realize I am wearing flip flops though, not hiking boots."

Ethan had pretty much just carried me in one hand and the blanket in the other all the way down their little mountainside. He never missed a step. Ethan is very strong. Being a cadet in the army hasn't changed him. The military is really taking all of his best traits and building them up. He's six feet tall and very muscular. He has dark brown hair and gray-blue eyes. Ethan is calm and thoughtful. He doesn't seem to have any unreasonable reflexes. Everything he does is with thought and intention. He's so level headed.

I guess I'm pretty calm too. I can hit an explosive point, but it takes a lot to get me there. I'm all reaction when I'm really angry, sort of like a firecracker. We have our similarities and our differences.

We stepped out of the trees onto the white sand. Without hesitation or thought, I kicked my flip flops off flinging them as far as I could down the beach. He laughed and rolled his eyes at me.

"I'll find 'em later," I said to Ethan laughing. "I just love being barefoot in the sand!"

I ran in little circles scrubbing my feet deep into the cool sand. While twisting and grinding my heels in too, I said, "This is by far the best way to exfoliate for your feet Ethan! It feels so good. You should try it."

He responded while laughing, "Uh, I like my feet just the way they are thanks. No exfoliation needed at this time."

I laughed at him and stopped digging with my heels.

"The air feels amazing tonight," I said as I raised my hands out by my sides, closed my eyes and turned my face towards the water to feel the fresh air brushing my skin. "Aaaaaahhh…"

I snapped my eyes open, lowered my hands and looked at Ethan. "Don't you feel like you're in Heaven?" I asked him. "Lake Everclear, like Heaven on Earth!" I said.

Ethan smiled and shook his head. He was silent. He bent down and took his shoes off too. He was so calm. How does he stay so calm? He was still smiling at me, probably thinking, "She's such a child!" I didn't really care what he was thinking. I was just happy to be there and to be there with him.

There were two lounge chairs on the beach. "Do you want to walk or sit?" he asked pointing to the chairs.

I replied, "I just want to sit, but not in the chairs. You brought a blanket. Let's lay it out on the sand and sit on the ground."

It was around 9:30 now and the sun had gone behind the mountains. The sky was grayish. The color right before darkness takes over. I didn't have anything that I wanted to say to him. In the back of my mind I was very curious about why he was here with me and why he wasn't with Hannah if he was going to be leaving again on Sunday. To remain calm, I let our brothers' words ring through my ears, *"Evi, he's only nice to you because he's your friend."* Okay, got it Jarren, got it Brody.

Ethan and I sat down on the blanket with only a few inches separating us. I had my legs crossed in front of me and was leaning back on my hands, letting the wind blow my hair off of my neck. He had his knees up with his hands grasped around them. I could feel him looking over at me every few seconds.

Finally, without looking at him, I spoke first, "I'm okay just sitting here for a while not talking if that's okay with you."

"Sure," he replied.

I turned over onto my hands and knees and starting smoothing the sand out under the blanket. I was making a very slight ditch. He was watching me. Then, using the blanket, I started making a small pile of sand underneath that I would use for a pillow.

"What are you doing!?" he asked me in a tone that was to let me know I was crazy.

"I'm getting comfortable. I decided I don't want to sit. My back will hurt. I want a comfy bed if we're going to be here a while."

"Evi, I've lived in this house my whole life and no one has ever done this down here on the beach."

"Well, you have not had very smart people over then have you?" I said. He laughed out loud. "So are you going to try it?" I asked him.

"No, not this time. I can get comfortable anywhere after how I've been living for the past two years."

"Suit yourself."

I lay back into my little ditch. I pulled my hair up off of my back and neck draping it above me. Almost as soon as I placed my head on my little sand pillow. Ethan was lying beside me. We both relaxed peacefully and stared at the sky.

"Don't let me fall asleep Ethan. I have a big day tomorrow."

"I won't."

After a few quiet minutes, he turned onto his side facing me and propped his head in his right hand. He placed his left hand on the blanket by his stomach. I knew he must have something that he was dying to say so I turned my head to look over at him. Quietly, I then rolled onto my side so I could face him.

He didn't speak though. He just continued looking at me. I was looking at his hand as it rested on the blanket. That was easier than trying to look him in the eyes.

My nerves were beginning to activate. Up to that moment, Ethan and I were just two friends talking, walking, goofing around, having ice cream, whatever, but he changed. He looked serious.

I watched him stretch out his right arm and lay his head on his upper arm. Then, he put his hand in my hair. With his left hand, he reached across my waist and scooted closer to me. He was lying right next to me. His entire body from his head to his feet was right next to me. His face was inches from mine. I could smell him, feel his exhales, feel his muscles, everything.

I was sure he could hear, or feel, how hard it was for me to breathe. Unbelievable, I wasn't scared at all of having him this close to me. I was so happy my heart was racing. I trusted him completely. He knew me. He knew how I felt. He wouldn't hurt me.

Ethan rested his left hand on my abdomen, and I placed my hand over his to let him know I was fine. Neither of us spoke. He was pulling my heart back into him. He knew I was in love with him. I wasn't afraid to smile at him. He returned the warmth.

We remained in that position for a while. Eventually, we closed our eyes. I think we both were afraid the moment would end if we moved. Although, we both knew it would have to end very soon.

I don't know what he was thinking about, but after the initial elation of having him next to me subsided, my mind wandered back to Hannah. I wondered if they had broken up and that was his way of telling me? Or were they still together and that was why he was not moving any closer to me? I had to know. Regardless of interrupting that perfect moment and causing its end, I had to ask.

Gently, I wrapped my fingers around his and held them. Then, I slid his hand up closer to my neck. It felt like I was grasping a security blanket. I pressed it hard to the bones in my chest. It was giving me strength to ask, "Ethan, why are you here with me?"

It took him, what seemed like several minutes to respond. He finally whispered, "Because I want to be here. This is what I want. This is where I want to be, next to you." Then after a pause he said again to me, "I keep you close, so I can keep you close."

I wasn't satisfied with that answer, so I reworded the question this time. "Okay, I'm still not really sure what that means Ethan." I asked, "Why are you here with me and not here with Hannah?"

Halfway through asking the question, my voice cracked. I couldn't believe it. *Oh my god, he's still with her!* was all I could think. He couldn't lie to me, and I knew he wouldn't lie to me. He had truly done nothing wrong to that point. He had not actually cheated on his girlfriend. But, he had managed to tear my heart out again. I waited for his answer.

"This is what I want Evi. I just don't know how to have this."

I squeezed his hand to my chest once more. I could hardly speak because the lump in my throat was paralyzing my voice. I turned my head away from him. I was embarrassed. Then, I released his hand and pushed it away from me. I was furious! I sat up, put my forehead on my knees and took a deep breath. I put my hands over my face. Then quickly, I turned to him.

"I told you I have to be the only one Ethan! I don't think that is asking too much of anyone. You know how I feel about you and you bring me here to tease me. How can you of all people be so heartless?" Taking another deep breath I continued, "I trust you. I trust you! Please stop letting me down! Stop stringing me along! Stop playing games! Please!"

I didn't get up and storm off. I just sat there beside him with my head down. There was nothing he could say in response. Absolutely nothing. He reached for me. He put his hands on my shoulders. I looked over at him. I could see that he was truly sad that he had hurt me more deeply than ever this time. Then, I turned toward him and let him take my hands hoping maybe it would somehow make us both feel better. I wanted to let him know that I love him, therefore I will always forgive him, but I was still furious.

Ethan looked at our hands. He sat silently. I waited for him to speak next. Then, he said again, "I don't know how to have this... with you."

I didn't feel sorry for him. I was mad. I said to him, "It is very strange to me Ethan that you don't have a problem wanting me, calling me for the past three years, bringing me here, hurting me, but you can't seem to be open with your girlfriend about anything. How is that possible? I can't even and don't even want to imagine what you two must have in common. Why are you two still together?"

I didn't want an answer. I just wanted to be heard.

Instead of leaving him there, I raised up on my knees and hobbled myself between his legs so I was facing him. I pulled his hands to my stomach and thought about what I was going to do next.

I released his hands and placed mine on his shoulders. Then slowly, I leaned and I kissed him very carefully on each cheek. He lightly placed his hands on my waist. I pressed my face against his and tried to breathe slowly so he wouldn't think I was weak. I felt his fingers press into my lower back and a gentle pull. In a deep soothing voice, he said, "Closer, please Evi."

With our faces still pressed together and our lips almost touching, I processed his words. I closed my eyes and exhaled. I was going to be the strong one here.

"Hey Ethan, hey Hannah!" Brody's voice yelled from just down the beach.

I dropped from my knees to sitting on my hip between Ethan's legs. I pressed my face into his chest. I heard Brody's footsteps getting closer to us very quickly.

"Please make him leave Ethan. Please," I whispered, begging, completely petrified.

"Oh! Evi! I'm so sorry." Brody was breathless and clearly upset by what he'd just said and probably what he was seeing.

I couldn't look at him. I was facing the other direction down the beach. I squeezed Ethan's shirt, and he wrapped his arms around me with such a gentle strength. I knew he wanted to erase my humiliation. He's had to protect me before from people's whispers, and he had been keeping my secret safe too.

"Brody, can you just leave us please?" Ethan calmly asked.

"Evi, are you okay?" Brody called out to me.

I certainly did not want to upset Brody, so I barely whispered again, "Please Ethan. Please make him go."

"She's fine Brody. We just need a few more minutes." Ethan was reassuring and protective.

Brody said nothing else and politely obliged. I knew he was worried but I also had a feeling he didn't really want to face me yet either.

I had been so strong until that moment. I looked up into Ethan's eyes and I burst into tears. I wrenched his shirt in my hands as I cried so hard. He held me tightly with his lips pressed to the top of my head. I wondered if Brody had gotten far enough away or if he could hear my uncontrollable sobbing.

Ethan reached his hands under my knees and pulled both of my legs over his left thigh. "It's okay babe. It's okay. I promise Evi. It's okay."

"It's not okay Ethan. I've done everything wrong by just coming here with you. You… have… a girlfriend! I love *you* and you have a girlfriend." Three years of tears were falling.

His grip tightened. "I know you do sweetie. It's going to be okay."

I figured I'd get all of my tears out while I was there with him. I certainly didn't want to go home and cry. I wiped my face over and over again on his shirt. It had gotten dark by this time so I can only imagine what kind of mess I had made.

Finally settling down, I twisted my torso a little. I leaned to the side so he could cradle me in his arms. My head was resting on his chest. It took one breath for me to realize that in my squirming, my dress had slid all the way up my thighs, and I was essentially sitting on Ethan's lap in just my underwear. To make matters worse… for me… he had his hand placed gingerly over my hip bone on my skin. I felt his fingers soothing, learning.

I took a snapshot of the moment in my mind, then I pushed myself out of his arms and off of his chest. I moved so I was sitting between his legs, all the way down on the blanket with my feet now out to my side. I looked up at him and wanted him so badly. I was brave enough to touch his stomach. I said to him, "This hurt Ethan. Don't do this to me again. You will always know where to find me. You will always have my number, my address, and anything else you could possibly need to find me in this world. I want you to myself Ethan. When you are ready, you can come for me, but please do *not* do this to me again. I will not *let* you do this to me again. Do you understand?"

He nodded and asked, "Will you wait for me Evi?"

Looking in his eyes I replied, "I don't know Ethan. Will you come for me?"

He gave me no response so I knew it was time to end the evening.

"Ethan, one more thing before I go, I hope I don't have to ask you this next question, but tonight, will you talk to Brody and make sure this is our little secret?"

"Of course Evi and you're right, you did not have to ask me that question."

"Thank you."

I stood up, wiped my face one more time, turned, looked down the beach, put my hands on my hips, and said, "Now, do you want to sit there, or do you want to help me find my shoes? I am leaving you now! And I am leaving here tomorrow! I need to go home. And, since you do not have steps, I need my flimsy little shoes to climb up that dangerous mountainside."

We both smiled and laughed a little. Ethan got up and we found my shoes.

"Now sit back down soldier," I said in a commanding voice. "I'm leaving and I don't need an escort. I'll see you when I see you, and I thank you for an enchanting, an *enlightening* and then, an awkward evening."

I walked to the edge of the trees and started climbing up the hill. I stopped for a second and turned back to Ethan. I called, "Ethan?"

"Yes Evi."

"I have one more question for you before I go."

"Yes Evi."

"Are there any snakes in these woods?"

He burst out laughing and said, "No Evi! You've lived in this area your whole life and you don't know it's too cold for snakes here? There are no snakes. You're perfectly safe."

It was dark. I stumbled clumsily up through the trees, tripping on rocks, sliding on pine needles. I knew he was listening and certainly laughing.

I yelled back again, "You're sure, right?"

"Yes Evi, I'm sure. There are no snakes." For fun he added, "It's the bats you need to worry about."

I screamed, "No! You're lying!"

"Be careful Evi, they love to get tangled in long blonde hair. Yours will be an easy target. There's a lot of it."

I screamed and began trying to run up the hill.

"You're a jerk Ethan!" I yelled back down to the beach as I reached his yard. And more laughter rang out from below. *Ugh! Why do I love him so much?* I thought laughing too, and I went to my car.

I left this time in my life behind me.

I guess that was the best way for me to leave home for college. I knew that Ethan did, on some level, truly love me. I knew that I did not have a "crush" on Ethan. I was in love with him. And, when I left his house, I wasn't feeling hurt. I couldn't wait to get up the next morning and start my new life.

Chapter 8

I don't think I need to go into many details about my move to Charleston. We had a great family vacation. My brother flew from Charleston back to his school in Washington the day I moved into my dorm, and my parents returned to Idaho the next day.

Jarren was starting his third year of college. I had spent a lot of time with him at his school, so I knew what to expect of the so called college life. The moving into my dorm room, meeting my roommate, buying books, finding my classes, figuring out my favorite places to eat, and so on, that was all routine for me. Jarren and I were very close, and I had walked through the process with him for two years. I loved hanging out in his dorm with him and his friends when I was in high school. I was excited to start my own adventure.

Blessed is how I truly felt about my roommate. Not only did she and I adore each other and get along really well, but we became fast friends with all of the girls on our hall. We compared class schedules and started figuring out who was going to eat with whom throughout the week. We figured out which of us had classes nearest to the other and where the best place to eat was located. There was a group of eight of us who got along perfectly, and we all became our own little family very quickly.

My roommate's name was Piper. She was from Florida. Her dad had grown up a surfer, so he named her for the word "pipeline." Her dad was blonde and blue eyed and her mom was South American. She had the most beautiful skin tone and she also had hair to her waist, except hers was very dark brown and very straight and smooth.

I told her my name was Everclear but people call me Evi. I also told her that I was named after the lake in my hometown. I loved her name, and she loved mine. We got a kick out the fact that both of our dads had named us after water! We also thought it was strange that we went to college there for the same reason. Her family, like mine, had vacationed in Charleston since she was a child, so choosing to go to school here was easy for her.

Classes started and the fall semester moved along. For fun, we would all either go downtown or we often went to the Citadel football games. Sometimes we were lucky and my friend Byron would be working the door at a bar called The Venue. He would let us in so we could dance. We gave him our word that we would not drink. I, of course, didn't drink anyway. I just wanted to dance.

The Venue was in the historic shopping district by the market. It was a fairly large place by Charleston's standards. You could dance inside or outside. It was our favorite place to go on the weekends.

As I mentioned before, the fall moved along smoothly. There were no monumental moments worth mentioning. There were no guys to date and no calls or texts from Ethan or even Kieron. Brody and I stayed in touch for the first few weeks, but once we both were in our school routines, we stayed preoccupied with our own social lives.

I often thought about every moment I had ever had with Ethan, especially our last night together, but instead of dwelling on my memories every day, I was only thinking about him a few times a week. Why should he call? After all, I was the one who told him to leave me alone until he decided I was the only one. I figured he had not made that decision yet.

I was also proud of myself for never having told Piper about Ethan. She knew Brody was my best friend and she knew about Kieron, but I was too embarrassed to try to explain Ethan. Piper had seen pictures of Kieron and I, and she had seen dance pictures of me with other guys, but no pictures exist of Ethan and me. Along with not sharing the story of Ethan, I also never bothered to explain to her that I had still never kissed anyone. I just let her assume that my relationship with Kieron was "normal" by today's standards.

Thanksgiving Break arrived and I flew home for the entire week. As soon as I got back to Idaho, Kieron was at my house. I walked in the front door and he screamed, "Let's get packing Everclear! Grab your gear. Mountain's open. We'll be on it for the next five days baby!"

My parents, brother and I all laughed and said, "We like the way you think!"

The snow had arrived and the slopes were open. Home. I was home!

Kieron and I were so happy just being buddies again. Brody was glad too. He didn't have to feel like a third wheel that week when just the three of us were hanging out on the mountain together and watching movies in his basement together. Kieron's brother and Jarren are the same age and had been friends their last year of high school, so they skied with us the whole break too. I did miss that so much, but I didn't miss it enough to want to move back, yet.

That first night after skiing the five of us headed over to the Parkers' house for Ethan's big homecoming party. They loved hosting the gatherings so they could keep Ethan home. Seeing him so rarely must have been difficult. I completely understood them wanting him and all of his friends at their house for the few times he visited.

Entering their home, the first people in my line of vision were Hannah and Ethan, so I just gave Ethan a quick "welcome home" hug like he was my brother. He looked at me and opened his mouth like he was about to say something, but before he could speak, I simply said, "It's great to see you Ethan." Then, I looked over at Hannah and said, "Hi Hannah."

I observed that they didn't look overly happy, but I didn't recall them ever acting significantly affectionate with other people around. I guess that was nice of them. He loves her the way she is, and their relationship seemed to have been working for them for years.

I fled the area after my casual greeting, and spent the evening sitting in one of the other family rooms with my friends. Because the snow had fallen and it was very cold, there would be no outdoor walks this trip. Around midnight, Jarren and I left. Nothing about that night was significant other than how proud I was that I did not have any hard feelings over seeing Hannah and Ethan.

I wondered if Ethan would call me during break, but I didn't expect it. He did send me a text saying he was happy to see me and Jarren and that he looked forward to seeing us again at Christmas. I didn't bother telling him that none of us would be in Ponderosa for Christmas. My brother and parents were coming to Charleston. We were going to get a condo in Myrtle Beach for a couple of weeks and enjoy the weather.

Often in South Carolina, during the winter months, it is still fairly warm. They get cold spells, but they don't last long. We have family photos of Jarren and me swimming in the ocean in December when we were kids. The locals thought we were crazy, but they had no idea how seriously cold the Idaho water is in July, so their ocean water temperature was nothing to us. I figured if Ethan asked for more details around Christmas time, I'd explain then.

Jarren and I went back to our schools, and we both worked and made it through our finals.Only three weeks passed since Thanksgiving and we were all together in South Carolina for Christmas. When Ethan texted me the dates he was going to be home during December, I told him we were staying in South Carolina. He wished us all happy holidays and said he'd get back in touch with me around Spring Break. That was that.

I was still in love with him, but I was not going to try to stay in touch with him. He knows too much about me so trying to go back to the "we're just friends" place in our non-existent relationship was too uncomfortable. I had decided that I could be friends with him, just not yet.

I never fathomed that I would be so elated to return to school and move back into my dorm after the holidays. Piper, our friends and I picked up where we left off. We compared our new schedules and figured out when and where we'd be meeting for meals. Classes began.

I loved my new life with my new friends, and I loved my new home. I was ready now for whatever this semester was going to bring.

Chapter 9

I realized I was young. I turned nineteen in October of 2011, but I was still always amazed at how life could deliver some of the most amazing, and sometimes interesting, surprises to you. It seems like you can make your plans, and be moving along perfectly in the current you have created for yourself, and out of nowhere, something completely unexpected will come crashing into your world.

I mentioned at the beginning of this story that life changes in an instant. One moment, one single little moment is upon you, and it can change your entire world as you know it. There is another life-changing moment coming for me in my love story, and at that point, I still had no idea it was even on the horizon.

Late January, on a typical Friday evening, my girl friends all decided to go out. We were going to do it different though. We were giddy and excited. Byron was working the door at The Venue so we were ecstatic to go dancing for the night. We got dressed in our tight, ripped up jeans, slipped into our favorite tops, buckled on our favorite heels, styled our hair to perfection, and off we went, looking simply smashing.

Before dancing, we went to dinner downtown. There not going to be any cafeteria or deli food for us that night. We were going to have a nice dinner at an actual restaurant. So, we did!

After our dinner date, we were ready to dance. As we were sharing stories, giggling, and squealing on our way to The Venue, a group of cadets from the Citadel was walking toward us. Two of the girls from my hall knew a few of the guys, so we stopped to chat with them for a while. None of us was in a hurry. We were all enjoying the evening. I was standing near the back of our group beside Piper. Since I didn't know anyone, I waited patiently to continue our walk to the bar.

In a sort of serendipitous way, I felt a pull on my attention to the group of cadets. I felt drawn to something. A voice was telling to me look up, so I did.

Standing in the group was a guy who caught my attention. He was already looking at me, and perhaps that's why suddenly I couldn't help searching their faces. Maybe I felt his attraction to me. Once he saw that I had noticed him, he moved from his group directly to me and stood in front of me.

"My name is Clark Ravenel. I'm from Atlanta, Georgia. I'm a first year cadet at the Citadel. What's your name?" He didn't hesitate. He wasn't afraid. He was focused and warm. I gaped, then smiled. My heart first stopped, then started pounding. Here I was again, just trying to breathe.

Before I told him my name, my mind scanned him from head to toe. He was in uniform. I have no idea which uniform. I just know they all have a purpose. This one was gray with a black banded collar and a black line down the center. He was wearing a hat. I had learned by now, being around friends who date cadets, that they have to wear their hats at all times when outside. He had very blonde hair and blue eyes that called me. He wasn't very tall, perhaps five-eight or five-nine. This was the perfect height for me since I was wearing heels that night. Clark wasn't overly muscular, but very fit and … and … just perfect. I seriously thought I was going to faint. No wonder girls around there were so silly for those guys. I got it. I finally understood.

"Um… my name is Evi," I said still focused on his eyes.

"Her name is Everclear!" My sweet, funny roommate chimed in quickly.

"Well, yes. It is Everclear Jordan. I'm from a tiny mountain town in Idaho. I was named after the lake in my hometown. It's the most beautiful thing you may ever see." *Okay, I need to stop talking*, I thought.

It may seem like a cheesy thing to say, but staring directly in my eyes, Clark immediately and softly replied in a hypnotizing southern accent, "There's no way a lake is the most beautiful thing I may ever see. That's not even possible."

So this is what I've always heard about. All the country music songs in the world are about moments like that. I had just met a southern gentleman and holy cow, he swept me off my feet. It was real. That actually happens in this world. I felt like screaming with joy and dancing right there in the middle of the street. I felt like there should have been flashing neon signs in the shapes of arrows all pointing at him, at us, saying, "Here it is folks, the real thing! This is it! He's here! He's here!"

Regardless of the excitement going on in my head, through much restraint, I took a deep breath and simply said in a soft tone while exhaling, "Clark, it is really, really nice to meet you." His presence instantly healed every hurt I had.

Clark offered me his left arm and asked if I'd like to walk with him for just a short while. He needed to be back on campus soon, but his friends said they would meet him at their car in twenty minutes. I told my friends I'd meet them at The Venue after our walk.

"I only have twenty minutes to get to know as much about you as possible," he said.

I just smiled at him and responded, "You better start asking questions then and you better choose them wisely. If we are only ever going to have *this* twenty minutes together, I hope you make it count. I think I'll work on getting to know you by the questions you ask me. That way, you can do most of the talking." I just wanted to hear his voice. It was comforting.

"Is there a possibility that you would someday give me another twenty minutes then?" he asked sweetly.

"Let's see how this first one goes before we start making wedding plans if that's okay with you." I replied in a flirtatious voice, rolling my eyes and regaining eye contact.

That retort, caught him off guard. He was speechless for a split second. Then, he gave me a big, sweet smile and said, "Okay Everclear, you're in charge of letting me know if we're heading to the altar after this twenty minutes is up."

I laughed out loud and squeezed his arm.

We walked and talked, but mostly watched the time. He was escorting me to meet my friends, but he still had to have time to get to the car for his ride back to campus. We talked about our families, where we grew up, and things we did back in our hometowns, like sports and church.

I kept my hand hooked through his arm the entire time, and every now and again, I'd realize that I was holding onto him with both hands. We were never afraid to look directly at each other. I wasn't scared. I wanted more time with him. He was the air I needed to breathe. My heart continued pounding with excitement.

As we arrived at The Venue, Clark put my phone number in his phone, and I put his number in mine. He explained briefly the rules of making personal phone calls, but it all went in one ear and out the other… so many rules.

I told him, "How 'bout *you* call *me* whenever you want to hear my voice, and I promise to always answer when it's you if I am able. If I don't answer, leave me a message and tell me exactly when I can call you back and I will."

Gosh I was feeling bold. I thought to myself, *I don't even know this guy. What is wrong with me? Perhaps I should back off a little. I just met him twenty minutes ago.*

"Thanks for delivering me here safely," I said to him. "Before you leave though, I want you to meet Byron. He's my friend." I opened the door and introduced Clark to Byron.

"Byron, this is my new friend Clark. He's going to make sure I'm safe."

"And happy," Clark added looking me in the eyes.

I'm sure I must have grinned ridiculously at him.

"Nice to meet you Byron," Clark said returning his eyes to me.

Byron knew Clark wasn't interested in going into the bar. He was in uniform, and besides that, he was clearly underage.

Before he left, Clark turned to Byron and asked, "Byron, would you mind taking a picture of us?"

"Sure man, be glad to."

Clark stood behind me and put his arm around my neck grasping my shoulder. I held onto his arm with both of my hands. He put his other arm around my waist. I leaned my head towards him and he slightly rested his cheek on my hair.

"Got it," Byron said.

I squeezed Clark's arm and gently hugged it just before he released me.

"Thanks Evi. I need this."

Flattered, I asked, "Why do you *need* it?"

"It gives me reason."

"Reason for what?"

"Just reason… a reason to smile, work, get up, run faster, pray. Just reason."

"Then make sure you send it to me Clark. If our picture serves so many purposes, I may *need* it too."

"I will. See you soon Everclear. I'll call you," he said in a loving tone.

Then, he left.

I stood at the door watching Clark walk away. I was waiting to see if he would turn around, and of course he did. I smiled and waved.

"Clark!" I suddenly yelled out. He stopped and turned toward me. I ran and jumped into his arms. He hugged me back so tightly.

"Sorry 'bout that. I don't know what came over me," I said as he put me down.

With a sigh of relief and a laugh, he replied, "Don't be sorry. I'm just glad you did it first!"

I waved again and watched him until he went around a corner, not wanting him to leave.

"Clark!" Once more I yelled.

He came to me this time. "Evi, this isn't going to be easy for us is it?"

I shook my head. He hugged me. We smiled. He kissed my hand, but before I let him go, I said, "Maybe." He knew what I was talking about. He winked at me and left.

I went back to the door of The Venue and Byron immediately asked, "How long have you been seeing this guy? I didn't know you were dating someone. I've never even seen you with a guy!"

"Um, I guess we've been dating for oh… about twenty minutes."

"What! Not months? That guy looks at you like you are the only one in this world for him. You just met him twenty minutes ago?"

I kissed Byron on the cheek and said, "I'm going to dance!" I took a few steps when Byron's words "the only one" hit me right in the gut. I was motionless with my hand pressed to my abdomen.

Piper was working her way over to me. "What's wrong with you?" she asked.

I had a quick flash of telling Ethan I deserved to be the only one for someone. I suddenly missed Ethan for the first time in months, or did I?

"Evi, what's up?" she asked again concerned.

"I think, I really, really like Clark," I stuttered.

"Well I certainly hope so!" She screamed and laughed. "He's perfect! He clearly wants you, and you haven't dated anyone since last summer. It's not like you're unavailable Evi." Our favorite song suddenly blared through the speakers. "Come on Evi, let's go dance!"

My friends and I danced and danced. We stayed at the bar until closing at two a.m. We went home, and I hoped to sleep at least until noon on Saturday.

Clark went back to campus Friday evening and immediately put in a formal request for leave for all day Saturday. I'm guessing it nearly killed him to wait until nine in the morning to call me, certainly he was up long before that.

Right at nine, my phone buzzed under my pillow. I knew it wasn't family because they are all two time zones away and probably still asleep too. I was trying to figure out which friend it could be since we all were out together. They should have all still been asleep too. Slowly coming to my senses, yet very groggy, I checked the screen. It was Clark calling. I had promised him I would answer when he called if I was able, and I wasn't going to break that promise. I didn't want to break that promise. I was actually happy it was him.

"Good morning!" I sang into the phone in a raspy voice. "You sure do sleep late on Saturdays," I teased him.

"Well I would have called much earlier, but I figured *you'd* still be sleeping after a long night of working out on the dance floor." Clark joked back.

"Noooo… Clark, not me. I've already gone on a five mile run and been to the gym. I'm not as lazy as you must think. What have you done today?"

He was laughing because clearly I was lying. He replied, "Well I *have* already gone on a five mile run and been to the gym. I'm not sure if I should believe you or be worried that you may be lying to me already."

"I think you'd be safest to believe me then," I told him snickering quietly since Piper was asleep, and I really didn't want to wake her.

"So I am guessing you are calling me this early because you have made big plans for us today. Am I right?"

"Yes. How soon can you be ready?" he asked excitedly.

"Please tell me you're still at school Clark and not sitting downstairs at my dorm. If you're still at school, I have at least thirty minutes before you can even get here to me."

"I'm at school. You never told me where you live."

"Whew! Thank heavens I had at least one moment of clarity after meeting you yesterday. I was smart enough not to lead a perfect stranger to my doorstep."

"Yes Evi, you followed your Kindergarten stranger danger lessons very well, except the phone number part."

I laughed at him.

He suggested, "How about I pick you up at ten?"

"Sounds perfect. Should I look like normal me or a slightly better version of me? I guess what I am asking is: are we going to be working out, or are we going to go on an actual date where I will be seen in public."

"You should be ready to be seen in public. No more workouts today since it seems that we both have already run five miles and been to the gym, right?"

"You're funny Clark. I like that you can keep up with my sense of humor. I'll see you in an hour. I'll try to make myself *beautiful* for you." I droned dramatically.

"You shouldn't have to try too hard."

I gave him my address and room number since we can have boys in our dorm after nine a.m. I didn't bother giving him directions because he knows the city better than I do. I got up quietly and went to the coffee shop in our lobby. I didn't plan on eating, but I was going to have my coffee.

I had an entire hour to get ready. That seemed like days. Being a tomboy, I could wrap my hair in a bun and throw on most anything and feel successful. So, having a whole hour to get ready was a breeze. I showered, then dried my hair. I figured I'd assess how frizzy it was after drying. Turns out it was pretty bad, so I had to straighten it. I decided to wear my hair down and parted in the middle like a hippy. Doing my hair took quite a chunk of my time, so I was only left with a few minutes to choose something to wear and put on makeup.

It was late January, so we were in the few cold weeks of winter. I heard they usually only last until mid-February. Of course, South Carolina's coldest weather wasn't near what I was used to coming from the Northern Rockies. Back home, it was nothing for us to have ten or more inches of snow on the ground for months at a time. Not to mention all the times I had been skiing in below zero temperatures for hours on end.

I decided to wear something warm but comfortable and still appropriate if we were to go out to lunch or dinner. I put on a pair of jeans with no holes in them, a pink, thick, fuzzy, off the shoulder sweater so I would look feminine and not boyish, and my comfy, furry boots.

Clark texted me when he arrived outside my door. He was so polite and thoughtful. I was glad he didn't knock. I had managed to not wake up Piper, and I didn't feel like explaining where I was going and who I was going to be with at that time. I left her a note saying I'd be back later and I had my phone with me if she needed anything.

I stepped out the door and closed it quietly behind me. As soon as I stepped out, I looked at him and probably had a surprised look on my face. He was in his uniform again.

"Why are you in your uniform Clark?" I whispered.

"I have to wear it if I am within ten miles of campus. I can't change into civilian clothes downtown since I am a first year cadet. I can change into civilian clothes if I cross the bridge to Folly or the Isle of Palms bridge. I wasn't sure how far we were going today, so I packed a bag just in case though."

"Ah, makes sense," I nodded.

We took the stairs to the first floor. He didn't offer me his arm, we simply walked side by side. I was expecting a hug from him probably because that has become such a standard greeting for anyone these days, but I wasn't going to instigate one. I didn't mind any of this, it was like we had been together for years, and I think I loved him the way he was right then and there. My next, and most logical thought was there may be uniform rules that I don't know about, so I'd let him do the leading on any types of affection. Well, with my one exception of course. Perhaps seeing someone who has uniform rules is the perfect way to start a friendship that has potential. I didn't have to insult him by being myself and following my beliefs. Somehow though, I knew from the moment we met, that I could completely trust him. I wasn't concerned about how he'd feel about my standards in relationships.

Clark opened the door for me to get in his car. I stepped back before getting in. I couldn't believe how nice his car was. If his family had enough money to buy him a brand new Lexus convertible coupe, why did he need to go to college at all, and why would he choose a military school. Why not enjoy a relaxed college experience? Anyway… I got in and anxiously awaited news of where we would be going.

Clark didn't drive towards downtown. He drove over the Cooper River Bridge to Mount Pleasant. There was a little diner there where we had a huge breakfast. Although I don't normally eat breakfast, if I've been taken out, or one of our moms cooked, I ate!

After brunch, we came back over the bridge into downtown. He drove us to the Battery and parked his car. Clark offered me his arm as we walked along the waterfront, and through the park for at least an hour. I held onto him with both hands as we talked about high school sports and our families. I talked about snow skiing and how I hate swimming in Idaho's cold water. He's a middle child and does plan on working for his dad when he graduates. The Citadel was his choice for college because he grew up always wanting to go to there. I had learned that that mindset was very common in the south. The big picture statement was, I loved being with him.

Our next adventure was a tour out to Fort Sumter. You take a boat to get to that fort. I hadn't been out there since I was about five years old because Fort Moultrie had always been my family's favorite fort to visit. Since you drive to Moultrie, our parents usually took us there.

The Fort Sumter tour took a couple of hours and when we were done there, I told Clark I was seriously tired. I wasn't sure if he had more plans, but it was around four o'clock and I needed a nap. I wished there was some way we could just go sit somewhere together on a couch and watch TV or take a nap, but circumstances did not allow this. I didn't want him in my room and my dorm lobby was too loud and busy, especially with a coffee shop in it.

"Clark, I don't really want today to end yet, but I am too tired. Can we see each other tomorrow? I want to rest."

"Sure. I didn't actually have anything planned for today. All I wanted was to see where it would lead us. I'll take you home now and of course we can see each other tomorrow."

He opened the car door for me again. When he sat down, I reached my hand across to his. I pulled it to my cheek and told him I had truly loved every minute of the day. Then, with our fingers intertwined, we lowered our hands onto the console as he drove me home. We arrived at my dorm and as I got out of the car, I almost, as if it was some sort of instinct, kissed him! I quickly turned my lean into a hug.

"Tomorrow?" I asked.

"Yes, tomorrow," he softly replied smiling.

＊ ＊ ＊

Through February and early March, Clark and I spent almost every weekend together. Every now and then, he had a required event or inspection, so our time together was cut from two days to maybe just an afternoon or evening. But, we made sure we were together every chance we had.

When we went on dates, we mostly went out to eat or to a movie or on long walks, we even went to church sometimes. Occasionally, I thought of Ethan and wondered if it was time to let him go forever. I hadn't heard from him since Christmas, so it was becoming easier to forget him.

Clark and I had only been seeing each other for a month and a half. He was quickly becoming all I needed and wanted. Clark made me happy and comfortable. He chose only me. I knew he was in love with me, I knew I was in love with him, and Clark never pushed the issue of wanting more from me.

Chapter 10

One evening in early March, Clark and I were talking on the phone before bedtime. We tried to keep our calls short because Clark didn't get much sleep as a first year cadet. We were talking about what to do during our upcoming weekend together.

"I still haven't seen you out of uniform Clark. We could go to the beach for the entire weekend. Can you do that?"

"I'll make sure of it," he said.

I made the plans for us to go to Folly from Friday to Sunday. I wasn't sure I was doing the right thing, but I booked a double room so we'd have separate beds. I suddenly heard Kieron's voice in my head, "Yes Evi, two sleeping bags!" I laughed out loud for several minutes. I probably would have looked drunk or high to a passerby, but I had not changed. I had made it that long sticking to my virtues. I didn't see any reason to turn away from my beliefs.

The next thought that came to mind was the evening I had spent with Ethan before I moved to Charleston. I felt his hand in my hair. I felt his other hand draped across my stomach. I felt his breath on my neck and face. I felt the excitement of being with him. Then, I felt the sadness of him misleading me.

I reassured myself that I was doing the right thing. Maybe Ethan is not the man I'm going to marry. After all, for years I had been feeling like I was the one being cheated on by him. Maybe my feelings for Ethan were an overwhelming crush. I put him out of my mind.

Friday evening, we checked into our hotel room at the beach. Clark went into the room first to change into his jeans and a sweatshirt. I knew we would work out the logistics of trying to be modest later, but for those first moments, I figured it was best for him to go in alone.

When he opened the door to let me in, I couldn't move. I stared at him. He was so real. He didn't look like a puppet or like he belonged to something else. He looked like he was there with me, for me. I finally felt like he was all mine. I sat my bag down and threw my arms around his neck. He wrapped his arms around my ribs and held me tightly. He kissed me on the neck, and I nuzzled my face into him. I started realizing I was going to have to make a big decision that weekend.

Clark picked up my bag and held the door open for me. He closed the door behind us and set my things down. I plopped right onto my bed and said, "I'm starving Clark!"

"Well okay Evi. There is plenty of food to be had. There's an entire ocean of food right outside the door. You'll get fed. I'll make sure of it."

I puffed out a laugh at him. Then, within a second, I realized the room was dark. I jumped off the bed and ran to the curtains. "Clark! Help me!" We each clasped a curtain rod and pulled back the drapes. "AGH! We're at the beach!" I screamed. He opened the sliding glass door so we could step out onto the balcony.

He inhaled, "Oh, smell that air. This is my favorite smell, other than the marsh. This is why I came to the Citadel. I wanted this view and the smell of the ocean as close as possible."

"Me too!" I said. "My parents begged me not to go so far from home. I grew up in the mountains, serious mountains, but I really always wanted to be near the ocean. This is where I feel at home."

We stood and watched the waves, listened to the breakers and the seagulls, and felt the chilly breeze blowing.

"I hope it is a bit warmer tomorrow. Maybe we can swim," I suggested with raised eyebrows.

Clark looked at me like I was crazy and said, "Swim?"

"Yes, swim. It's March. The sun will be shining. The water is probably about sixty-five degrees. The rivers in Idaho are around fifty degrees in mid-summer. We could swim." I assured him.

"Huh… maybe. We'll see."

The gnawing of hunger was growing stronger so we decided it was time to go eat. When we left the hotel room, Clark took my hand. He had never held my hand in public before then. It was as if I had been given a precious gift. I was really liking the no uniform thing. I smiled at him, squeezed his hand, and rubbed my cheek with it. Once I did that, he pulled his hand from mine, put his arm around me, and hugged me. Then, he held the back of my neck while we walked.

We ate seafood at a nearby restaurant for dinner. Afterward, we decided to walk on the beach and look for seashells. The evening was perfect. I think we both could see our forever together.

When we got back to our hotel room, surprisingly, there was no awkwardness in getting ready for bed. We took turns changing in the bathroom. And we each climbed into our own bed.

I watched him watch me walk to my bed. I wore a little pair of shorts and a tank top. Though I tried not to appear overly interested, I observed him as he walked past me to his bed. He was wearing only a pair of sweatpants.

After propping his pillows and settling his sheet so it covered him only to his waist, he got up right back up. I watched to see what he was doing. He walked to the balcony and slid the door open about two inches so we could hear the ocean all night. I secretly admired him as he walked across the room back to his bed.

When Clark was settled again, I told him he could have the remote; I was going straight to sleep. He turned on the TV and seemed to be so happy knowing he was going to get a full night's sleep. He was going to be able to sleep as late as he wanted the next morning. No one was going to wake him up screaming at him in an hour. No one was there who would force him to stay awake for hours until dawn. We were tired and both glad to have our own safe space together.

"Good night Clark. Thanks for spending the weekend with me."

He looked at me and with his sweet, accepting voice, he said, "Night Ev, and I should be thanking you."

We smiled.

I awoke around nine Saturday morning. Clark was still sound asleep. I quietly put on a pair of leggings and a sweatshirt and walked to the coffee shop down the street. As I was ordering, I realized I had absolutely no idea if Clark even drinks coffee! How do I not know this? I love coffee! I'm pretty sure he must know that about me. I got him a black coffee and a water, just in case, and I went back to the room. He was so out of it, he didn't hear me leave or return. *Boy, he must be really tired*, I thought making a shocked facial expression.

I sat out on the balcony and enjoyed my coffee in the warmth of the sun listening to the sounds of the world. I thought I could have sat there forever, except I do get bored fairly easily. I think all of my years of competing in sports and being outside have molded me into a very active person. I don't like to just sit for too long.

I looked into the room through the curtain. I had kept it mostly closed so the sun didn't wake him, then I sat back down again. As ten-thirty approached, I couldn't take it anymore. I decided I was really bored, and I wanted him to be awake with me.

I quietly went back into the room, tiptoed to his side, and slowly climbed onto his bed on my hands and knees. He was sleeping on his stomach. The sheet was still around his waist, and since he wasn't wearing a shirt, his back was completely exposed. I hovered above his face looking down at him, once again secretly admiring him.

"You're staring at me Everclear."

Okay, not so secret anymore. I bit my lip to suppress how seriously attracted I was to him. I whined, "I know! I can't help it. I'm so bored and hungry again! I got you a coffee, but it's cold now."

"I don't drink coffee."

Ah, good to know, I thought. "Well, that's fine, because I got you a water too."

"Why'd you leave without me? I would have walked you to the coffee shop."

"You were in such a deep sleep, you didn't wake up when I left or when I returned. I figured you must need a lot of rest. I've been sitting outside for an hour waiting on you to get up." The whining continued.

"I'm up," he mumbled into his pillow.

"Then turn over."

Clark turned over, grabbed me with both hands and wrapped his arms around me. He held me on his chest. Ah, forever. I felt like I could stay here forever. "Don't let me go Clark," I whispered. I wasn't sure if he heard me, but if he did, he didn't respond.

We stayed there for about five minutes just breathing. I was wondering if he was motionless because he was feeling my heartbeat. My heart was pounding… for him.

His release came after he heard my stomach growl. We giggled.

"I told you I'm hungry."

"You'll get fed. I'll make sure of it. Let me get ready Everclear."

We both got dressed in something presentable and went to breakfast. Facing Clark from across the table began to ignite desires within me that I was not certain I could restrain any longer. He knew it. His eyes told me his body and soul were ready for more, for everything from me. I was glad we were in public with a barrier between us. I loved him! And he loved me.

It was almost noon by the time we finished eating. We managed to complete that meal without having a real conversation about where we were headed physically and when we were going to get there. As we walked back to the room, we could not let go of each other. In an attempt to side track the encounter that I thought was to come, I asked Clark if he was feeling brave enough to swim with me.

"Heck yes! Since you put it that way Evi, of course I *have* to swim with you now." He squeezed my shoulders and kissed me on my temple.

When we got to our room, we changed, grabbed our towels and headed to the beach. Crisis averted in my mind.

Generally, people run and dive into the ocean. This was not to be the scene for us. We walked to the edge, and as the shallowest waves retreated to the ocean, we stepped in. The wind was blowing and the water was quite frigid! However, I wasn't going to pass up swimming. Clark hesitantly followed me, complaining the entire time. We waded out and squealed as each wave crashed into our bare stomachs. I had felt colder water, but this was pretty cold. Determination was going to win though.

Clark held me for about fifteen minutes in the water. Our combined body warmth was probably the only thing that kept us in for that long. When we couldn't take it any longer, we ran to the showers by the dunes.

Thank heavens the hotel was piping warm water through the showers this time of year. We each turned one on and began rinsing the salty water from the tops of our heads to our feet caked with sand. We were laughing and enjoying one another. I didn't want to leave the shower.

As I was splashing water onto my neck, I looked over at Clark. His eyes were closed and his face was in the warm stream. Looking at him, I took a deep breath, then did something I never thought I would do. I turned off my shower and joined him in his. My fingers on his waist startled him, and he looked directly into my eyes. This was very unexpected. I really didn't know what I was going to do

95

next. I wasn't sure if I was ready to end my promise to myself. *Maybe Clark is my one. Maybe he is the one I've waited for.* I pondered the thought peacefully in my mind.

I moved my hands to his shoulders and pulled myself up onto my tiptoes. When my lips were merely an inch from his, I turned my head and kissed him on his neck. I held my lips on him, feeling the warm water on my back. My heart beat uncontrollably in my chest. He wasn't responding. His hands were placed lightly on the center of my back. I knew he was only going to let me go as far as I was comfortable. I could trust him not to push me.

To my surprise, and probably his, my lips moved down his chest as I lowered myself. Slowly, I took his hand and placed it over my heart, right in the center of my chest. I pressed it hard against my skin. Trying to take a deep breath, I looked down at his hand, then I looked him in the eyes and asked him softly, "Can you feel that Clark?"

"Yes," he whispered.

"That's my heart beating for you. You're a part of me. You make me happy." I smiled at him.

"Forever," was his response. Then he whispered, "Forever, I hope." He kissed me on my forehead.

When he added the words "I hope" I felt like he knew I had given my heart to someone else years ago. I think that's why he never pushed me. Maybe he was thinking I had been hurt by another guy and was recovering. His words made me think of Ethan again for an instant. Suddenly, I felt such guilt because I wished for a second that Ethan was standing there with me instead of Clark.

I looked back into Clark's eyes and he said to me, "I think we've gotten the ocean off of us." He turned the water off, took my hand and we walked to our towels. He picked mine up, shook the sand off of it, and draped it over me before reaching for his own. He was always looking out for me, taking care of me first.

Wrapped up in our towels, we opened our arms and hugged standing there on the beach. I placed my head on his chest and closed my eyes. It felt so right being there with him.

When we released our embrace to walk back to our room, I decided to lighten our serious mood. I smiled and asked him, "Clark, would you like to see something that I can do?"

"Uh, yes!" Clark threw his arms out to his sides joining me in our attempt to focus on something other than the cravings we needed to control.

"Okay. I don't know if you know this about me, but I want to show you something."

I used the wind to help me lay my towel out on the beach. The wide open space was calling me. I felt like I needed to run so fast that I was about to burst. The surface of South Carolina's coastline is firm. It is easier to walk on or run on than the beaches of the west coast. I sat on my towel, stretched, then eased into a straddle split. I twisted to my right, then to my left. With my hips loosened, I turned face-down and did a few pushups. After my muscles were warmed, I moved back to straddle position. I did a press handstand being sure to keep my legs tight and straight and my toes pointed. I held it steady, turned my torso, did a right side split, bent my left leg, posed, and then walked over out of my handstand.

Clark yelled and cheered.

"Wait, I'm not done yet," I said with excitement.

I jumped up and down for a few seconds to get my adrenaline going. Next, I took three strong running steps and I power hurdled into a tumble pass. In my mind, I was competing. I did a round-off, back-handspring, into back tuck, then turned and powered stepped into a front walkover aerial. My show for him concluded with a gymnastics salute toward him as if he was a judge.

"What's my score Clark? How'd I do?"

I ran full speed to him, jumped into his arms, and wrapped my legs around him. I leaned back, then screamed in his face, "Did I win?"

"Holy crap Evi! That was amazing!"

"But did I *win*!?" I said in my old vicious, competitive tone, scrunching my nose.

"Oh yes! You win! Always sweetie."

"Yay me!" I kissed him on his neck as he swung us around laughing.

"I can't wait to hear and see what else you can do. Do you want to see what I can do?"

"Oooo, I'd love to," I told him.

Clark put me down. I grabbed my towel and he handed me his towel too. "Jump on my back Evi." I obliged. He said, "I can carry you all the way up to our room, using the stairs not the elevator, without stopping."

"Seriously!?" I was intrigued.

"Here we go!"

I laughed and held on tight as he headed to the third floor. A few times, I squealed and begged him not to drop me. In the end, he was absolutely right. He was able to carry me to our room without stopping or dropping me. I was impressed. It was so much fun having someone to play with that day.

Once in our room, we put our lounging clothes back on and watched the television with the curtains and door open. Neither of us needed a lunch. Our breakfast had been late and filling.

At dinner that night, I filled him in on my skiing experience and I told him about modeling a little bit. He said he was going to search for me on the internet. I told him he should be able to find plenty of information about my high school days. We laughed and enjoyed our evening and getting to know each other even more.

That night, when it was time for bed, I felt like we had made a lot of progress together. After I put on my shorts and tank top, I looked at my bed. He acted like he wasn't paying any attention to me, but I knew he was watching me using his peripheral vision.

I stepped between our beds and asked shyly, "Clark, can I sleep in your bed with you?"

He responded softly, "Of course you can," and he lifted his covers inviting me to his side. I crawled into his bed and scooted up next to him getting as close as I could. Clark put his left arm under my head so I could use it like a pillow. I rolled over onto my side and laid my head onto his chest.

I didn't waste any time telling him why I was there. My hand caressed his taut stomach while I said, "I want to talk to you Clark, and I want to be close to you for this."

He adjusted. He turned onto his side. Facing me with his head still on his pillow and mine on his arm, he commandingly replied, "Okay. Talk."

I was nervous and he knew it. To help me relax, his fingers gently stroked long strands of my hair. I carefully informed him, "I'm not pretending to like you Clark, and I'm not trying to tease you. I know we've only been seeing each other for six weeks, but I feel like we've been together for years. I want you to know that I don't want to string you along. My intention will never be to hurt or confuse you in any way with how I feel."

"Okay," he whispered.

I continued, "I need you to know that," a deep breath, a long pause, "that I have never... ever... ever been intimate in any way with a guy."

"What do you mean by 'any' way Evi?"

"Clark, I've never even kissed or been kissed by anyone. I've only gone out with one person on more than one date. In high school, no guy ever asked me out more than once, because they all knew a relationship with me would go nowhere. I've worked really hard to keep a promise to myself that I would only kiss my husband. People these days get so wrapped up in physical relationships, then they are devastated when they end. My friends cry and cry when a guy breaks up with them. People get so serious. I've never wanted that."

I buried my face in embarrassment. What was he going to say? Whatever it was, I really didn't want to hear it.

"Well, that explains *a lot* Evi. It makes sense to me. I couldn't quite figure out why you seemed to always be avoiding me. At least now I know. I would also like to know though, how on earth are you ever going to know who your future husband is if you are not willing to at least kiss the person you're dating?"

He was right. He made a good point. I tried to answer without having to look at him, but he pulled my chin so my eyes would have to meet his. Our lips were so close and our noses actually touched.

I answered, "I don't know. I'm hoping I'll just know, and lately, I've been thinking you could be the one for me. But Clark, we're only nineteen, and we have three and half more years of school. That's why I always pull back from you."

"You're right, I could be the one. When I tell you I want to make you happy, I mean that forever. I cannot even imagine loving anyone else the way I love you. I want you to know that I had a serious girlfriend in high school. We broke up last summer before I left for school. We dated for two years. I loved her, but now I see that how I felt about her was nothing compared to how I feel about you. I regretted breaking up with her for a long time, but my relationship with you, after just six weeks, heck after the first few minutes, has been more real than two years with her."

I let his words sink in for a short while, then still resting on his chest I asked, "Did you sleep with her?"

"No Evi. She's a year younger than me and neither of us were ready for that."

I didn't know why I asked him that. His answer really didn't make a bit of difference to me. I was just curious. I smiled and said, "Oh. That was wise, and mature of you two."

He puffed a small laugh with me.

I was feeling so relieved that I had told him how I feel. I think he was relieved too. He breathed in a deep breath, then exhaled.

"Can we go to sleep now?" I asked.

"Sure babe. I was thinking the same thing. I won't get much sleep once I go back to school tomorrow night. Besides, if I *don't* go to sleep, I may not be able to control myself. You have some decisions to make, soon, Evi." We both giggled a little, but I knew he was right, and he meant what he said.

I rolled over onto my other side. Clark cradled around me keeping his left arm under my head. He wrapped me tightly with his right arm and again I held onto him with both of my hands. We slept peacefully in that position all night.

Since we slept wrapped up in each other, we woke at the same time. He kissed me on the side of my head just above my ear and whispered, "Time to wake up babe." Then he kissed me again, this time on my neck. As I opened my eyes, I felt his hand caressing me gently from my waist down past my hip, to my thigh and back up again and again. Every few seconds he would press his entire body against mine. I was so comfortable with him. I knew he was showing me I could trust him. I squeezed his arm, and while kissing it I leaned back into him letting him know I didn't want him to stop. I wanted him so badly.

"Evi," he said in a clear voice, "decide now."

I held my breath, tears came and my body naturally did the exact opposite of what my words said. I turned over so I was facing him. I placed my left leg over his hip. I pulled him on top of me and shifted so he was lying right down the middle of my body. I held onto him with all of my strength. We rubbed our bodies against one another. Then, I pressed my face into his neck and I cried, "I can't Clark. I just can't. I do want you so badly, but I can't yet! I'm so sorry!"

I became painfully aware of what I was doing to him. He was truly so perfect though. Still on top of me, with his hands clasping my shoulders from under my back, Clark whispered over and over in my ear, "It's okay babe. You're not ready. I'm fine. I love you."

Giving me time to calm down, Clark slid his body down and rested his head on my chest below my chin. We stayed there until we both could breathe normally and regain our composure. Before he released me, he said in such a mature way, "Evi, I don't want you to worry or feel embarrassed. This is just part of our relationship. Okay?"

I mumbled, "Mm, hm."

After having such an emotional start to our day, we actually went ahead and got up early that morning so we could spend as much time together as possible. We remained in each other's arms in his bed until we needed to eat again.

By the time we got up, our relationship was back to normal, and we were chatting casually while we packed. We walked to breakfast with his arm around my shoulders and mine around his waist. Returning to our lives was a dreadful feeling. A few short hours were all we had left until he once again belonged to something else. Clark would be leaving me for his other commitment.

Anticipating the next few weeks brought uncertainty because we weren't going to be able to see much of each other. Our Spring Breaks were coming up and they were different weeks. Mine was the week before his. I had already told him I was going home. Plans had been made and a ticket purchased back in December for me to go to Idaho for the week. Clark was going home to Atlanta for his Spring Break, basically the same plans had been prearranged by his parents months prior as well. I pushed the thought of the next few weeks out of my mind and savored every single moment remaining of our weekend together.

Chapter 11

Guess what? That next big moment in my life, the one I keep mentioning, well it still hasn't happened yet. It's coming up. I promise.

After breakfast, when we got back to the room, Clark put on his uniform. I could still hug him because we weren't out in public, so I did. "You're going to have a great week," I told him. "You look amazing. Don't go finding any sexy cadet girls okay?"

He laughed out loud. "Not a chance! Not a chance. I'm following you on this road Evi. I can't wait to see where we end up. I'm not the least bit curious about any other girl in the world! You are it for me, the only one."

I couldn't believe he just used those words. I smiled at him without telling him how important those three words were to me.

Clark drove me back to my dorm. Once he was parked on the curb, he jumped out of the car to get my bag and open my door for me. He held out his hand to help me out of the car. I stood in front of him and he hugged me. Almost in a whisper he said, "I'll call you soon, really soon. You know how I feel. I'm not going anywhere Evi."

Before releasing me, without giving me a choice, he placed his hand on my mid-back, pulled me towards him, and he kissed me very softly on my bottom lip. I didn't respond at first. I just looked at him and smiled. Then, though insecure, I whispered, "Once more?"

Clark pressed his forehead to mine, closed his eyes, and nodded. He dropped my bag and put his other hand on the back of my head. Gently his lips touched mine and moved slowly from side to side. I was being hypnotized by him. He wanted it to be perfect. He pressed. It felt so good to finally connect with him. Clark took complete ownership of my heart in that moment. Without moving away from me, he whispered again, "I'll call you soon."

I wanted more.

Piper was in our room watching TV when I got home. "Have a good weekend Everclear?" she said it in a seductive voice. She still assumed my relationships were like everyone else's.

"It was great Piper. I wouldn't change a thing." I proceeded to tell her a brief and vague version of the things we did like swimming, and sitting on the balcony, or eating really good food. I offered no other details.

Then she asked, "Did you sleep in two beds?"

Just as I was about to answer her, my phone buzzed. Fully expecting it to be Clark, I grabbed it without even seeing who was calling and cheerfully sang, "Helloooooo!"

"You certainly sound happy and energized."

"Ethan!?" I sort of screamed in shock.

"Yes. Were you expecting someone else?"

Oh my God! Yes, oh my God, was all I could think. Not in a disrespectful, sacrilegious way, but in a true, heartfelt, "Lord please help me" way.

"Um, no. I'm just surprised, no, shocked, that you're calling me."

Piper was off to the side of me mouthing, "Who the heck is Ethan?!" I was waving her off and pacing frantically. I had one hand on my forehead and the other was holding the phone. Trying to be calm, I forced myself to stop pacing. I sat on my bed and told myself to settle down. Within the span of three seconds, I was up pacing again.

This means nothing. This means nothing. He always calls when he's on his way home.

I tried to sound casual, "So how have you been? What's up Ethan?"

"I've been great. I'm calling to let you know that I'll be home next week. Will you be there?"

Like I suspected. I replied, "No. I'll be home for Spring Break, but not until the next week. Jarren will be in Ponderosa when you are there though. Make sure you call him too."

"I always do. So when will you be coming home? Maybe our paths will cross by a day or two."

"I'll be there late Friday night."

"Okay, I'll see you early Saturday. I don't leave until late Saturday night."

"That sounds great. Are your parents having a party?" I was asking because I wanted to know if his get together meant all of us as usual, including Hannah.

"I'm not sure yet. I'll let you know more when I see you in a couple of weeks."

"Okay. I'll talk to you soon. Thanks for calling Ethan."

And just like that, I was second guessing everything again! How did he do that to me? Or more important, why did I let him do that to me?

The proverbial cat was out of the bag. I had to fill Piper in on who Ethan was. I still tried to avoid telling her much about him. I didn't know why I needed to keep how I felt about him a secret. Perhaps it was because I was afraid people would think I was crazy for wanting someone I couldn't have for so long. The most significant part of the truth that I shared was admitting that I had a difficult time dating anyone because I was that girl who had been hung up on someone she couldn't have for almost four years.

"Does Clark know about Ethan?!" she asked.

"No! I haven't told him because there's really nothing to tell."

"Nothing to tell? You are in love with some guy from home who breaks your heart year after year and you don't feel that is information worth knowing for Clark?" Piper was lovingly lecturing me. Her tone was sort of like she felt sorry for me and for Clark.

"I don't know how to explain this Piper. Besides, there's really nothing to explain. I've never even been on a real date with Ethan. He has a girlfriend. The way I feel about him makes no sense to anyone other than me. I don't think it even makes sense to Ethan."

"Ethan knows how you feel about him? Are you kidding? And he still never asked you out?"

"Well," I stalled. "He knows how I *felt* about him, yes. It is really a long story that has no point. Please try to understand that I just don't understand it myself. There's just always been a part of me, a big part of me that is drawn to Ethan. Until I met Clark, I couldn't seem to let him go! Now, I'm confused all over again. I'm still trying to figure out if Ethan is just a high school crush." I spoke sounding frustrated and confused. In my mind I reasoned, *I still feel like Ethan's my one.*

I thought we had dropped the whole conversation, but almost as if she knew, she asked, "That picture right there of you in high school," She pointed to a picture of me in my cheer uniform at a basketball game. In the photo I am looking over my shoulder and I appear to be staring off into space. I'm not smiling, I'm just staring. "What are you doing in that picture?"

I answered, "My mom took that picture and printed it for me. She put it in my things to bring to school with me."

"Why would she take a picture of you not smiling, just looking off into the distance, then print it for you to bring to school?"

"It's a picture she took of me staring at Ethan. She, my dad and my brother all know that I've been in love with him since I was fifteen. She thought it was cute and a good reminder to me to… well… a reminder for me to stick to my values. There *is* someone out there for me, so I shouldn't go wild looking for, nor waiting for that person. God will send the right guy for me when that guy is ready for me and when I am ready for him. This picture tells me to be strong in my faith and *wait* for God's timing. *He's* never going to let me down."

"Well, I sure can't nor will I ever try to argue with that Evi. Good luck." She laughed a little but in a sweet, she accepts me way. I was relieved when the conversation was finally over.

Piper was on Clark's side all along. She never pressed me about Ethan, nor did she linger on Clark discussions for very long. She wanted me to make a decision for myself.

Two more weeks passed. Clark and I had only had a chance to spend time together during one weekend. The time with him was different now because I could only think of whether or not I was being fair to him. I was sure he sensed my distance and I was sure he wanted an explanation as to why. I tried to feel as close to him as I did when we were at the beach together, but admitting my history to Piper changed my path, it changed me. It had weakened me.

In an attempt to comfort Clark, I asked him to drive me to the airport when it was time for me to leave for Idaho. He gladly obliged.

Parked on the curb, before I got out of his car, I asked him, "Will you come see me before you leave for Atlanta next weekend?"

"Absolutely Evi. There's no way I plan on leaving without spending at least a few minutes with you."

"See you next weekend," I softly said to him.

"See you next weekend," he replied.

We gently pressed our foreheads and noses together. I turned slightly and we kissed each other on the cheek at the same time. I was not ignorant, I sensed his frustration. He looked away, and I got out of the car.

After closing the door, I tapped on the passenger side window. Clark looked at me, turned the car off and got out. I walked around to him and feeling guilty I said, "Clark, I know how you feel. I promise."

"No, I don't think you do Evi." I didn't respond. He continued, "There's no way we are going to be able to get any closer if you are always intentionally working to keep a distance between us." I placed my hand on his upper arm and looked down. "Evi, your beliefs just don't make any sense to me."

I finally had something to say, "Clark, we have three years before we can make any decisions about our relationship. I have to keep my distance because you have no idea how frustrating it is to feel the way I feel about you."

He abruptly stopped me and in a deep and raised voice he said, "Evi! Don't even talk to me about frustrations! I know I'm winning the restraint competition between us by a landslide!"

I loved that he made me laugh so hard. I clearly understood his innuendo. He laughed with me and kissed me on my forehead.

"I have to go Clark. I just couldn't let you leave without seeing your smile." I placed his hand over my heart.

"Go Evi, but think about us this week. No ultimatums. I'm just asking you to think about us. Call me, okay?"

"Clark,"

He acknowledged me by tilting his head and nodding his chin.

"I do love you."

"I'm glad to hear that babe," he replied as he touched my cheek with the backs of his fingers.

And, as if it was the most natural motion in the world, I stood up on my tiptoes to kiss him. He wasn't going to miss the opportunity so simultaneously he pulled me into him. It was quick, but it satisfied us both, for the time.

❀ ❀ ❀

I arrived in Ponderosa late Friday night and went straight to bed after catching up for a little while with my parents. I figured I'd tell them about Clark later.

The next morning, my buzzing phone woke me up at ten. Ethan was texting me. "What are your plans for today Ev?"

"Don't have any right now. Will you just call me Ethan? It's too early to type."

"Are you serious? Too early? It's ten! Are you still in bed? Get up!"

"Oh my gosh Ethan! Call me! I can't focus right now."

"No, I think more texting is just what the doctor ordered to make sure you are good and awake."

"Ugh! What do doctors know? I'm done Ethan. Call me or this conversation is over!"

I was lying in bed laughing now. Geesh, it's no wonder I love him so much. I took a deep breath and very slowly released it. *Darn it*, I thought, *why do I still feel this way about him?* He was calling me. I answered. But before I could speak, a gleeful, "Good morning sunshine!" came through the phone.

"Hey! I miss you so much Ethan!"

I thought, *Oh crap! Did I just say that out loud?*

"Evi, did you just say you miss me?"

Think. Think. I buried my face under my pillow.

"Evi? Hello? I heard what you said. Say something."

I couldn't lie to him. "Yes, I said I miss you. I'm sorry. I'm so sorry and so embarrassed. I shouldn't have said that," I whined.

"Evi, I can barely hear you."

"That's because I have my face buried under my pillow Ethan. I'm humiliated now. Maybe calling wasn't such a good idea either!"

"Well throw the stupid pillow on the floor and talk to me."

"I can't. I'm really too embarrassed."

Soldier mode kicked in for a few seconds. "Don't make me come over there and yank the pillow from your hand and throw it on the floor myself! And don't apologize. Talk to me." Then, his tone softened a bit, "Besides, if it makes you feel any better, I miss you too. There, it's over now. You're okay."

I mumbled, "Well, I will be okay, but it'll take at least a few more minutes."

Changing the subject I asked, "What time do you leave today?"

"I'm leaving at five. I really want to see you Evi. We haven't spent any time together in over six months. Can we get together?" He was so sincere. I absorbed the sound of his voice for a moment. It was familiar, comforting. It was a sound I'd known and heard many times over the past several years.

I began thinking that I really didn't want this conversation to have to get serious. I recalled how hurt I was when we were on the beach together the night before I left for school. Ethan makes me laugh. I loved joking and playing around with him, but I was not ready to get roped into having to face that he and Hannah were still together. In addition to that, I had been seeing Clark and wasn't sure where that relationship was going. Basically, even though I didn't want to have a serious conversation, I knew I was going to have to face one.

Regaining ownership of my emotions I asked him, "What do you plan on us doing Ethan? You know I would love to see you. I always look forward to seeing you, but do you remember the last time we were alone together?"

"Of course I do Ev. It's just that, since we've met, we've never gone this long without spending time together. I really do miss you."

"Ethan, you promised to never hurt me again the last time we were alone together. I trust you, but I think I may need to help you keep that promise. You leave in seven hours. Seven hours! What difference will having lunch together, or getting coffee, or sitting at my house, or sitting at your house, or making out for a few minutes make? I want you to be sure you are ready to be with me and only me."

Ethan interrupted me, "You make out with guys now Evi?"

"What?" I asked completely confused.

"I said, do you make out with guys now Evi?"

"No! Why would you ask me that?"

"Uh, because *you* said what difference would making out for a few minutes make? That is definitely what you said." He was laughing.

"No I didn't!" I thought for a second then asked him, "Did I say that?"

He roared. "Yes! You did say that. Don't misunderstand Evi, I would not have a problem with that option. As a matter of fact, I can't think of anything I'd rather do before I get on a plane today."

"Okay, I really should not ever speak to you again Ethan. I can't live with this much embarrassment in one life time."

"Oh, now I really want to see you today. I have got to see your face. I want to make sure you aren't lying to me about *making out* with other guys."

"No. Leave me alone Ethan. I'm serious. Do not call me just so you can pop in and say hi. That's not what I want from you. I'm not the same person I was last summer. A lot has happened in the past few months, and I can't see you today Ethan. I am so sorry. I just can't."

"Okay Evi. I can see I'm not going to be able to change your mind right now. I understand. When do you go back to school?"

"I leave Friday morning. I'll be back in my dorm first thing Saturday morning. I'm staying with one of the girls from my hall Friday night."

"Okay. Hey, have a really good week. The mountain is still open ya know so don't break anything skiing you clumsy goober! I've still never met anyone as clumsy as you. I don't how you've survived this long."

"Hey! There is nothing clumsy about me on skis! You're just jealous because you've never been coordinated enough to figure out how to ski."

"Yeah, yeah, tell yourself that sweetie. Have a good week and a safe trip back. And I really do miss you Evi, believe it or not." He said it so lovingly that I truly believed him.

"I miss you too Ethan. I really do, but we're young, we'll get over it right?"

"Maybe Evi. Maybe."

"Bye Ethan."

"I'll call you again soon. Bye babe," he said softly.

That was new. His words went in through my ears and filled my soul like a warm vapor. He did it, and I know he did it on purpose. He grabbed ahold of my heart once more and I craved him again, probably even more than ever. My thoughts... *Ugh! How does he do that?* and, *Why do I let him do that?*

I wanted to call him back and tell him to come over as quickly as he could, but I had to turn off my emotions and think. I would see him in June when he came home for his summer break. I'd make sure he told me once and for all if he was ready to be with only me. Time was coming for me to put Ethan behind me. For the time being, I'd continue in my comfortable world and enjoy my week in Ponderosa.

Spring Break was fun. Turns out that Kieron and Brody were both home the same week as me. We skied and hung out at my house, then at Brody's for a few days. The three of us were inseparable. We even watched movies, ate junk food, and had sleep-overs together. Then, the middle of the week, my parents and I went to see Jarren. He was home the week before me and since his school is only a few hours away, we had planned on going to see him all along.

After a fun visit, a lot of skiing, and two days with my brother, I boarded a plane for South Carolina. My friend Ginger picked me up from the airport. I wasn't ready to see Clark yet, so I told him I'd be back in my dorm Saturday. I stayed the night with Ginger, and we moved back into our dorm rooms first thing the Saturday morning.

Chapter 12

Piper wasn't going to be back until Sunday, so I had the room to myself for the night. Saturday afternoon, there was a play at the theater on campus. If we went and brought our tickets to our professor, we would get extra credit. After getting settled back into my room, I got dressed up but left my hair down and shaggy. I had let it dry naturally so it was very curly that day.

Just after I got ready, someone knocked on my door. I suddenly remembered that I had told Clark to come see me before he left for Atlanta. I felt horrible about forgetting that. I opened the door and sure enough it was him. He looked amazing. He wasn't in uniform. He wore a pair of khaki shorts, a light blue polo and flip flops. He looked like a breath of fresh air. I wondered how he was able to make me forget my name just by looking at me.

"Clark! Come in!" I pulled him by his hand.

He stepped in and we gave each other a strong hug while he kissed me on my cheek by my ear. Holding tightly to him, I exhaled.

We stood near the door as I spoke first. "I didn't realize how much I missed seeing you until I opened my door."

"Well I've missed you like crazy every minute of every day."

I felt bad about the way I worded what I said, so I tried to explain my comment. I asked him to sit with me and I said, "Clark, I'm sorry.

All I meant was that since I was out of town, at home, for the week, I've been busy and distracted. I missed you. I just kept moving so much that I haven't thought much about anything except what I was going to do next."

"So you were busy huh? Too busy to call me, even once?" He looked sad and mad at the same time, but he reached over and held my fingertips.

"Clark, I'm not trying to make you jealous, but I wasn't actually alone this entire week. I didn't call anyone."

"So if you weren't alone, who were you with all week?"

"Well, I've never told you this, but my best friends are guys. We spent every day on the mountain until closing, and the three of us spent every night together at one of our houses. Then, I went to Washington to visit my brother. I stayed in his dorm room with him, so I was *never* alone."

"So you sleep all night at other guys' houses? In the same room with them?"

"Yes Clark. We have for years. We're just friends. Our parents know it, our brothers all know it, kids at school all know it. It's not an issue."

"Fine Evi. So why didn't you have me get you from the airport?"

"I had already made plans to stay with Ginger. Clark, I'm sorry." My heart was hurting for him.

"I understand." He replied trying to sound casual, but I knew he didn't. I knew he missed me, and I never even told my parents about him.

We spoke a little more about my trip home, seeing my brother, and skiing all week with my two best friends. He wanted more information. I had nothing to hide, so I was very forthcoming and truthful. We talked a little about the things he had planned for his week with his family. No part of our conversation was deep. It was all small talk. He asked why I was so dressed up and I told him. He told me I looked beautiful and that he really did miss me while I was gone and he'd miss me this coming week too.

I think that was the moment I felt a complete sense of guilt and dishonesty. I couldn't stop thinking about the fact that there was one more person I had never told him about, Ethan. The problem was, I still didn't want to tell him about Ethan. Ethan was in my heart. I was afraid Clark would try to talk me out of my feelings for Ethan, and I was becoming more certain that that was never going to happen.

I realized that just like being home was a distraction for me, Clark was also a distraction for me. He made me forget everything about my life. He was my perfect distraction. He was perfect, and I didn't face reality when I was with him. I sat there wondering if I truly loved him or if he just kept me busy so I didn't think about Ethan. I was suddenly aware that until I figured it out, I was not being fair to Clark.

I looked at Clark deeply and quietly. He was quiet too. I took his hand and placed it in the center of my chest. "Do you feel that?" I asked him.

"Yes Evi," he whispered looking at our hands.

"You make my heart race. You make me forget the world around me. You make me happy."

"So is that a problem? Why do I get the feeling this is about to go south quick?" He moved his hand away.

"Clark, I told you I'm not pretending or trying to string you along, but I think that maybe I'm not being completely honest with you either. You are my fantasy world. I don't face reality with you. You are perfect. We are perfect, but…"

He interrupted, "Evi, there's nothing wrong with being happy with someone, with me. I don't know why you can't seem to let yourself completely love someone. You're so insecure about something. You worry about promises and marriage. I know we have three years ahead of us before marriage is a possibility, but I can and do promise you that I will be here for you forever. Some days will be bad, you'll see, but I will be here for you. I am not going to abandon you, ever! There's nothing wrong with us starting out perfect for each other."

Although it may have been unfair, I let Ethan's voice drown out everything Clark had said to me. "Clark, please enjoy your Spring Break with your family. I want this to be over. I'm not… not right for you, at least not right now. If you want to go out with another girl, I want you to do that. Do whatever you want Clark. Please don't think about me right now." I got up and opened the door for him to leave.

He rushed to me, grabbed me and hugged me. He buried his face in my neck and said, "Don't do this Evi."

I gasped in an attempt to hold back tears, and I began to hug him back. Immediately, I pushed him slightly away and I let him go. He looked right at me for a few seconds, but I couldn't bear the pain in his eyes. He studied my expression, my tears. I turned away, and he left.

Once the door closed, I let my tears flow. I sat on my bed again furious with myself. I couldn't believe I just ended that relationship all because I couldn't be honest with one of the most trustworthy people

I would probably ever meet. He would understand. Clark would understand. I thought about going after him, but I needed to sit and cry. I needed to breathe. I needed to be reasonable. I knew that running to him would not help me get over Ethan, and I knew it would never be fair to have him in my life if I was still thinking about someone else.

When Clark left, anyone would be able to see he was very upset. He went downstairs with his head down and was moving quickly for the door. As he crossed the lobby of my dorm he bumped into someone entering.

"You okay man? Sorry 'bout that."

Clark responded, "I'm okay, excuse me."

"You don't look okay."

"My girlfriend just broke up with me."

Just then a girl from my hall walked by them and said, "Hey Clark, you here to see Evi?"

"Um, yeah," he responded.

"Evi? That's a different name."

"Yeah, her name is Everclear."

"Well you seem like a great guy, a gentleman, I'm sure she'll either come to her senses or you'll find someone even better." The stranger replied politely.

"'Perfect guy' is how she put it, but you don't know her. There is no one better."

"Have you been dating long?"

"Only about two months," Clark said.

"Well if she's not the one, then there's always someone better."

"No. There's really no one better. Can I show you a picture of her?"

"Uh, sure. I have a few minutes."

Clark always took lots of pictures of us. Everywhere we went he wanted to take pictures. He showed this stranger the very first picture we ever took together, the one Byron took of us where I was smiling so big with his arms holding onto me. Then he showed him a picture of us at the beach after our shower. I was facing him wearing only my bikini. My forehead was pressed into his chin, my hands were holding onto his waist, my eyes were closed. I was thinking about how much I loved him. He looked at the camera with a serious expression. He had one arm wrapped around my back with his hand on my shoulder, and he snapped the picture with the other hand.

"Isn't she beautiful?" Clark asked.

"Uh, um, yeah… she is. A rare beauty my friend," the stranger replied.

"She's not rare. Girls like her are not rare. They are extinct. She's the last one on earth. She's sweet, hilarious, and affectionate."

The guy asked Clark, "Um, I'm not from around here. Where was this picture taken?" He pointed to the one of us as the beach.

"Oh! Yeah! That was taken out at Folly Beach. We spent an amazing weekend together there."

"Amazing huh? You seem to really care for her. I uh, I have to go." He was now trying to end the conversation.

Clark continued anyway, "She makes you feel like you are the only person in the world when she looks at you. Have you ever met a girl like that?"

"Yes, just one. Hey man, I'm sorry she's broken up with you. I hope everything works out, or I hope you find a girl who will show you she loves you apparently the way this girl has."

"Oh no. It's not like that. She doesn't believe in being physical in anyway. I'm sure this is way too much information, but she's one of the good girls."

"Are you trying to tell me that after two months, and spending a weekend at the beach in a hotel alone, this girl has still never done anything with you?"

"Nope, nothing. She says the guys from home are not interested in her because she's not a 'fun girl' to date. Must be a bunch of idiots. Why would any guy not want someone like her?" Clark was trying to stall. He didn't want to leave my dorm.

"Wow. I agree. Idiots. Hey, I need to go. Again, I'm sorry to hear about your girl. I do hope things get better for you and you find your 'Miss right.'"

"Hey, real quick, what are you doing here? I've never seen you around here before." Clark asked.

"Oh, I'm here to ask a girl out on a first date. Aren't we a pair?"

They laughed, then Clark said, "My name's Clark Ravenel. What's your name? Maybe I'll see you around again."

"My name's Ethan, Ethan Parker. Good luck to you Clark." And he left the conversation there. Having heard enough, he was actually hoping they wouldn't cross paths again.

They shook hands and parted ways.

Up in my room, still crying, I was talking myself out of chasing Clark. Then, I jumped up, grabbed my key, and ran out my door. Just as it closed behind me, I got a sick feeling and knew I was making a mistake. I leaned against my door and thought, I may not be Ethan's only one, but he is still mine, for now. I turned around and scanned my card. I was opening my door when I heard a voice behind me say, "Going somewhere?"

I almost collapsed. That was the voice of my forever. I put my head on my door, closed my eyes, and started shaking. I was afraid to look. Ethan walked over to me and pushed the door open. He moved me into my room. With his hands on my waist, he used his whole body to hold me up and help me walk. In every way I was his. He carefully closed the door behind us. Then he turned me around so I was facing him, and he hugged me so tightly.

I needed him to be my best friend, my protector, and my boyfriend. There's just something that words can't describe about having someone from home, someone who has known you for years, hold you when you are sad.

With his face pressed against my neck Ethan softly said, "I need to breathe you." He took a deep breath and walked me to my bed. I was still in shock. I was confused and elated, and I was feeling a little embarrassed because I was seconds from chasing another guy. I pushed my face into his shoulder and gripped his shirt in my hands. Was this real?

"What are you doing here?" I asked with tears still falling.

"I came to get a kiss from the one and only girl for me. And, since you wouldn't see me last Saturday, I figured I'd have to fly all the way from New York to Charleston to get it."

I would not have pushed him away for anything in the world! He leaned me back onto my pillow and stretched out beside me. He put his right arm under my head and his left hand slid across my abdomen onto my hip. We were lying in that exact same position seven months prior.

"Now, I *am* truly all yours," he whispered in my ear.

He pulled my chin so my face was about an inch from his. We were breathing the same air. He reached down and slowly pulled my leg from behind my knee over his thigh. He slid his hand from my knee, back up my body to my face without ever losing contact. All of him pressed to all of me. I think we became one person in that moment. The one moment that changed my forever had arrived. Ethan kissed me, and kissed me, and kissed me.

We stayed wrapped around each other kissing. I was so glad I had waited for him, for this. I had never wanted anyone else but him. I knew I would never want anyone else but him. Ethan was the man I was going to marry someday. He was finally my only one, my forever. I was never going to let him go.

Chapter 13

Ethan didn't ask me about Clark. I guess he got all the information he needed about us and our relationship in the few minutes they spoke. I would have told him anything he wanted to know. I had nothing to hide from him. My priority in life was making sure I would have nothing to hide from my husband and nothing to be ashamed of with my husband, whoever that was going to be. It can be done. It's old fashioned. It's very difficult sometimes, but it can be done.

Ethan and I eventually stopped kissing. However, I did not make it to the theater. I didn't really need the extra credit anyway.

Still lying together on my bed, Ethan softly brushed my hair out of my face and off of my neck. He looked so sweet and serious too. "Evi, I don't want you to feel like you have to tell me why you are crying, okay?"

"Okay, I won't, but I do want you know that, I, I said goodbye to someone."

"Fair enough babe. Let's focus on us now, and let's go."

"Where are we going?" I asked wiping my tears.

"You decide. You're in charge."

"Anywhere, anything?" I was able to form a smile.

"Yes," he replied nodding and smiling at my childish excitement.

Feeling more energized I responded, "Oh boy! How long do we have Ethan?" I asked grabbing his shirt.

"Twenty-four hours."

"Twenty-four hours? That's all?" I said to him.

"That's a lifetime in my world," he said as he leaned down and kissed me like he had done it a thousand times. Maybe he had, in his mind?

I couldn't think about tomorrow. I wanted every minute with him that day, and all that night, and the next day.

I left Piper a note, "I'll be home late Sunday. Do not worry. Tell my mom not to worry if she can't get in touch with me. I'm leaving my phone!" I started packing some things for the night.

"Do you have a bag packed?" I asked him.

"I have everything at my hotel room. I flew in last night. I took a cab to my hotel, got some sleep, woke up this morning, and waited for you to have a chance to get moved back into your room."

"You flew in last night? From New York?"

"Yes, you said last weekend when you *wouldn't* see me that you'd be moving back into your dorm this morning. I knew I would have this weekend off, so I did some research, found a great hotel, booked a flight, and here I am. I really love this city. No wonder you wanted to move here. It's beautiful, so historic, right up my alley."

"I'm sorry about last Saturday. I just wasn't ready to see you yet. The next time I faced you, I wanted to either be over you completely or I wanted, well, I wanted this. I'm so glad I ditched you." I said laughing at him.

"I'm glad you did too. I wasn't sure what I would have said to you last week. It probably would have been really difficult only having a

127

few hours together anyway. I know it may sound strange, and I won't go into details about why, but I feel like I know so much more about you today than I knew even a week ago. I didn't have doubts last week, and I certainly have no doubts this week. I just feel closer to you now. I've wanted you with me for a long time. I'm sorry it took me so long to come for you."

"It's okay. Everything happens in the right time. Maybe we both had things to learn about ourselves and about other people before we were going to be ready for each other."

I think he knew I was talking about Hannah, and he probably assumed I had been seeing someone too. He didn't ask though.

I added, "I loved being friends with you. I got to know a side of you that I may not have ever seen if we had started dating when I was fifteen! Gosh that was so long ago."

"That's true," he said.

"Okay, let's go," I urged.

Ethan put his hand on my lower back as we walked out of my room. We passed one of my friends in the hall and she gave me a look that said "Who the heck is that?" I waved at her subtly and kept walking. I wasn't ready to introduce Ethan to anyone. I just wanted to get somewhere alone with him.

We took my car to his hotel. He was staying downtown in a hotel by the waterfront park. "Do you want to go for a walk, eat or get settled a bit?" he asked me.

"I want to do all three, but let's put my bag in your room first."

Ethan carried my bag for me. We went up the stairs to the second floor. He scanned the key card and opened the door for me. Again, he placed his hand on my lower back and escorted me into the room. He tossed the key onto the dresser and placed my bag on the floor.

The first thing I noticed was that there was only one bed. *Time to grow up Evi,* I thought to myself. "This room is beautiful Ethan!" I walked to the window to check the view and sure enough, he was in a room with a view of the water.

"That's the Cooper River," I told him. "That enormous bridge over there is the Cooper River Bridge. Legend around here is that the Atlantic Ocean is formed where the Ashley and Cooper Rivers meet. That's actually something I've known most of my life from vacationing here with my family."

Looking out the window with me he asked, "Are you going to be comfortable here tonight Evi?"

I responded confidently, "Yes, very comfortable. There's nowhere else I could even imagine being. This is where I belong. Can you see that?"

Ethan stared out at the view. I'm sure he was nervous. He looked like he had just brought home a new toy and he couldn't decide if he wanted to put it on a shelf and look at it, or take it back to the store. As the "toy" in this scenario, I didn't like either of those options. I could sense that I needed to take control of this weekend.

I turned him so he was facing me and softly asked, "Ethan, since we only have one night together, our first night together, can we spend it right here? The whole day and evening, then tomorrow too, until I take you to the airport? We can eat here and spend every minute with nothing to think about but each other." I had waited for that, for him, actually my entire life. I wanted every minute of it with no interruptions.

"Yes. Let's do that." He smiled approvingly.

"Alright, we need food. Should we go for a quick walk and order food to go, or call room service?" I asked.

"Let's walk, I want to smell the air," he replied.

"Okay, let's take a quick walk out onto the pier, sit in a swing for a little while, then get our food to go."

I thought to myself, *So much for spending every minute in the room.*

He agreed, "Yeah, that sounds good."

My hope was that Ethan would be more talkative when we returned. He really seemed terrified. We had never had a difficult time talking to one another, quite the opposite in fact. Maybe opening this new door made him feel like his role with me had changed. I would get him loosened up soon.

We exited the hotel and stepped onto the cobblestone street. The stroll to the pier was a very short distance. Once there, we walked until we found an unoccupied swing. When we sat down beside each other, he reached over and pulled both of my legs over his. I was so glad he was feeling more confident about us. Maybe he was just in shock for a little while.

Settling together, I rested my head on his chest and asked him how many times I was going to get to see him over the next few months. "Just for now, all I can give is time during weekends and holidays Evi. I can come here for one weekend in April and one in May. Then by June, we should be able to spend at least three weeks together at home."

That sounded wonderful to me. I heard 'three weeks together at home, and for the first time in months, I couldn't wait for the school year to end.

"That sounds great. Can we stay at this hotel when you come visit me?" I asked eagerly.

"Sure, I really like it here," he replied.

"I really like making plans with you," I said.

"Me too, this is different. It feels good. I'm sorry I'm so quiet right now. I have just been processing this, just trying to understand it. All of a sudden, I feel like we just met."

"It'll pass. I feel like we've been together for years, so don't worry about being quiet. Besides, it's no secret that I talk enough for both of us."

Ethan smiled in response and looked out toward the water, then back at me.

That entire time, we had been facing each other as we talked. He finally leaned towards me and kissed me. Then he kissed me again and again. I felt like he was trying to decide if I was real.

He didn't need to worry. I didn't need to worry.

"I'm ready to get something to eat now," he said.

Ethan stood and pulled me to my feet holding both of my hands. I guided us to a local sandwich shop nearby. We enjoyed the cozy restaurant, and after we ate lunch, instead of going back to our room, we decided to walk around the market and tour one of the historic buildings downtown.

Despite the initial plans we had made to spend all of our time in our room, we didn't actually return to the hotel until early evening.

And by then, it was time to eat again. We ate a light, quick dinner before going back to our room.

When we walked into the room, Ethan asked again, "Are you sure you're going to be okay here tonight Everclear?"

I replied with conviction, "Yes. I'm fine. I really am glad to be here with you. I do want to get ready for bed though if that's okay with you."

"Of course it is."

I went to the dressing area and changed into a little tank top and a small pair of boy-shorts that I usually sleep in. I washed my face and brushed my teeth.

After a few minutes, I came out with my hair wrapped up on top of my head. I liked that I didn't feel uncomfortable with him seeing me in my natural state. I had spent the night many times at his house. My usual look when I was around Ethan was a ski bum style; messy hair, baggy clothes, and no makeup were a norm for me in Idaho. Stepping toward him, I smiled, shrugged my shoulders holding my hands out to my sides, and I simply said, "This is me. I'm done."

Ethan was sitting at the foot of the bed with the remote in his hand. When he looked my direction, he seemed surprised. I loved that his expression made me feel like this was the first time he'd ever really looked at me. He stood, put the remote on the bed, and walked over to me. There was no way for me to distinguish between feelings of fear and excitement.

Ethan pulled my hair down, then brushed my cheeks gently with the backs of his fingers. He kissed me so softly. I didn't know if he was scared or if his years with a serious girlfriend left him feeling very comfortable in this situation. I believe he was giving me a few more minutes to relax though, because after he kissed me, he said, "Why don't you just rest for a little while. I'm going to go take a shower." He kissed me one more time and said, "You're beautiful Evi," before walking away. I kissed his hand.

When the door clicked, I scanned the room for some distraction. Not being interested in the television, I went to the window to see the view at night. Elegant was the word I chose. I pressed my forehead against the glass and stared at the water. The view relaxed me and made me realize I was quite tired. I turned, picked up the remote, and crawled into the bed. Once I was propped and comfy, I searched for something that would hold my interest.

Ethan came out of the dressing area wearing a pair of shorts. I sat up, stared for a few seconds, then, I turned off the TV. I wanted him to know that he could come to bed. I was fine and completely comfortable with him.

Once he was in our bed, I turned off the light. The room wasn't completely dark because there was light coming in through the curtains. I could still see his face. We pulled each other close. He rolled us so he was on top of me, and I naturally shifted him into a more *personal* position. He kissed me like he had waited his entire life for me. His hands explored almost every inch of me. We never let go of each other the entire night. I wished those hours could have lasted forever.

Sunday morning, I awoke to Ethan rubbing my back and my neck, and he was stroking my hair. He slid half of his body over me and whispered, "I don't want to memorize anything about you. I want learn everything about you. I won't get to touch you again for a few weeks, so I need to make sure I know how you feel and how you look when you go to sleep and when you wake up. I've always dreamed about your eyes, but now, your expressions are mine. I have to keep you close."

His lips moved across my back and down my arms. My body could not, or would not, move. I soaked up every second of his affection. Finally, I whispered, "Whether you know it or not, my expressions have always belonged to you."

We forced ourselves out of the bed early so we could enjoy our time together. After having breakfast, we returned to the room. Ethan showered first and was sorting his things when I got in the shower. When I came out, he was standing in his uniform. I was speechless, completely speechless. I know most girls swoon over a man in uniform. I get that, I really do. However, in my mind, I think because I loved him so much, I saw a man, I saw Ethan, and I got that familiar feeling that he didn't belong to me. He was on his way back to West Point because he belonged to them. That was the instant I realized I wasn't going to be his priority for at least another six years, or probably even more. I was only going to be able to cherish the few moments we could steal together.

Fear set in to my heart. He read my body language and put one hand under my chin. When he turned my face up towards his I said, "Ethan, I don't want you to go. You're going to be so far away. It scares me. You're leaving!"

I had been conditioned to say goodbye to him and every time it hurt, but after having him with me for a night, it hurt more than ever before.

"I'll be back soon, I promise. You're mine now. You're all mine. We belong together. I'm not going to let much time pass before seeing you again. Trust me."

His words and his deep voice made me feel a little better. I had to accept that he would get back to me as soon as he could. The situation left me no choice but to believe him. He kissed me and we left. I drove Ethan to the airport and went back to my dorm to face the next few weeks. I had plenty of work and studying to keep me busy, and so did he.

Chapter 14

Ethan's next visit in April was much like the one we had had together in March. He flew to Charleston late on a Friday night. I got him from the airport, and we went straight to the King Charles Inn for the weekend. We stayed close to the hotel for those 2 days, although I did take him to tour my campus. We held onto each other every minute of each day and we fell asleep each night with our bodies intertwined.

When Ethan left Charleston after our second weekend together, I anxiously awaited news from him about our upcoming May weekend. I joyfully went about my life dreaming of our times together.

At the end of April, another Friday night was upon us, so of course my friends and I were ready to go have fun. This means we were going to The Venue. The weather was very warm and Byron was working, so we couldn't wait to go dancing. Ethan had already told me he wasn't able to visit that weekend, nor had he mentioned when he would be coming back. I wasn't too concerned; I was aware that school kept him endlessly busy. I was also becoming more and more accepting of the fact that he belonged to something else, with the exception of the few hours I got him on the occasional weekend. Ethan and I both knew we would be together in June though. There was no taking that away.

Piper and I slipped into very short, cutoff denim shorts. My top for the night was a sheer, short sleeved, poncho styled shirt that tied at the waist, and my cowboy boots pulled the ensemble together perfectly. I was going out with my hair down, style courtesy of the current humidity level. Also, no boyfriend, no one to impress, meant very little makeup.

The eight of us got to The Venue around nine, which was pretty early by going out standards. We wanted to stake our claim on a couple of tables before the thickest of the crowd showed up.

A little while after we arrived, my phone buzzed. "Ethan!?"

"Hey babe, where are you?" he asked.

"I'm at The Venue with my friends."

"Oh, okay just call me in the morning."

"No! I'll step outside. You're way more important than the next song. Or at least I think you are right?"

"Maybe, I'll let you decide."

"Give me one second." I stepped out the front door to the sidewalk. "Okay, I can talk now," I said to him.

"Good. We don't have to talk for long, I just wanted to say I love you and good night."

"I love you too. I miss you. You sure are going to bed early."

"Well, I called this early thinking I'd reach before you went out with your friends, guess I was wrong. I'll be up a little while longer."

"Oh… So do you know when you'll be able to come down here again?"

"I'm planning it now. I'll let you know next week sometime."

"Okay, sounds good."

"I miss you so much Evi."

"I miss you too Ethan. Just think, we'll be home in a few weeks. We'll be together every day! I can't wait!"

"I love you babe."

"I love you too."

We hung up. I pressed my phone to my chest just under my chin. I was trying to hug it because it was my only connection to him.

"Evi," a familiar voice behind me called my name softly.

Surprised, I turned, "Clark! Um… how are you? What are you doing downtown this late?"

"My friends and I just had dinner. We're going back to campus now. I saw you standing out here on your phone and I wanted to say hey, so I told them I'd catch up in a minute."

We hugged. "It's really good to see you Clark."

"You too Evi. Hey, I am not going beat around the bush. Have you even thought about calling me? We haven't spoken since the day I left for Atlanta back in March. It's been four weeks."

I had to tell him. "Clark, I'm seeing someone. It's pretty serious."

"You're seeing someone? Are you kidding me? How could you be serious with someone else after only a few weeks? I thought we were pretty '*serious*' too. Did our relationship mean absolutely nothing to you?"

Clark was really upset. I looked over my shoulder at Byron. He was waiting to see if I needed help. He knew Clark, so he wasn't too concerned, but he was watching. I gave him a slight wave so he knew I was fine, just needed privacy.

"Clark, I don't want to explain myself to you. You just have to trust that our relationship meant everything to me. It did! What we had was real, but now, it's over. I'm really happy with this guy. He really loves me and, and… I don't know what else to say Clark. You have to trust me."

"He really loves you? He *loves* you? And, *trust* you? How on earth could you have moved this fast in four weeks Evi?"

Ugh, this was not happening. His question was valid. He deserved to know the truth. The truth may be more painful than not knowing though. Sometimes, maybe we don't need to know everything. If Clark knew how long I'd been in love with Ethan, he'd think our time together was meaningless. I didn't want him to think that I didn't truly love him, but I just couldn't tell him about Ethan yet.

"Clark, I'm not going to try to work through this with you right now. I'm going to go back inside with my friends. I hate seeing you like this. Please, don't make me continue this conversation, it is crushing me."

Clark raised his voice, "Fine, you can go, but you don't know what being crushed feels like Evi. You've never been serious about anyone. I meant it when I told you I loved you!" He whispered looking down, "You said you loved me too." He paused, then said sadly, "You have no idea how this feels."

I replied calmly, "You're wrong. I have been hurt, and I do know how you feel. And now Clark, standing here with you, this doesn't feel good either." I touched his arm lightly, "You're going to be okay Clark. I'll see you later. I'm going back inside."

I wanted to hug him and tell him that everything was going to be okay. I wanted to tell him that he was important to me, that I did care about him, that I did love him. But instead, I looked quickly into his eyes, then turned and went back into the bar. Byron took my hand gently as I walked through the door. He could read our body language because he knew our story better than anyone in the world. He knew we were both hurting.

Clark looked at me through the glass, then walked away. As he went around the corner, someone had been standing there listening.

"Hey! Ethan right?"

Ethan replied, "Yeah. Clark? Um, nice uniform Clark."

"Oh, thanks. I'm a first year cadet at the Citadel."

"A plebe?" Ethan asked.

"No, we're called knobs. How do you know about plebes?"

"I'm a third year cadet at West Point."

"Wow! That's great to know. So, did you hear that conversation?"

Not wanting to admit it, reluctantly Ethan said, "Yeah, I did. Sorry man. I just couldn't interrupt. That would have been even more awkward than *this*. Soooo..."

"So, apparently my ex-girlfriend is *happy* with someone else. It doesn't even make sense. Who the heck could she be seeing after only four weeks? She didn't waste any time. God, I'm an idiot. I thought she cared about me and just needed 'space' or something stupid like that. I'm such an idiot."

Hearing the word 'ex-girlfriend' made Ethan cringe a bit, but he stayed focused and non-reactive. "Clark, you're not an idiot. Was what you two had real?"

"It was. I'm sure of it. But how could she meet someone else so quickly?"

"Was she honest with you the whole time you dated?"

Clark shrugged while looking down, "As far as I know."

"She said to trust her. Maybe there is a reasonable explanation that she's not ready to give. Maybe, I don't know, maybe she was already hung up on this other guy. Regardless, I think in order to keep from going insane, you're going to need to believe that she cared about you and never cheated on you. You need to believe her. Weird things happen all the time. You'll be okay, and you'll find someone else. I'm sorry 'bout all this, but I have to go. Good luck to you Clark, and good luck finishing up your first year. Stay strong!"

Ethan shook Clark's hand and walked around the corner to The Venue. I was still standing in the front room, but my back was to the door.

Byron carded him and yelled over the noise, "Oh, an Idaho boy and a soldier. Welcome my friend."

"Thanks man. Hey, by any chance do you know a girl named Evi?"

"Yeah! You're here for Evi? She's great!"

"Thanks, she is great. I *am* here for her. Do you know where she is?"

"Yep, she's standing right on the other side of that group of people there." Byron pointed toward my direction.

"Thank you sir," Ethan offered as he shook Byron's hand.

Ethan worked his way through the crowd and grabbed me from behind. He spun me around fast and forcefully, then kissed me. He about scared me to death! It all happened so quickly, I hardly had a split second to even see who had ahold of me. When I pulled back to focus, I saw him, this man I love so much. I was so happy to see him. I held back tears. I was already emotional over seeing how hurt Clark was, but to have this surprise holding onto me, I almost couldn't control myself. I was hoping he was thinking I was more surprised, than feeling upset about something.

"Let's get out of here now Ethan?" I yelled.

"No, not yet. Let's have a little fun together first."

"Okay! I'm staying with you tonight right?"

"You better be. I didn't come all this way for the weekend to admire the scenery. Well, only your scenery!" He stepped back and looked me up and down like I was dessert. "Evi! I can see straight through your shirt!" he yelled.

"I know! That's why I bought it. Isn't it great? I love this shirt!" I sassed back laughing out loud.

"Evi! I can... Evi, *everyone* can see your bra!"

"I know. It's a cute one too!"

Though not angry, Ethan gaped.

"Relax!"

"Alright Evi. Keep your shirt on... or don't. It won't really make a difference." We both laughed, and he hugged me again.

Making our way through the crowd, I introduced Ethan to everyone I knew. We danced for a couple of hours, then left.

"Night Byron," I said as I hugged him on my way out the door.

He whispered in my ear, "Clark came back and saw you with your new man. Just letting you know."

At first, my eyes shown my concern. Then, I smiled and said, "Thanks Byron."

"Also, Clark and your new man had a few words outside. I don't know how honest you've been with everyone, but you may want to start making sure things don't go crazy on you. Just watching your back Evi."

I whispered near his ear, "Thank you. Thank you so much. I think I'm okay. I'll talk to Ethan for sure. I have nothing to hide."

"What was that all about Evi?" Ethan clearly had noticed our lengthy exchange.

"Can I tell you when we get back to the room? I promise I will. It'll give us something to talk about."

"Well, I wasn't planning on *talking* when we got back to the room, but okay."

"Oh, it can wait babe, it can wait!" I said laughing and holding onto him like he was my very life. Our fingers locked, and I clenched his arm tightly with my other hand. I kept my head on his shoulder for most of the walk to the hotel.

The instant we got into the room and the door closed behind us, Ethan grabbed me. He put one hand behind my head and the other around my back. He lifted me up off of the floor, and I wrapped my arms and legs around him. I hooked my feet, squeezed him toward me and held onto him with every bit of strength I had. He lowered me onto the bed then pulled my boots off one at a time. Next, he slowly pulled my shirt up over my head. I let him. He looked at me to make sure I was okay and he sarcastically said, "It's not like you really needed that on anyway."

I laughed so hard I couldn't breathe for a minute.

Stealing back the romantic moment, he took off his own shirt. I smiled, and to let him know that I wanted him, I pulled on his belt buckle and shorts.

"Are you sure you don't want to just talk?" I asked in a flirty voice.

"Uh, yeah! Very sure," he replied nodding with his eyes widened.

143

I scooted backward to rest my head on a pillow, and I held onto it with both hands. My knees were bent, my feet were together. Ethan slowly crawled to me, raised up and placed his hands on my knees. I looked at him waiting to see what he was going to do. He pulled them apart, so I slid my feet to match the position.

Ethan moved his body right up against mine. Both of his hands slid very gently down my inner thighs to my shorts. I got light headed. Looking into my eyes the whole time, he unbuttoned them. Then, he unzipped them. He stayed focused, being certain he had an invitation, as he pulled them open. His attention moved lower causing me to inhale a deep breath. Resting in his touch, I wan't sure what I should do.

"Close your eyes if you want babe," he whispered.

I did.

Ethan placed a hand on my abdomen and caressed with his fingertips. Slowly, he slid it up my body exploring each curve. He positioned himself over me. I opened my eyes as he lowered himself, then pressed his hips into me. I gripped his waist and pulled.

"You are never getting away from me Ethan."

"Don't worry babe, I don't ever want to get away from you."

He kissed me so deeply and passionately, I could have floated to the stars. His hands and lips never left my body. I wanted him, all of him so badly… but… he hadn't asked yet.

Chapter 15

We exhausted all of our energy being twisted around each other. Looking back, I can't believe how quickly I seemed to grow up in just matter of weeks with Ethan. I think because he was twenty-one, had almost finished his third year of college and had been through so much military training, he seemed a lot more mature than most guys his age. I guess I was just maturing faster all of sudden to catch up to him.

I loved having him touch me. I loved having him on me. I needed him within reach at all times when we were together. Regardless of how much I wanted him though, we still had only kissed. After all, technically, we had only been on three dates. Well sort of, we'd spent three weekends together. I'm not sure how long couples usually wait before they decide to be completely physical, but at the time, I knew I was still planning on waiting until we both agreed that we were heading towards marriage.

Ethan never tried to push me to go any further than I was comfortable. He knew when to stop, even though I sometimes wasn't sure I wanted him to stop. In hindsight, I have to be honest, I probably would have given him all of me the very first weekend we were together if he had persisted.

Dear God, I loved him!

Since we both felt sweaty from the dance club and our time together, we decided to shower. He said I could go first. Just before I stepped into the shower, it occurred to me that I didn't have a change of clothes. That visit had been a surprise, so I hadn't packed any clothes.

"Ugh! Ethan!" I yelled frustrated as I grabbed a towel.

Thinking something was wrong, he ran to the door and opened it without knocking. "What?!" he asked with urgency.

Frustrated, I whined, "I don't have anything to wear. All of my clothes are in my room."

He laughed out loud like I had said something hilarious. "Geez Evi, that's not a crisis! I guess you'll just have to wear nothing then won't you?"

"Ethan! Seriously. I don't want to put my dirty clothes back on. That's gross. They're all sweaty."

"Well, what the heck do you want me to do?"

"Did you rent a car this weekend, or did you take a cab?"

"I took a cab."

"I don't even have a way to get to my dorm to get clean clothes then. I rode downtown with my friends, then walked here with you. My car is back on campus in the garage. Will you fix this please?"

"Well, do you want to shower?"

"No, not yet. I'll wait."

I came out of the bathroom with just the towel covering me. Ethan took the opportunity to flirt, tease, laugh, and put his hands on me. I was frustrated and tired, but of course I didn't mind at all.

"Look at me Ethan. I'm a mess."

"Where else do you think I would look? My girlfriend, the one love of my life is standing in front me wearing nothing but a towel. Seriously! Where else would I be looking? Ya know, if you were here with anyone else Evi, you'd be in a heap of trouble!"

"Ethan!"

"As a matter of fact…" he said slyly.

He took the opportunity to kiss me and carry me *back* to the bed. Again, I was not bothered. I trusted him completely. I was smiling and giggling with him.

After kissing for a few more minutes with nothing but a towel between us this time, I asked, "Did you figure this out yet?"

"Figure what out Everclear? I have a *lot* of things figured out here."

"I want a change of clothes!"

I laughed at him again, and pushed him off of me. I said, "We will get to *this*," and I pointed to the bed "very soon, I promise, but I'm tired right now, and we didn't think through this very carefully tonight."

"We're not fighting battles or creating complicated war strategies Evi. We just need a ride to your dorm. We'll call a cab babe. Now stop whining, put your sweaty clothes back on, and let's go. Oh! Wait. Here put this shirt on. You can get rid of that other one, or just wear it around me." Ethan tossed me one of his t-shirts.

"Aw, thanks sweetie." I smiled, glared and put *my* shirt back on.

He shook his head at me.

I guess he was right. The situation wasn't complicated, it was just inconvenient. The concierge at the front desk called a cab for us. It arrived quickly and drove us to my dorm. Once there, Ethan had to wait in the lobby since I couldn't have anyone of the opposite sex in my room or on my hall after eleven p.m. How strange that rule seemed to me in those moments. I had just been in a hotel room, naked, with the man I planned on marrying and he was not allowed in my room. Strange.

Piper was still out. I didn't need to leave her a note. She had met Ethan at the bar, so she knew where I'd be. I packed a bag and left.

Ethan drove my car back to our hotel. We shuffled to our room. I showered first and was deep asleep before he came to bed. I didn't even feel the bed move when he got in.

Ethan runs on very little sleep, and he knows exactly what kind of coffee I always want, so he got up early and took care of the coffee run for us both. Not one minute was going to be wasted. As soon as he got back to the room, he woke me up.

"Here's your coffee Ev. Wake up."

I shifted and squinted at him.

He was all energy. "Hey! Let's drive out to the beach today. Do you know the way or which beach is best?" he asked.

I took my cup from him and with a scratchy voice, I replied, "Yeah… I do,"

"I heard Folly Beach is close and a good place to check out."

Still groggy, but getting better with my coffee in hand, I said, "Um, yeah… I'd rather take you to a different beach though."

I looked at the lid to my cup afraid to make eye contact until I processed his intentions. As soon as he said Folly Beach, I knew I needed to tell him about Clark. I wondered if he was asking because in their brief meeting on the sidewalk, Clark had mentioned our weekend together. It was strange to know he knew about Clark, but he wasn't asking. Ethan didn't really seem to want to know. How the heck did those two happen to meet the night before? I felt like he should at least hear my side of the story of us dating for those few weeks. I was trying to keep my hands from shaking.

"Where *should* we go then?" he asked.

I responded right away, "Sullivan's Island. There's a quiet beach there with places to eat, and a fort, and a museum. I'd love to show you that part of the area. I've been there more times than I can count with my family. I love it there. I know you will too."

"Okay, Folly some other time?"

"Sure babe," I raised my eyebrows and nodded trying to hide my discomfort.

The soldier emerged and we were dressed, fed and at my car by eight-thirty Saturday morning.

Ethan absorbed every image, scene, and landscape as I drove us out of town. Taking him over the Cooper River Bridge and out to Sullivan's Island for the first time was invigorating. The entire drive was refreshing. I didn't want to say this to Ethan, but I was convinced I was born to live by the ocean. There is no feeling like being in the mountains, they are beautiful, but I was really becoming accustomed to the smells of the marsh, the salty air and the expanse of the seemingly endless ocean.

The weather was perfect and we were anxious to be outside so we toured Fort Moultrie first. It captivated Ethan and held his attention. After wandering through the Fort, we walked across the street to the museum. Most of my time was spent lingering, watching him, or looking at exhibits. Ethan studied.

My dad is a high school History teacher and my mom teaches middle school English, so I had read the placards many times. I made a mental note to take Ethan to Fort Sumter as well.

The war history and the history of South Carolina in general was fascinating to him. I broke his concentration and asked, "Now do you see why I love it here and why I wanted to come to school here?"

He half smiled, "Yeah, I do. You get to have three more years of this. I'm jealous."

I think Ethan was realizing, from a different perspective, what he had given up by making a commitment to the military. He had lost the freedom of a 'civilian' college experience, the freedom to sleep late, the freedom to go to the beach anytime he wanted. He had given up so much for his family and soon our country. Ethan's third year was a month from ending and he only had one more year of school. He was bound to his commitment for at least another five years after that. I stopped to wonder where I fit into all of it. I was reminded, he didn't belong to me.

The melancholy thoughts were erased, and I cheerfully said, "Let's go back outside. There's a path leading out onto the beach. We can go for another walk. Hey! I don't even have to fall down a wooded mountainside to get to this beach!"

Ethan laughed out loud, "Ah! I totally forgot about that. I still can't figure out why you can't walk down that tiny hill."

"Kieron suggested I try skiing down it. He figured I'd be safer on skis."

Ethan replied, "That's hilarious. He's a smart guy underneath all of his crazy."

A curiosity must have been triggered, because as we walked towards the beach Ethan asked, "How did things go when you two dated last summer?"

The question didn't seem odd to me at the time. I answered, "Fine. No, good. It was good. We've been friends for so long though that dating wasn't ever going to go anywhere serious for us. We played and camped. The usual."

"You guys went camping? Alone? In the woods? Just the two of you?"

"So many questions!" I repeated Kieron's words to Ethan from the last summer and laughed at him before answering. "Yes, I figured he would've told you. It was no big deal." I looked at Ethan and his expression screamed that he wanted to know more so I added, "It was no big deal Ethan." I repeated, "We... camped."

"So where'd y'all sleep?" I noted his discomfort.

"In a tent!" I was laughing so hard in my head and I knew my face had to show my hysteria. The conversation was exactly the same as the one I had with Kieron on the topic.

"One tent?" he asked with concern.

"Yes, one tent!" I yelled back.

"So you both slept in one tent? Together? For an entire weekend?" Ethan's voice was raised an octave with a hint of panic in it.

"Well, several weekends actually."

"What?!"

"Yes, several weekends..." I paused, "but *two* sleeping bags in case you're going to ask that next. I did!" I sort of screamed a laugh.

"What?"

"Yeah, I asked Kieron if he at least planned on us taking two sleeping bags. He assured me that he was not... oh how did he say it... 'out to steal my virtue' I think is what he said." Ethan laughed out loud now too.

"So you never kissed him either?" Ethan asked.

"Um, no, not really Ethan, only you." I paused and made a curious expression. "Wait a minute, what do you mean by 'either' Ethan?"

"What do *you* mean by 'not really' Evi?" He raised his eyebrows and made the same curious expression back to me.

I jumped right into the conversation we should be having. I informed him, "I mean that I didn't really kiss Clark."

"Evi, you either did or you didn't."

"Mmm... no, there's an in between. My answer is still not really. You are still my only one." I was trying to lighten his mood, but he was serious. I took a few seconds to read him. He was silent. He turned and looked away. I knew it was time to tell him the truth about my relationship with Clark.

"Let's take our shoes off and walk in the water," I said to him.

"No, I'd rather sit and relax."

The temperature was in the low eighties on the beach and the wind was blowing enough to make Ethan's untucked, button down, shirt fill with air. He was looking out towards the ocean with his hands in his pockets. I could tell he was thinking, wondering and imagining. I couldn't tell if he was worried though.

"Okay, let's sit then."

We sat.

I began, "Ethan, I know you know who Clark is. I don't know how you know, but you do. I want to tell you about him."

"I don't really want to hear it Evi or talk about it. I think I have all the information I need, and I probably know more than I should. You had every right to date someone, anyone. As to be expected, you dated a guy. He's still hung up on you. He'll get over it. The end."

"Okay," I said simply, but I still wanted to tell my side of the story, and I felt like Ethan was robbing me of that. I wanted to tell him because I had no idea what Clark had told him. So, I persisted. "Will you at least listen while I tell you a little bit about the few weeks we dated?"

"No Evi. I really don't want to hear about or talk about you spending time with another guy. You are with me now. You and I, we are meant to be. I don't need to think about you dating anyone else. It's irrelevant."

I respected his request and didn't say anything else. I wanted him to know that I had nothing to hide, but I restrained. I nodded and looked at the waves rolling onto the beach.

After a few moments, to my surprise, he asked, "I do have one question though. Will you answer me truthfully?"

"Of course Ethan, what is it?"

"Did you love him? I mean *really* love him? You said you two only went out for a few weeks. Right? I want to hear the truth."

This was not the question I wanted to hear. Okay, be honest, be honest. I searched my thoughts and emotions and answered.

"I hope this doesn't make you angry, but yes, I did really fall in love with him." Then I continued, "But it faded very quickly. No matter how hard I tried to commit to Clark, I couldn't because you are the only person I truly love. You are the one I have truly loved with all of my heart, since I was fifteen, for almost four years, etcetera, etcetera." I was trying to break the tension.

"For four years?" he asked seeming very surprised. "Four years Evi?"

"Yes Ethan. I've been in love with you for almost four years. I thought you knew that."

"No, I didn't know that!"

"Don't be mad, but, when we were sophomores, Brody told me that you said you want to marry me someday. I have held onto to those words for dear life since I was fifteen. That's why you going back to Hannah was so difficult for me. You have no idea how seriously hurt I was when I found out that you two got back together a couple of years ago. I was able to *act* like I didn't care, and after a while, maybe I didn't care as much anymore, but I was really devastated and felt betrayed for a long time. Brody stayed by me though. He was always rescuing me from my emotions and protecting me from myself."

"What's that supposed to mean?"

I think I struck a nerve by bringing his brother into the conversation. I didn't have anything more to offer though, so I looked at him and shrugged my shoulders.

"Evi, that morning when I surprised everyone by coming home for Spring Break, I saw Brody grab you and kiss you. I saw his reaction to you and Kieron holding hands. I saw the way he looked at us on the beach the night before you left to come here. I can't even count the times I've seen you draped over his back asleep in our basement. Tell me, do I need to be worried?"

"Everything you mentioned was all about you and my feelings for you. Brody grabbed me and took me to your basement so no one would see me cry over Hannah showing up. He begged me not to date Kieron because he knew how I felt about you. His expression that night on the beach, I guess was one of shock. He was probably mad at you because you still had a girlfriend. Finally, as for sleeping on his back, I don't know. I think Brody loves you so much that he protects me for you. He's just another brother to me."

Although, his eyes looked like they were focused on his hands, I could tell Ethan was picturing Brody in his mind. "So he keeps you close too huh?" he mumbled with a half smile.

I smiled.

"Evi, deep down I knew you probably liked me, but since I was leaving and you were still in high school, I just figured there was no point in us dating. I really don't think I would have ever gone back to Hannah if I had any idea how much you truly cared about me."

I felt like I was punched in the gut. Had we wasted the past four years? Why did he have to wait so long to come for me? I placed my chin on my shoulder and looked down the beach to my right. I stared into the distance imagining how different my life, our lives, would have been if we had been together those past few years.

"Ethan, can we just be done with this conversation? I can't dwell on what could have been if you weren't with Hannah, or if I would have been brave enough to tell you how I felt about you years ago. Thinking about you and Hannah carries me backwards. I feel like this is our life now. Let's just appreciate that we've been blessed to be friends these past several years, and now we can focus on being us! I already feel like nothing can ever come between us."

"Yeah. Okay. But please know, I believe you about Clark… and Kieron… *and* Brody. I trust you Evi."

Offering a very soft smile, I said, "I love you Ethan."

"Oh! I love you too Everclear, probably more than you know." He leaned over and softly kissed my cheek.

God I love the sound of his voice. I hooked my arm under his and leaned my head onto his shoulder. He kissed me on the forehead and then on the lips.

We sat for a while longer before we got up, walked a bit more, and drove back to the hotel.

Chapter 16

Late afternoon, Ethan and I arrived back at our room. Since we had gotten such an early start to our excursion, there was still a lot of time left in the day.

We took off our shoes and Ethan collapsed on the bed. I went to the window because I always do. I love staring at the outside no matter the view. I can even find something interesting about a parking lot or rooftop view. In that moment, people were going in an out of the ice cream shop across the street. People were chasing their children who were headed straight for the fountain in the park. People were sitting beneath trees on concrete benches. And, people walked along the pier looking out at the water.

My mind envisioned the lake view from Ethan's home in Ponderosa. The peaks kept their snowy caps well into the summer. The two views were so very different and both so very dear to me.

"I want more with you Evi."

Ethan's voice broke into my daydream. I looked over my shoulder at him.

Staring at the ceiling from where he was lying on the bed, he didn't look at me or make eye contact when he added, "I'm sorry if you aren't comfortable with that yet, but I want more. I only have one more year with you, and I don't want to miss a minute that we are able to have together. I want to be with you and only you."

At first, I heard "only one more year" ring through my ears and my soul. Then, I knew what he was asking. I let his words sink in. I said softly, "I want the same thing Ethan and I'm ready, but I need to know that we are forever. I have always known that you are my forever, but am I yours?" I almost felt like Ethan was already my husband, but I needed to hear him say he felt the same way.

"I want to marry you Evi. There's no question for me. I can't believe that I've actually wanted to marry you since I was seventeen years old. I know it so clearly now." He was still not looking at me.

"Then I'm ready."

Ethan turned over and faced me with a slightly surprised look on his face that was somewhere between "Oh boy!" and "Oh crap." I smiled at him because I didn't even think he realized that his expression was so full of... expression.

"I'm ready," I repeated it again so he had his reassurance from me.

There was too much love and too much passion between us to discuss it anymore. We made a decision. We were committed, so we didn't waste any time.

I walked on my knees to him on the bed, and he kissed me so sweetly. I swear if I hadn't known better, I would've thought that was *his* first kiss ever. It was like he was starving and couldn't get enough of me, and I must say, my feelings were right in line with his. His hands were moving from my face to my back, then to my face again. I just held onto his belt loops and pulled him towards me.

"Ethan, I don't know how to do this," I nervously whispered.

He whispered back, "You don't have to know anything. We work through this together. Just focus your eyes on mine. Okay?"

I nodded.

He whispered, "I mean it, look at me Evi."

Even though it was difficult, I did as he asked.

When our eyes were locked, Ethan took a deep breath, slipped the straps of my dress off of my shoulders, and he kissed me on my neck.

I looked into his eyes again and slowly unbuttoned his shirt. I pulled his shirt open, then slid it down his arms, dropping it onto the floor. I ran my hands up his arms to his shoulders, then back down his chest to his stomach. He was so perfect.

"Do you promise that we are forever Ethan? Do you promise?"

"Yes! I promise."

I smiled, placed my hands on his chest again, and pushed him down onto the bed. We laughed, and together we pulled back the sheet and blanket. Settled on the pillows, we resumed our passionate kissing as we finished undressing each other. Although he can melt me with one look and stop my heart with one touch, this process was much more mechanical than our encounter the night before, perhaps because we had a mutual goal in mind this time? Periodically, our eyes locked and I wondered what he was thinking. All I could think about was how much I wanted to be with him.

When we had finally positioned ourselves to make this commitment to one another, and the moment was upon us, I suddenly got so scared. I never planned on backing out, but I really needed a minute for my mind to run around the room twelve times. If you could have seen inside my thoughts at the moment I was lying there with him, you would have seen that half of me was peacefully saying,

"You're ready for this. You love him. You're okay." And the other half was screaming, "You can't go back after this Evi. You can never go back."

Ethan sensed my fear, therefore tried to hold me tighter. "Are you okay?" he whispered so softly.

"Yes, I'm okay."

Then with our lips touching he asked again, "Evi, are you sure you're ready?"

"Yes, I'm ready." Then another pause while I looked away and took a very deep breath.

I turned back to him. He wasn't afraid at all. How was he so sure through this? In my mind, we were making an eternal decision. He was so calm. I begged him, "Ethan, *please* say something. Please."

He took my head into both of his hands so carefully and pressed his lips on my ear. He was steady. His breath was the only thing in the world that existed, not our bodies, just his breath. He whispered "Everclear, will you marry me?"

I instantly relaxed. I thought, *This is my husband*. I wanted him. I kissed him.

"Ethan, I'm ready to close my eyes now."

He looked so intentional as he kissed me one more time. He nodded. I turned my head. He pressed his lips behind my ear. I grasped his shoulder with one hand and the back of his neck with my other. He *barely* whispered, "I love you."

I listened to him breathe while he made love to me. I remember nothing else but the sensation and the rhythm of his breathing. I was so focused on him, that I didn't feel like I was part of it.

I think that even though intimacy with someone is supposed to be about becoming one, I felt more separated during that time. Being in that position with someone is so personal that I couldn't help but feel uncomfortable, exposed, vulnerable, insecure.

Now this next part is very important, so listen carefully.

I keep saying we have moments that change us, moments we feel forever. Sometimes they're happy. Sometimes they're sad. This was another one of those moments in my life. Every human emotion I could possibly have had at the time was produced: birth, joy, fear, sadness, anger, death, hope, faith, *love*.

There is a reason that making love should be saved for marriage. I am only sharing this because someone out there may make a life changing decision based on my experience. So, here's my thoughts on why waiting is important…

At the end of our time together. I could never have imagined that I would ever love anyone on this planet more than I loved Ethan Parker, and I didn't. God, I loved him! But, within one minute, lying there, in bed with Ethan still on me, holding me, I turned my head to the side so I was facing away from him. I pulled the pillow beside me over my face and I cried so hard I couldn't even inhale. There was nothing in me but a grinding cry. I held the pillow tightly. I couldn't let go. I even screamed very silently in anger and frustration.

I can't even image what Ethan was thinking and I… didn't… care! This was my life, my decision. I had broken my most beloved promise to myself and I felt destroyed.

Ethan kept repeating, "Evi, it's okay. You're okay."

But I kept crying.

As I began to settle, he took the opportunity to take the pillow from me and throw it on the floor so I couldn't get it. Then he threw the other pillow on the floor. *Then,* he pulled the sheet down to our waists so I couldn't hide there either. He forced me to face him. I put my hand over my eyes and more tears fell. All I could think was, *I can't change this. I can't go back. I can't fix this. I can't undo this.* And then the dreaded, *What if he leaves me?* All of these words played over and over and over in my head and I thought, *This is why you were supposed to wait! This is it. You cannot undo this. You can never go back!*

However, Ethan was *not* going to let me do this to myself or to him, and he was certainly not going to let me destroy the moment that was ours to remember together forever. He gently clasped my wrist, pulling my hand from my face, and he pinned it down to the bed. He made me look at him.

"Evi, look at me. Look right at me. I told you to keep your eyes on mine."

I opened my eyes and cautiously looked at him while I tried to inhale.

"You're okay. I love you. I love you. I love you. You're okay." Then he kissed me, small little healing kisses.

I suddenly realized that I could be destroying him. Gasping for air and sniffling, I started kissing him back.

"Ethan, what have I done? What have I done?" I whispered in desperation.

"You made love to me Evi. *This* is forever. We are forever. This can never be changed, and I wouldn't ever want it to be changed. Allow what we've done, what we are, to sink in. Understand it. Embrace it. It's done." He rested his head on my shoulder.

How does he always know the exact words to say to me? It felt like a weight the size of the moon had been lifted off of my stomach. I could breathe again. Then, the beauty of the moment set in and I felt so good about, not the realization that I hadn't waited until I was married, but I *had* waited for him.

I looked at him and said in a quiet voice, "I guess you know just the right words to say to me because you've already been through this before."

He lifted his head and looked at me with surprise. "I've never been through this Evi... with anyone... but you. Everything I say to you, is because I love you. This is about you and me. This has nothing to do with anyone else! You have to know that. You are truly my only one and always have been."

I couldn't believe it! I was so excited, so happy, so relieved. *He's all mine!* I rolled onto his chest, my hair draping all over his face and I kissed him so passionately, a team of horses could not have pulled me away.

"I'm not okay Ethan, I'm good, really good. I love you too."

We relaxed for a few minutes. We were still wrapped up together but I was facing away from him, looking out the window at the blue sky. I started thinking about cloud animals, about pizza, about finals, and about how dang hot and muggy it was in our room. The windows around there always have condensation on them, and it was so hot.

Ethan asked, "Do you want to shower?"

"Yes, but not with you," I replied laughing.

"Okay, so do you want to shower *alone* then?"

"Yes, I do. I want to be alone. *Then,* I really want pizza. Then I want to dance."

"Sounds good."

While I went back to daydreaming and looking at the sky, Ethan got up and brought me my robe. I went into the bathroom and got in the shower. I tried not to think too much while in there. I was afraid I might begin crying again. This was a big day, no, this was a big moment.

Chapter 17

Pizza! A slice of heaven!

We chose a booth and sat on the same side together. Next to him, I felt like we were holding the most wonderful secret in the whole world. I was surprised that we were just talking and having a normal conversation after all we'd just experienced together. We talked about our routines, grades, classes, roommates, and friends. He took the opportunity to mention that he wouldn't be able to visit in May since he had surprised me that weekend. I didn't mind that at all.

During the entire conversation, I had a burning question for him that was sitting in the back of my mind. There was something I wanted to tell him, and it was serious. I was actually afraid of what he was going to think or say. Another reason people should wait until they are married to be intimate is… I blurted out my question, "Ethan, I've *never* had to think about what we just did. You know that. So, um, aren't you concerned about me getting pregnant?"

You see, a married couple has adult conversations before they put themselves in those situations. We did not. I didn't get pregnant that day, but there was a reason. That is not usually the case when people are as careless as we were with our emotions in that moment.

Ethan explained West Point's rules on marriage and pregnancy. He was simply not allowed to parent a child. It was sad, but made perfect sense. I kept telling myself, he doesn't really belong to you, and this is just one more reminder. He's married to something else, not someone else, and he was certainly not married to me.

Then, I told him, "Ethan, I started taking birth control pills in August before I ever left Ponderosa. You don't have to worry."

He looked a little shocked and a little irritated. He asked, "Why did you need to be on birth control pills Evi? And why didn't you ever tell me before now?"

"My mom and I talked about things like boyfriends and schedules and just the whole convenience of it before I left home. We decided it would be a good idea. As far as not telling you about it before now, I'm not really sure why. I have kept it a secret from everyone. I guess I didn't want to be judged."

His demeanor became a bit possessive, "Well, I'm not sure how I feel about that. Shouldn't we decide this together?"

"Ethan, it's taken care of; we don't even need to bring the topic up again. Would you rather us always be at risk of getting pregnant?"

"No! But, I don't like knowing that you made a decision like that without me. This is our life now Evi. I want to be a part of the choices that affect both of us."

"Ethan, I made the decision with my mother nine months ago!" I laughed, then added, "Look babe, it's done. I was worried about how you'd feel when I told you. Somehow, I knew you were going to be upset. There were times over the past few months I debated not taking them anymore, but I changed my mind each time, and now, I am so glad I did. It has worked out perfectly. There's no way I would ever let your career and all you are working so hard for be destroyed."

I knew there was more he wanted to say, about it. I realized he felt out of control. Ethan is someone who is in charge of situations. He was uncomfortable with the news, but he let it go and I was glad. I leaned over to him, he pulled me and kissed me several times. Then he simply said, "Okay, okay."

After that, the mood significantly lightened. We talked about June and made plans for our upcoming three weeks together. He knew the day he was going to be released for leave. I was going to be home two weeks before him so my schedule was irrelevant. We agreed he was going to tell his mom he'd be home on Saturday and offer no other details. She would want to get him from the airport, but he was going to tell her a friend was getting him. Mostly true. I would actually be picking him up from airport Friday afternoon. The airport's two hours from where we live so we'd get a hotel room, see a movie, have dinner, then have a relaxing morning before our drive up in the mountains to Ponderosa.

My parents trusted me completely, so I'd just tell them I was going to get Ethan from the airport and I'd be home Saturday. We laughed about how simple that was going to be for me. The only person in my life I'd have to handle was Jarren. We agreed that Jarren wouldn't judge me or Ethan, and he certainly wouldn't spend a second thinking about what we *might* be doing. Then, we laughed again.

After our pizza, our planning, and our serious talk, we were done, and I was ready to go dancing. I had my boots on and I couldn't wait to get moving. Even though I had just eaten a ton of pizza, I felt light as a feather and had the energy of a Jack Russell terrier in a wind tunnel with balls flying everywhere. I was so happy, and I knew Ethan sure was glad to see me happy after my meltdown a few hours earlier. We headed to The Venue to see if I was going to be able to get in.

On the way to the bar, we found ourselves face to face with Clark and his friends.

I greeted first. Casually but sweetly I said, "Hey Clark."

"Hey Evi. Hey Ethan." Clark replied clearly feeling betrayed.

"What's up Clark," Ethan added with caution.

I felt a need to explain myself, "Clark, Ethan and I went to high school together."

"I get it," he replied. Clark wasn't afraid to look directly at me. He never took his eyes off of me. It felt like in his mind, I was still his. He stared at me as if Ethan wasn't even there. He was the same confident guy I met on that street a few months earlier.

Then, time seemed to slow down. Clark reached for me, and just before he touched my hand, Ethan instinctively stepped in front of me. He very slightly shook his head at Clark. He was letting Clark know that I belonged with him.

I was surprised. Clark and I looked into each other's eyes for an instant before I had to turn away. I was afraid he'd read my mind and know all of my secrets.

Clark wasn't daunted though. He was angry, and before we walked away, he looked past Ethan and asked me, "So is Ethan one of the guys you said is just a *friend* Evi?" He stressed 'friend' like I had been lying to him.

Ethan looked at me. Clark's tone irritated me but my expression to Ethan let him know I could handle the situation.

"Clark, please don't do this. I don't have to justify myself to you."

"Then don't Evi!" Ethan insisted.

I continued anyway, "If it makes you feel better Clark, Ethan is actually the brother of one of those guys with whom I am *just friends*."

"Hmph," was his only response.

I knew he was hurt, but I also knew he was done.

I carefully squeezed Ethan's arm and pulled his hand to my stomach to let him know it was time to leave.

As we continued our walk, Ethan said to me, "You didn't need to tell him anything Evi. Who I am to you is none of his business. Don't you dare give him any power over you."

I defended myself, "Ethan, it's not what you think. He doesn't have power over me. I was not going to let him make me look like a liar or a tramp." That last word felt excruciating coming out of my mouth.

"How the hell does he know you spend the night at my house all winter anyway?"

"Well, he was pretty upset when I didn't call him the entire week I was home for Spring Break. I told him I was never alone because I was with my friends the entire week. I have nothing to hide, so I told him Kieron, Brody and I always spend nights together and that even our parents and brothers know about it. I told Clark you are one of the brothers so he wouldn't bother trying to turn you against me."

"Okay first, some ex-boyfriend of yours could never turn me against you. I'm above that. And second, your Spring Break story sounds too weird even for me Evi. I think your days of sleeping with Kieron and Brody are officially over don't you? Uh, it makes me sick to even put all of those words in one sentence. I guess I can see why Clark would have been angry about that."

I covered my eyes with my free hand and laughed. Ethan and I looked at each other with facial expressions that just acknowledged he's right and we smiled.

Ethan said, "I like that Clark just made my evening interesting. He kept me on my toes for a few seconds. I like him."

I didn't reply, I just thought about how I hated to see Clark hurt.

When we got to The Venue, a different guy was working the door, but he let me right in because he'd seen me there so many times. He assumed I was 21.

"Hi! I'm Evi! We've never met. What's your name?" I asked.

"I'm Trever, nice to meet you Evi."

"Yeah, you too. I'll see you around Trever," I said to him.

Ethan got carded, and we both giggled again like we had a secret.

"That guy wasn't even interested in knowing my name," Ethan said in a sarcastic voice.

"Well, just a hunch here babe, but I'm guessing that's because he can tell you don't live here. He's never seen you around before. By this time of year, if you lived here and went to school here, he would have seen you hundreds of times. Don't get your feelings hurt Ethan. You'll be okay!" I said laughing and yelling in a condescending voice.

He rolled his eyes at me and took my hand like he wanted everyone to know I was his. We kissed several times as we worked our way through the crowd. I loved how he walked close behind me and guided me with his hands on my hips. Ethan kept his body pressed against mine, every now and again wrapping one of his arms all the way around my waist.

As we shuffled along, I spotted Byron. He was working inside, so I ran to give him a big hug and a kiss on the cheek as always. He asked me, "So, you're with your new man tonight? You get everything worked out nicely? And please don't give me details, because I don't want to hear them, and I don't care?"

I replied, "Yes, thanks to you! Good enough?"

Byron gave a simple, "Yep."

I formally introduced him to Ethan, and we went dancing.

When we got back to the hotel that night, we showered, together this time. I was surprised at how easy it was to be natural with him. After showering, we went to bed. He rested on his back. I draped across him, and he wrapped his arms around me.

"I loved this day and this entire night with you Evi. Every minute, every word, everything we did together was perfect."

"Me too Ethan," I whispered.

"Evi?"

"Yes?"

"I even loved your reaction after we made love. You were so real. Thanks for not trying to hide your feelings from me."

I buried my face in his chest and moaned in embarrassment, "Ethaaaan, don't."

"I loved it and I love you." Then, "Evi?"

"Yes?"

"One more time before I leave tomorrow?"

I smiled and replied, "I'll be here, and I don't have any other plans."

A small laugh from him, a kiss on top of my head, and he whispered, "Night Hun."

"Night Ethan."

We went straight to sleep. It had been the longest day of my life, and to that point, the best.

Chapter 18

During the next few weeks, Ethan and I didn't talk much. I missed him desperately, but I needed to focus on school. Studying for finals kept us both distracted. In addition to finals, I had to pack my things in my dorm room and load them into my car. I was taking my car to my cousin's house in Florida so I could leave it there for the summer. Then, I was flying back to Idaho from there. I had lots to do. Ethan and I had a lot of work to do before we went back to Ponderosa. Knowing we'd be together soon was satisfying enough.

Jarren was home the first week that I arrived in Idaho. Our family went on a short camping trip, then we relaxed the remainder of that first week together. I told my parents and Jarren that Ethan had come to see me a couple of times in Charleston and that we were dating. I didn't offer any other details. My mom's input was that it was about time. My dad's, "I really don't want to hear about it." And Jarren's point of view was that he wondered if Ethan was ever going get the nerve to ask me out. I agreed with Jarren. I had wondered the same thing for years.

The second week I was in Ponderosa my schedule was full. One day, my mom and I traveled to Boise to shop. Several other days I spent time looking for a summer job. The remainder of the week I got to hang out at the beach and go hiking with Kieron and Brody. It was so nice and quiet in Ponderosa. I was realizing how much I missed my quiet, small town life. It was comforting to feel like my old self again.

Finally, the day came for Ethan to come home. I drove to the city to pick him up from the airport the last Friday in May. I arrived early so I could meet him as he exited the terminal. I wanted to take pictures of him for his mom. Since she wasn't there, I wanted to be able to text her photos, the next day of course.

Ethan was in his uniform. As he came walking so confidently through the glass doors toward the waiting area, I almost fainted. I literally felt light headed. I had only seen him in uniform once and that was when he was leaving me. Being there in that moment was the first time I had the feeling of seeing him coming *home* to me! I put my phone in my back pocket, ran to him and threw my arms around him. I hated, for just a second that I had stolen that moment from his sweet mom. However, the pure elation of being in his arms made me forget all about anyone except him.

Ethan dropped his bags and picked me up in a big bear hug. We held each other and kissed. When he put me down, I told him I had to take pictures of him for his parents, so he graciously posed for me. Before we left the airport, we had a stranger take a few photos of us together.

Ethan and I were staying in a hotel in a complex nearby that had a theater and restaurants. We went straight to the room so he could get changed. We stepped in, closed the door, and quickly enjoyed some time alone in each other's arms. When he released me so he could get ready for dinner, I slipped off my shoes and crawled onto the bed. I fluffed the pillows and stretched out. I turned onto my side, propped my head on my hand, and looked at him. Ethan was standing perfectly still, watching me, one eyebrow raised.

After a few seconds, Ethan put his hands on his hips and looked at the ceiling. He said, "Evi, you can't just lie there. Get up and go stand by the door."

"What? Are you crazy?" I laughed as I replied.

"No, I'm not crazy! There is no way I can stand to be in this room with you if you are going to be lying in bed like that staring at me."

With a puzzled expression, I gaped at him. "Seriously? You want me to stand by the door while you change? Are you really that modest Ethan?"

"Oh no! This is not about modesty at all. This is about getting you off of the bed or we aren't going to leave the room."

Butterflies fluttered in my stomach. "Oh." I blushed a little. "Well, what's wrong with spending time alone together before dinner?"

"Evi, I want to go to dinner first. We have all night to be alone babe. I can hardly wait."

"Why can't we be *alone* before *and* after dinner?" I asked in a very flirty tone.

"Evi, stop it. Get off of that bed and go stand by the door. Now! Please. I want to wait until after dinner so we have all night together. You're not making this easy." He looked expectant of my accommodating his request. I really liked his bossy side. It felt like a challenge.

"Fine Ethan. If me lying here on this bed is that *irresistible* to you, I'd hate to torture you for another second. But, I am going to watch you change your clothes."

I put my shoes back on and stood against the door dramatically acting like I was being held to it by restraints. He laughed at me and rolled his eyes.

Ethan started changing quickly. I was giggling at him losing balance and being so hurried. As he was putting his shorts on, he was moving so fast, I finally burst out laughing.

"What the heck is so funny Everclear?"

Barely able to speak through gasps for air, I yelled, "Ethan, I never, ever thought I'd be a girl whose boyfriend would be so adverse to being with her, that he's willing to actually put his clothes *on* his body like he's in a fast forward movie! My goodness, you can't seem to get dressed fast enough. I've always thought this scenario would be in reverse. I figured if I wanted to make love to you, like I do, you'd be taking your clothes *off* at this speed. If this weren't so hilarious, I'd probably be offended!"

Ethan was laughing too, "Evi, stop it! I just want to get to dinner."

"Geez, you sure are obsessed with dinner tonight." Suddenly a strange thought entered my mind, and before I could think about it I asked, "Ethan, you aren't going to break up with me tonight are you?" I was joking with him, but like I said, the thought did cross my mind.

"God no Evi! Would I be standing here half naked if I were breaking up with you? Don't be ridiculous. I love you. You know that!"

"Ah, just checking." I smiled and winked at him, but I was getting impatient.

"Ethan?"

He paused to look at me, "What now Evi?"

"I want you to know that I don't need a bed to make you want me. I can get you over *here* to me with one word." I smiled in a sly way.

"Evi, don't. Can you please just let me get ready?"

"Ethan, stand still and look at me." He had put his shirt on, but he hadn't buttoned it nor his shorts yet. He paused.

"Okay, fine Evi. I'll play. Let's see who is stronger."

I shifted my position against the door, arching my back, sliding one foot up, and pressing my hands flat on the surface by my sides. I whispered in a sultry tone, letting him know how much I truly wanted him, "Pleeease…"

He didn't hesitate. Ethan rushed over to me, dropped to his knees, lifted my shirt, and licked my stomach. His lips, tongue and hands moved up my body. He stood, then pressed every part of him into me as he kissed me. He pulled my leg up over his hip and I held on. My hands were inside his shirt gripped to his back.

Once I was so dizzy, I could hardly stand, he pulled back from me. Slowing his panting to even deep breaths he said, "That was a good word Everclear, but I'm stronger. You're going to have to wait. Besides, no matter how that turned out, I was going to be the winner." He literally grinned at me, stepped back, pulled my top down, and buttoned his own shirt.

I was dumbfounded, but able to laugh. I didn't try again to lure him, after all, he was right.

Since my mood had been shut down, I decided I should pressure him to hurry. "Ugh! Ethan, let's go. Didn't the Army teach you to get dressed faster than this?"

"You're killing me Evi! Stop it. I'd be dressed by now if you'd quit interrupting."

When Ethan was finally ready, we left the room and continued our evening.

At dinner, we made plans for camping trips and we talked about all the things we would do together at home that we had never done before. The month was going to be so weird, and so fun. Suddenly, it occurred to us both that no one knew we were seeing each other except my parents and Jarren. We had never told anyone else that Ethan had been coming to visit me in Charleston. We decided we'd tell everyone, but maybe save how serious our relationship had grown for some other time.

When we left the restaurant and got in my car, Ethan asked in a quiet voice, "Mind if we skip a movie Evi?"

I answered, "Of course not. Are you tired from traveling all day? Do you want to go back to the room?"

"No, let's drive downtown. There's a bookstore I want to go to before it closes."

"Okay," I replied quizzically.

His suggestion seemed out of the ordinary, but I was fully aware that we hadn't had a *normal* relationship to that point, so I figured he liked bookstores. Ethan drove us downtown because he knew right where he wanted to go.

The sun was still up since it doesn't set until almost ten p.m. in Idaho during the summer. The stores were open until nine. We had plenty of time for Ethan to shop.

We parked. He opened my door for me, and we walked the few blocks to the shop of his choice. The little store was tucked between a deli and a bakery in a historical brick building. It's long and narrow with hardwood floors, wooden shelves, and it had a high ceiling with dropped warehouse style light fixtures.

When we walked into the bookstore, we immediately parted and wandered in different directions. Since this detour was his idea, I gave him space while I browsed for a few minutes.

The clerk tapping on a keyboard caught my attention. I saw Ethan at the register. I meandered a bit more making my way to him. When I stepped to his side I put my hand on his lower back to wait for him to pay. I glanced at the book laying on the counter, and I saw something unexpected and surprising. It was a Bible. It was beautiful. My brow pinched and I opened my mouth to ask about it.

"I'll tell you in a minute," he said smiling.

"Okay," I quietly replied.

After his purchase was complete, we went outside. Ethan stopped me at the nearest bench and invited me to sit beside him. He opened up the Bible and took a pen out of his pocket. He signed his name on the "Records of Family Marriages" page.

I started shaking.

Ethan said to me, never losing eye contact, "My grandpa told me that in his day, people didn't need formal certificates to say they were married. Couples were married when they agreed to love only each other forever, when they agreed to love only each other for richer or poorer, when they agreed to love only each other for better or worse, in sickness and in health, and, most important, when they said these vows and made these promises before God. They sealed marriages by writing their names in their family Bible. This is now *our* family Bible."

He took out two rings, a gold band for him and a diamond band for me and said, "I know you remember, quite well, the last time I asked you to marry me Evi. It was the most important moment of my life and I meant it. I promise you, I meant it. That single moment is one I will never regret, and one I will *always* love more than any other. Now, I want to ask you again," he held the diamond band out to me, "Everclear Jordan, will you marry me forever?"

"Yes!" I replied in elation. Tears fell out of pure happiness.

Ethan put the ring on my finger, then he put on his own ring. After I signed my name in the Bible, he wrote the date, 25th of May, 2012.

"Evi, you know I can't legally get married. I'd be expelled from school, but I want you to know that my promises to love you truly are forever. As far as I am concerned we are married now, forever. Do you understand me?"

I couldn't speak. There was nothing for me to say except, "Yes." I wrapped my arms around his neck as we kissed.

I took the little black velvet bag from his hand that had held our rings and I put it in my pocket. I mustered up, "I'll keep the rings safe and with me everywhere I go Ethan, I promise. And, I will keep the Bible too." And that I did.

Ethan's insistence that we wait until after dinner to be together now made perfect sense. He was so thoughtful and loving. At that point in time, we had only been together twice. Thankfully, we had the whole night and the next morning ahead of us. We went back to our room and thoroughly enjoyed being alone. We made love again, and again, and *again* the next morning, as a married couple, at least in our minds. We had another wonderful secret.

I took Ethan to Ponderosa the next afternoon. We decided to act casual around his family. We knew Brody and Kieron would be at his house and would probably give me strange looks since I was their best buddy. I also knew Brody would want details, but I wanted Ethan to give that explanation this time.

Confidently, we walked into Ethan's parents' house together. As suspected, strange looks were sent my way courtesy of my two besties. No one asked why *I* was the friend who had picked him up, and I was glad, because I would not have had a response.

Everyone was so excited to see Ethan, they didn't bother to ask questions. They jumped up, gathered around and hugged him. I had had the past twenty-four hours alone with him, including a marriage, so I let myself out quietly.

Backing out of their front door, I stole one more glance at the man of my dreams. Ethan was watching me. He gave me the most beautiful smile and a wink. It felt like there were magnets in my heart pulling towards him. I felt like I was truly leaving my husband behind. It didn't seem fair. I managed to blow him a little kiss, then I closed the door.

The Parker's were having a party that night, so we both knew I'd be back soon. Ethan would have time to pose for photos, eat treats that his grandma baked him, and answer all of his mom's questions before all of their friends began arriving.

A nap was on my agenda. I went home for a few hours, slept, ate, and got ready for my first public evening in Ponderosa with my boyfriend, no husband, no boyfriend.

Assuming I had given the Parkers ample time to catch up and enjoy Ethan as a family, I returned to Ethan's house that evening a little before eight. I parked and instead of going to the back gate, I was going to enter through the front door. Walking down the sloped, circular driveway, I heard a car door shut behind me. I looked back and Kieron had clambered out of someone's car. My instinct was to wait for him to catch up, so I paused.

Though I probably should not have been shocked, I was.

"Geez Kieron! I can not believe you! You're drunk! You can't go into the Parkers' house like this. What is wrong with you?" I scolded him, but it was pointless. Not much of anything was going to be comprehensible to him in that state.

Kieron draped his arm over my shoulders and started mumbling something in my face about us being together or dating again this summer. I wasn't sure what he was saying, so I sort of laughed then turned my head away from him rolling my eyes.

That guy had no idea how much I had changed in the past ten months, heck the past two months. I put my arm around his waist to try to hold him up, but he started getting a little too affectionate with me. He was trying to wrap his arms around me. He started pressing his nose to my ear and my neck as he continued mumbling.

When he started kissing my neck and trying to kiss me, I yelled, "Kieron! You need to stop. You also need to call someone to come get you. You should not be here like this."

Even though he was crossing lines, I was still trying to hold him up. He was getting too heavy, and I wasn't going to be able to keep his hands off of me much longer.

I texted Ethan with my free hand, "Get out front. Hurry!"

Ethan didn't hesitate! He was fast. He ran out the door to the driveway, grabbed Kieron and commanded, "Let him go Evi! Move!"

Ethan was angry at first. However, once he realized how drunk Kieron was, he relaxed a bit and seemed more annoyed than anything.

As Ethan hoisted Kieron from under his arms I yelped, "Ouch! Kieron! What the heck? You jerk, let go of my hair!"

Kieron laughed and in a groggy, incoherent way, mumbled to Ethan, "I love her man."

"Let her go Kieron, and no you don't."

I peeled my entangled hair from between Kieron's fingers. He shifted his hold onto Ethan freeing me from his grip. Kieron and I never had an issue with personal space, so I wasn't shocked at him for grabbing onto me. I looked at Ethan and shook my head.

"Two sleeping bags huh Evi? Wise choice," Ethan said to me. I bent over and screamed a laugh. Smiling and shaking his head, Ethan said, "Oh Evi, you and your *emergencies*! You scare me."

"Well did this one count Ethan? I couldn't handle him on my own? He was sliding all over me, breathing in my ear, trying to kiss me, and apparently attached to my hair!"

"Yeah! I'll give you this one babe." Ethan laughed, but he has been trained for real crises, so my constant "Help me!" messages were very amusing to him.

Without much effort, Ethan got Kieron into the house and put him in one of their guest bedrooms. It was evident that Ethan was not inexperienced with Kieron's state. He whispered in such a big brother way, "Kieron, dude, sleep it off. I put a trashcan right here beside you in case you need it. I'll check on you in a little while."

Just as he was passing out, Kieron grabbed Ethan's arm, and although he thought he was whispering, he was not, he said, "Ethan, hey make sure no one gets near Evi. We're dating again. I think she's saving herself for me."

Ethan and I snickered, and I made a quiet gag sound. Kieron was out. Ethan turned to me, put his hands on my hips, and pulled my lower body tight to his. I placed my hands on each of his shoulders. He said, "No Kieron, she saved herself for me," and he kissed me so slowly. Oh, another kiss that left me wanting to climb all over him.

We heard a slurred voice from behind us mumble, "I heard that."

We stopped kissing and Ethan turned to him and said, "Good!"

Kieron was out.

Hoping no one would notice, we walked down the hall to Ethan's room, closed the door and locked it. Although, in the back of my mind, I didn't really care because we were married.

We leaned against the door, and I stood up on my tiptoes so I could be close to Ethan's face. I whispered to him, "Exactly one year ago, we stood alone in this room. It was the first time I had ever stood face to face, alone with a boy. Right here, in this very spot, you broke an innocent young girl's heart by telling her you loved someone else. You broke her heart when you told her she should go find the one who was going to love only her and pursue only her." I was teasing him at first, but unexpectedly, it hurt at the same time.

"Oh, *please* don't remind me of that Evi. Please don't," he whispered and couldn't look at me.

"I'm sorry, but I have to know, did I find my one?"

"Of course you did. I'm so glad you waited for me. The instant you touched me that night, I knew without a doubt, that I was going to come for you. I just didn't know how or when. I'm here. We're here."

"Okay. I love you."

"I love you too."

Ethan bent down, scooped me into his arms, and carried me to his bed. He slid his hands up my skirt, but I wiggled away from him smiling. I wanted him, but he needed to be stopped. I reminded him, "Ethaaan, you have guests. This is going to have to wait a few more hours. Besides, we need to figure out how to have time alone now that we're home. I don't want to be with you in your parents' house *or* in my parents' house. It feels so deceitful."

Ethan whispered while kissing my neck over and over again, "Okay. We'll wait until we're alone. I think we'll be spending a lot of time down on the beach, and I know we'll be camping a lot over the next three weeks!"

I giggled, wrapped my legs around him and agreed wholeheartedly.

We went out and joined the party and had a great night with all of our high school friends. We ate, played games, sat by the fire, and slid down the hill to the beach.

Everyone figured out at Ethan's party that we were dating. After all, we couldn't keep our hands or lips off of each other.

Those three weeks we spent in Ponderosa, Ethan and I camped as many times as we possible so we could be alone. We hiked. We fished. We played in the rivers. We soaked in the hot springs. It was wonderful simply enjoying one another. We slept in two sleeping bags… which we zipped together of course.

We loved our camping trips because we wore our wedding rings when no one else was around. Otherwise, they were always with me, either in a pocket or in a purse. I didn't go anywhere without our rings. Every minute of the three weeks we spent together was perfect.

Chapter 19

The summer was dreadful once Ethan went back to New York. I got a part-time job and really didn't do much of anything. Since my parents were helping to pay for two college tuitions, there was no vacation money that summer.

The next school year with Ethan flew by. He came to visit me in Charleston and I even went to visit him several times in New York. I could write a book on just the New York trips alone. Our relationship was strong. We were happy. The weekends and holidays that we got to spend together at home during Thanksgiving, Christmas, and Spring Breaks were perfect.

We wore our wedding rings when we were together, and we pretended that his fourth and final year at West Point wasn't going to end. He was to be commissioned right after graduation. We had no idea what was going to happen after that. We just knew he was bound to a five-year commitment in the army.

Upon graduation, Ethan would finally be free to legally get married, but I still was only a sophomore and had two years of college left. I figured we'd work it out and be able to keep our routine of spending the occasional weekend together. I couldn't even think about this being our life together for the next five years though. I didn't know what we would have to deal with in the future, but I was willing and ready to face it, because I had him and I knew I had his heart forever.

I'm not intentionally trying to skip an entire year with him. I am just trying to stick to the big moments in our relationship for you. Our first few months together were so wonderful and we had so many important moments together, I felt sharing those would give you a perfect sense of how much we meant to each other.

The first weekend in April of my sophomore year Ethan came to visit me in Charleston. It was a surprise visit like his visit had been exactly a year earlier when he asked me to marry him… the first time. He took a cab to my dorm, and we drove my car downtown. We checked into our favorite hotel, went to our room and put our things down. Ethan was very quiet and he wouldn't sit down. I was preparing myself for him to tell me about his post graduation plans.

Ethan stood in front of me almost at attention. His posture was straight. His hands were in fists by his side. It was the first time since I had met him that I was starting to get scared. Ethan looked like he was trapped between completing an assignment and wanting to back out of whatever he was about to do.

He stood straight. Then he slouched a bit and looked at me. He stood up again and looked over my head at the wall.

"I have never lied to you. I have meant every single promise I've ever made to you and I will keep my promises. My feelings will never change for you. I need you to trust me." He paused, then continued, "I have six weeks left of school, then I go to work. I will be adjusting to a new life with new responsibilities. In order to do my job effectively and safely, I need to focus all of my attention on my duties. This year for us is now over. I will be returning to New York, and I will not be revisiting you here or at home. I do hope you will try to understand why I have to do this, just for now."

Staring at him like it was a joke I said, "What? What did you say Ethan?"

"I told you a year ago that we would only have one year together and this year is now over. I will be going to work in a few weeks. I must prepare for my final weeks of school, and I need to concentrate on my duties."

I looked down at the floor and then back at him, "Are you serious Ethan? Surely you're not serious. Have you met someone else or did you go back to Hannah again? Ethan, did you go back to Hannah?! There's no way you would just leave me otherwise."

"I have made promises to you, and I will keep those promises. I assure you I am not seeing anyone else."

As I sat quietly for a few moments, suddenly I was aware that he was telling me with his speech that I was *his* distraction from his life. It occurred to me, again, while he was trying to explain his reasoning that he was married to something else.

Ethan was strong. He didn't cry. He was one hundred percent a soldier when he broke up with me. I didn't even feel like I knew him. I was in such shock. I was reading his body language as he stood in front of me and I recalled his words and tone of voice. He was unemotional, cold, detached, not mine.

"This can't be happening. This cannot be happening. Ethan, look at me! Look at me! Do not leave me!" I tried commanding him without tears. I tried speaking in a voice to which he could relate.

I sat stoic staring at him. I was waiting for him to change his mind, apologize, say something. Dumbfounded and shocked, I just stared.

When he couldn't take my glare any longer, or perhaps he could no longer talk himself out of staying strong, he turned and placed his room key on the dresser. Still, without making eye contact he said, "I have booked this room for you for the entire weekend anticipating you may need to be alone after receiving this information."

As he walked toward the door, I ran in front of him to block him from leaving. "You're not leaving Ethan. You're not leaving me like this. I don't care about your job! The point of a marriage is to face everything together."

"Evi, move, I've made my decision."

"You don't get to make this decision for both of us Ethan! We are more than just two people who have dated for a little while. We are married. You promised me this marriage is real. This is not a relationship you get to just walk away from without considering my feelings too."

"I have considered your feelings. If I thought this was going to be too hard for you, I wouldn't be here. You will be fine Evi. I will keep my promises."

"Well you're breaking your promises by leaving me!"

"Evi, please move. You are making this more difficult than it has to be on both of us. You and I both need to face that I have to go to work. I have a job to do. Every minute with you makes my commitments harder for me."

I knew if I could get him to sit and talk to me, he would change his mind. When he reached for me, to move me from in front of the door, I slid to the floor, sat and put my head on my knees.

"No Ethan, you don't get to decide this for us."

He stood staring at the door. I leaned my head back and began to cry. "Ethan, I waited almost four years for you. Please don't let this be it. I gave you everything and you've taken everything from me. Please don't make me regret how much I've loved you for the past four and half years. I'm not strong enough for this."

"Evi, this isn't it. This is just for now. I will keep my promises. And you are strong enough. I'll love you forever. You will always be the only one I love. Please believe me. Trust me, but I cannot be with you and do my job."

"So I am nothing more than a distraction to you Ethan? Nothing more? You've just been stringing me along *again*!? You promised me you would never hurt me again! When we sat on your beach before I moved here, you held me while I cried and cried and cried for you. You promised me you wouldn't hurt me like that again Ethan!"

He looked away. I could tell he was trying to find a way to soften my words and ease my hurt and disgust. He had no words to offer.

I broke his silence, "Fine Ethan, I'll move, but if you decide to leave me, if you walk away, you will be ending us forever. I will find someone who won't leave me for an ex-girlfriend or for a job!"

I crawled to the side, rested my head on my knees again and cried uncontrollably. I knew he was going to go, and I couldn't watch him leave.

Before he left, I sat and prayed he would stay. I prayed he would come to his senses. I prayed he would fix this, he would love me. I prayed he would just touch me. But he didn't. He opened the door and walked out.

The slow motion of the door closing halted. I felt hope. Ethan pushed it open with one hand. "Evi," he said calmly. I looked up at him and for the first time he was looking right into my eyes. With sincerity he said, "I love you. I will keep my promises. You have to trust me. Wait for me Evi." He paused, "And Evi, I'm not worried about you. I would never have the strength to do this if I didn't trust you." Then he completely broke me. He handed me his ring and said, "Keep this please."

The door closed; I screamed and kicked it.

I was so hurt and so angry. I sat and I cried a lot, nonstop. I was that girl, or should I say one of those girls who let a guy get too close and who really paid the price. This happened. I broke my promises to myself, and he left me.

In the midst of my excruciating heart break, I had one moment where I had to decide that I was not going to ever regret my decisions. They were a part of me and even though he left me, our decisions meant Ethan would always be a part of me too. However, for that time, I had done something I promised myself I would never do, and I had to pay the price, in tears.

Curled up on the bed, I cried until I couldn't breathe. After a few minutes, I reached for my phone and texted Piper to come stay with me. I didn't want to be alone.

"I'm in room 212 at the King Charles Inn. Please come quick. Ethan broke up with me."

"Be there as fast as I can," she replied.

I hung up the phone, and as I placed it on the bedside table, I realized I was holding Ethan's ring. I took my ring off and squeezed my hand closed. I walked across the room to get the bag I always kept them in from my purse. I dropped the rings into the bag, pulled the satin ribbons to close it, and zipped them in the pocket of my purse. Hunched over, I went back to the bed and continued crying.

Within about ten minutes there was a knock on the door. I was still crying inconsolably when I opened it.

Clark! I didn't ask any questions. I knew exactly how he ended up at my door. I looked at him and barely pushed the words out through short gasps for air, "I … can't… breathe. He left me. He left me."

Clark grabbed me around the waist and closed the door behind us. Then, he picked me up and carried me to the bed. He put his arm under my neck and he wiped my cheeks with his other hand. I pressed my face into his neck and shoulder and I cried. I screamed. I cried more.

Several unchanging minutes passed with him holding me and stroking my hair. Finally he said, "Evi, breathe. Calm down. Breathe." I was still not talking, but I was slowly calming down. I was so glad he was there with me. My best friend had showed up. He had never hurt me. He was there for me.

"I'm here. I will fix this Evi. You are going to get better. You will heal."

"I can't Clark, I can't. You don't understand. He left me. Forever. He's not coming back for me. He doesn't want me." Then I cried out loud again just saying those words.

"Evi stop," he gently insisted.

"You don't understand. He left me!" I kept repeating it.

Suddenly, Clark understood.

"Evi! Did you sleep with him?!" he yelled at me. "Did you?" He grabbed my face and turned me so I had to face him. He moved my hair to the sides so he could see my eyes, but I wouldn't look at him. "Did you?!" he pressed once more.

I nodded.

Clark got up and pounded on the wall with both fists. I crawled off of the bed and stepped towards him, but he turned away. He paced with his hands on his hips in anger and disbelief. He yelled, "How could you do that?"

I stumbled and leaned my back against the wall. He moved to me when he saw me slump over. With each hand on one of my shoulders, Clark gently braced me against the wall behind the door to keep me from falling to the floor. Carefully, he eased his body fully to mine and pressed me against the wall.

Once he had me secured he asked, "Evi! How could you do that? You know you can't handle that. I know you can't handle that. Look at you. Look what he's done to you!"

"He said he loved me Clark. He said he loves me." More tears fell.

"If he loved you, he wouldn't have done this to you. He has known for four years that he has other commitments. If he was not going to include you in his plans, he should have never done this to you."

"He loves me," I repeated as I continued trying to convince myself that Ethan did truly care.

Clark said again, "I will fix this Evi. You are going to get better. You will heal." Then he added, "We will heal. I'll make sure of it."

I suddenly realized that I had hurt Clark deeply twice. The first time was when I broke up with him, and the second time was when he had to face what I had done. I was weakening and getting tired. My tears were drying up. I was exhausted.

Clark put his hands back in my hair so he could turn my face toward him again. Without any provocation or notice, he kissed me, passionately. He took our first kiss. I didn't move. I couldn't think. He stopped to let me breathe. He looked into my eyes to see my reaction, then he kissed me a second time. Once again, he stopped to let me breathe. Looking at me, he was asking with his gaze if he was okay. I stared at him briefly, and we kissed once more, but this time slowly, with my hands placed softly on his shoulders. I didn't fight him, or push him, or get angry with him. I invited him lightly pulling him toward me. I was beat. I had been crushed, destroyed. I needed his comfort and I needed to sleep.

Clark looked at me and put his head on my chest just under my chin so he could take a breath. Then, he reached for the top button of my shirt. I grabbed his hands forcefully, jerked them away from me and said, "NO!"

Not releasing his hold on the button, his eyes raised from my shirt to mine and he whispered, "You have to trust me Evi. You know you can trust me."

I released my grip on his wrists and he unbuttoned a few more buttons. He put his hand in the middle of my chest to feel my heart beat, just as I had placed his hand there many times before. With his hand pressed on me, he looked into my eyes and didn't speak. His eyes had so much to say. I knew his thoughts like I know him. He forgave me.

Very close to my lips he whispered, "Your heart is going to beat for me again Evi. I promise. It's already starting to now. I will help you heal from this. I mean it, we are going to heal together."

With his hand still on my heart, he kissed me several times on my neck, my chest, and my lips again. My flesh absorbed his touch like it was being quenched. I took a deep breath, wrapped my arms around him and exhaled. Then, as if by instinct, my ankle wrapped around his calf. He looked down at our legs and back into my eyes. I knew he was waiting to see what I was going to do next. I held onto him, nothing more.

After a few minutes of us figuring each other out, I said to him, "I just want to shower now Clark. Will you get me some ice so I can soak my face?"

"Yes."

"Clark,"

"Yes?"

"Will you stay with me tonight?"

"Yes."

"And tomorrow night?"

"Of course babe. I don't ever plan on leaving you."

How did he feel like home to me? He was my best friend.

I took a very long shower. I knew there would be more tears, lots more tears, but I was feeling a little better and a little hungry.

When I got out of the shower, I wiped the steam from the mirror and stared. A bucket of ice was on the counter. The curtain was closed behind me, so I knew Clark couldn't see me standing there in just a towel.

"Clark, will you get my blue and white fleur de lis bath robe from my suitcase please?"

"Your what?"

I giggled, "Just get my blue and white robe please!"

He handed it to me without opening the curtain and I put it on. I stood again in front of the mirror. I brushed my teeth and shook my hair out. I added water to the ice bucket and soaked a washcloth in the cold water.

"Clark, you never leave me alone for this long. And, you are never this far from me. What are you doing?"

"I'm just thinking Evi. Just thinking and letting you get yourself together. A lot has happened. I need to process it all too."

His voice was so sad. I felt like he was disappointed in me. He sounded like he had been hurt too and was trying to figure out how to save us both. I think he was in disbelief and felt like his own dream had died with mine.

I opened the curtain and sat on the floor. I leaned against the wall, lain my head back and put the cloth over my eyes.

"Clark will you come sit by me? I'm too tired to move."

Without saying a word, he slid his back down the wall and sat. Clark scooted next to me so our hips were touching. He put his arm between my legs and his hand rested on my knee so I knew he was there. I wasn't his, but he had taken a very small part of me that up to that point belonged only to Ethan.

I took the washcloth off my face and looked at him. His gaze was focused on the ceiling. I leaned and softly kissed him on his lips to say thank you and I'm sorry. He squeezed my knee and placed his other hand on my cheek. Then, he pulled me and kissed me back, a deep, slow, meaningful, forever kiss.

Clark softly said with conviction, "Please don't misunderstand my intentions Evi, I'm not here to help you get over another guy. I'm here to take you back. I've always known you belong with me."

I love Ethan, but is it possible that I still love Clark too? I thought to myself.

Confident and loving, Clark looked determined. A half smile, accompanied by one raised eyebrow, appeared for only a second before he leaned his head back and looked up at the ceiling again.

I stared at him. He was so unlike Ethan. His style so different. Ethan was powerful, strong, intelligent, level headed, rugged. Clark was smooth, clever, affectionate, forth-coming, accepting. Two perfect men had entered and parted from my life. One of them had returned.

I placed the cloth over my eyes again and processed Clark's words and his presence.

"Clark?"

"Hm?"

"I'm hungry."

He laughed quietly and said, "Well there's food to be had Evi. You will get fed. I'll make sure of it. I'm here."

Not wanting to waste anymore time, I pulled myself up and reached for his hands and pulled him up. Without asking him to leave the room, I discreetly got dressed and we shuffled off to eat with his hand placed securely on my lower back.

Clark did stay with me those two nights. We slept in the same bed but apart. I won't embellish the truth. I spent the weekend with Clark crying. When my tears fell, he would stroke my hair to comfort me and help me stop crying. He didn't push me in any way to heal faster. He accepted me and let me get the feelings of despair and betrayal out of my system.

Sunday morning came and it was time for us to get back to our lives. Clark drove me home. I was too embarrassed to go back to my dorm and cry there, so I sucked it up when other people were around. Piper and my girlfriends all knew that I was basically experiencing a death. They took care of me on some days and gave me my space on others.

Clark gave me every spare moment he had for the following month. He healed me. He was able to make me feel happy again over time. There were more tears, but never as severe as at first. I wasn't over Ethan. I thought about him, but I knew every thought was pointless. I had to go back to suppressing all emotions as far as he was concerned. I put Ethan back into his hiding place deep in my heart, right where he had been since I was fifteen. As long as I didn't talk about him, I could pretend I was getting over him or pretend I *was* over him.

Ethan went back to school, and he graduated without inviting me or calling me. He got commissioned and went to work. The way I understood it, as a cadet you hope to receive a deployment, something about getting promoted if you have actual ground combat experience. I didn't really understand it very well. Being the brilliant and mighty Ethan Parker that he was born to be, Ethan ended up being assigned a deployment to the middle-east. The news terrified me and I was often in a state of disbelief that he never called me or even tried to contact me, but I guess it made getting over him a little easier. I just kept telling myself that he really didn't love me That in turn made it easier to be closer to Clark.

Chapter 20

Classes ended the first week of May, but I decided to stay in South Carolina with Ginger for a few weeks. I wasn't sure if I wanted to go home to Ponderosa for the summer, or if I wanted to find a job and stay in Charleston. After a few weeks of searching for a job and looking for a place to live, the decision was made for me. I went home.

Clark and I were seeing each other, but we weren't in a serious relationship. He returned to Atlanta and I missed him. Clark was keeping me preoccupied, and I really enjoyed the time we spent together. I was still suffering on the inside and missing Ethan so much it actually hurt to stand or breathe on some occasions. I believe I was pretty good at hiding my true feelings most of the time now though.

The final week of May, I returned to Ponderosa. The manager of the clothing shop I had worked for during the previous summers hired me back. I worked through June and into July.

One late afternoon in mid-July, I left work and walked into the hustle and bustle of our streets. Living in a year-round tourist town numbs you to busyness and scurrying people. The shop where I worked sat up on a hill and our entrance was atop a set of steps. The day was bright, warm, and exactly like every other summer day. After scanning left, then right toward Lake Everclear, I descended the concrete steps. When my attention lifted from the placement of my feet, Clark was standing in front of me! I could not believe he was really there. He had to have gone to a lot trouble to get to me. Clark of course knew my home address because he had sent me cards and little gifts throughout the summer, but I never expected to see him in Ponderosa.

The only way I can describe my feelings at that moment is to say I slowly exhaled and felt like I could sleep for a week. As soon as I saw him, I realized I had basically been holding my breath for months. I carried so much tension in my chest, it hurt all time. Once again, my best friend showed up and he was there to hold me.

Clark hugged me and kissed me on my neck, then on my cheek, then on my lips. I could finally inhale fresh air. I was so happy to see him. I kissed him back pulling him to me over and over again.

"I missed you so much Clark. So much!"

After a few more minutes of our intimate turned playful embrace, I jumped back from him, and as if he'd been with me all along, I said, "Come on, let's go walk on Idaho's version of the beach!"

"Okay," he replied smiling, clearly relaxed and confident in his decision to come see me.

My hometown is so small that the waterfront park is only a block from where I worked. We reached the beach and immediately sat in the sand. I hooked my hand through his arm and put my head on his shoulder.

"So this is Lake Everclear? The lake you were named for?" Clark asked looking out at the scene before us.

"Yep. What do you think?"

"You were right, it is amazing here. It may be one of the most beautiful things I ever see. It's like a picture every direction I turn. It's July and the temperature is perfect. The lake is so clear, it's like a mirror. The reflection of the mountains that surround it looks so real. I can't believe people actually grow up in places like this."

"Well believe it. I've lived in this state my whole life and was pretty much raised in this town. It's very small though, so everyone knows everyone. You can hardly take five steps without running into someone you know. I was so ready for a big city like Charleston and the actual beach!"

"Yes, I guess I can see why you'd want to leave, but this would be hard to leave permanently." He was in awe.

I asked, "Why are you here? Certainly you didn't come just for the view."

"Before I tell you why I'm here, I have to ask," he paused and seemed nervous, "Evi, this is a small town, have you seen or spoken to Ethan?"

I answered in a reassuring and definitive voice, "No Clark. He was sent overseas right after his graduation. It's really over with him and I'm not surprised."

I decided to fill Clark in on my epiphany of my past with Ethan. "Clark, Ethan never really wanted me permanently. Our, so called relationship goes back to when I was only fifteen and he was seventeen. I never told you about him when we were dating because, I guess deep down, I always knew there was nothing to tell." I looked toward the water, then back at him and continued, "Ethan was never truly committed to me. He had a serious girlfriend for five years. I see now that I was just someone he dated in between his breakup with her and his deployment." I had been telling myself this since he handed me his ring. It was the only way I could get over him. I concluded, "It was never real Clark."

"Evi, it happened, so it *was* real. You seemed pretty serious and he seemed pretty serious too. I want and need you to be sure because... I came here to get you."

"Get me? What's that supposed to mean?"

"I'm here to take you back Evi. I've moved into my parents' condo in Oceanside and I want you to come live with me for the rest of the summer. School starts in six weeks and I don't think we should waste a minute. I'm living in a three bedroom condo alone, and everyday you are all I can think about. There is absolutely no reason for you to say no."

"Well, moving in with a guy is a huge reason to say no Clark, and not having money or a job are two more big reasons to say no."

"You'll have your own room, you can easily find a job nearby, and you won't have any living expenses. You will only need to buy food. Everything else you earn, you can save."

We were still sitting with his hand on my knee and I was holding onto his arm as if it were my lifeline. I couldn't take my eyes off of his.

"Evi, you need to come with me. We need to be near each other. I can tell how happy you are to see me. I can feel how relieved you are that I am here. You know you need to be with me right now too."

He pulled my legs over his lap so we were facing each other and he continued pleading his case. "You are almost twenty-one Evi. It is no accident that we met and that we are together. You believe in God having a hand in everything and so do I. You can't deny that what we have is special. We are meant to have this time together."

"I'm not sure I can make a decision in a few minutes Clark. I need to think about it."

"You don't need to think Evi. Let's do this." He kissed me like we were alone somewhere, then he said, "I'm not leaving without you." He kissed me again.

"Evi?"

I looked behind us.

Clark still had his hand on my face. I squeezed it as I slowly moved it down.

"Um, hi…" I couldn't think clearly for a moment. I wasn't afraid, I was just startled and caught off guard.

Clark saw my confusion. He kissed me on my forehead and jumped to his feet from his seat on the sand. He walked toward the person with his right hand extended. In his deep, polite Southern drawl, he said, "Hey, I'm Clark Ravenel, and you are?"

"I'm Brody, Brody Parker."

"Hey Brody, it is really nice to finally meet you. I have heard so much about you. Everclear here speaks very fondly of you quite often."

"Clark, it's nice to meet you too," Brody responded shaking Clark's hand.

I got up, walked to them and stood very close to Clark. He placed his left hand on my waist and pulled me. I put one arm behind his back and my other hand on his stomach. He kissed me on my temple.

"Brody, this is Clark. Clark this is Brody." I managed an introduction.

"Where you from Clark?" Brody asked politely.

"I'm from Atlanta, but I'm attending the Citadel in Charleston right now. Evi and I live only a few minutes apart."

I wondered if Ethan had told Brody anything about his encounters with Clark over the past year. I wasn't sure if Brody was just making small talk or if he really didn't know about Clark.

I asked casually, "Brody, what are you doing down here at the public beach? This isn't your usual hangout."

"Well, it's not your *usual* hangout either Ev," he replied with propriety.

I smiled and shook my head. Our mutual exchange was that we were usually at *his* house.

Not wanting to exclude Clark, I spoke up, "Yeah, I just got off of work and Clark was here to surprise me. So, we walked here to this beach to sit and enjoy the view and the fresh air for a little while."

"Everybody likes surprises. You sound like a nice guy Clark."

Clark raised his eyebrows, smiled and said, "Well, I try."

"So Brody, what's up?" I asked.

"Oh, some of my friends from school are up here staying with me for the weekend, so we took our boat over there to the marina to grab something to eat. I was just running to the bank real quick when I saw you two sitting here. I *had* to say hello." Brody offered a silly grin.

Clark spoke up, "You live on the lake huh?"

"Yep. You can see our house from here." Brody pointed around the edge of the lake to where their house is located.

"Wow! Beautiful." Clark complimented.

I knew Clark was just absorbing information. He wasn't intimidated at all. He comes from a family with a lot of money too so he would not have been comparing assets with anyone.

"Thanks man," Brody said civilly. Then he added, "Hey, so, I gotta run Evi. Clark, it really was nice to meet you. Um, Evi, can I talk to you alone for a minute?" Brody shook Clark's hand, nodded his head motioning for me to join him, and stepped away.

I made an annoyed facial expression at him, then looked to Clark. He placed his open hands on my back below my waistline barely above *PDA* considerations. He pulled me. I kissed him and whispered, "Do you mind? I'm actually very curious to hear what the heck he has to say to me."

Clark and I giggled a little as we kissed. He said, "Go. I'm fine. I'll enjoy the view for a few more minutes. Oh, but, I'd like an answer when you come back."

I kissed him again and said, "Mmm, I'm glad you're here."

I walked over to Brody with a flood of emotions. I wanted to run into his arms. I wanted advice only he could give. I wanted to punch him because for the second time in our friendship I was noticing he looked exactly like Ethan! I held myself together and very confidently said, "So my dearest, most loving and obviously protective best friend, what is so urgent that it can't be said in a few hours when you call me? Because I *know* you will not be able to stand not calling me tonight."

He laughed and kissed me on my forehead.

"Oh, I can still do that right Ev? Mr. Handsy over there won't get mad will he?"

"Brody! Control yourself. You don't have to be a jerk. What do you want?" I asked growing irritated.

"Evi, are you doing the right thing by dating this guy again? I know all about you and Ethan. I know everything. Ethan just left a month ago. He loves you. Seeing you with this guy, seeing him touch you and kiss you, it all makes me sick."

"Ethan left *me* three months ago!" I raised my voice furious that Brody would bring that up. "You obviously got one side of the story Brody. I haven't spoken to you at all about Ethan and me because I didn't know that Ethan has apparently been so open with you. But Brody, he broke up with me... for good! It's over."

"Evi, I know everything and probably more than even you know. You should not be dating anyone. You need to be patient and wait. Ethan trusts you."

"If you'll recall, you were the one who tried to convince me to get over him for two years! So now that I am finally doing what I should have done in the first place, you've decided I should go back to waiting for him again?"

"Evi, things are different now. You can't deny that. Look, I'll call you later. I'm just trying to help. I'm not going to tell Ethan about this. Please don't screw things up. I like having you in my life. I actually *love* you. Uh, I hate you for making me say that!"

I laughed hysterically at his disgust when saying that word. He grabbed the back of my head and kissed me one more time. Then, very softly, he whispered something in my ear that almost did force me to punch him, "Evi, read your *Bible*."

With his hand still holding the back of my head and our faces merely inches apart, I clasped his wrist and said, "Brody, I'm not going to react to that because I wouldn't be able to control myself if I did. Don't you *ever* say that to me again." I looked down, then back into his eyes, "Clark makes me happy. We make each other happy. He's my home now. But Brody, even as deeply as you just hurt me, please know, I'll always love you too."

We released each other and turned away without exchanging any more words. Brody wasn't apologetic. However, remorse reflected in his eyes. His mind game backfired.

Spine straight. Smile on. I walked to Clark completely aware that he never took his eyes off of us. He spoke first. "Evi, I'm not ignorant. I know who that guy is. Geez, he looks exactly like his brother. Not knowing them very well, it took a second glance for me to realize that he isn't Ethan."

I didn't respond. I just looked at him lovingly.

He continued, "Be honest with me; did Ethan always know how close you two apparently are, and was he trying to get you to stop seeing me?"

"Yup and yup! My relationship with Brody never bothered Ethan at all until he and I dated. Then," I smirked, "Ethan said he was one hundred percent on your side when it came to me spending nights with Brody. He ended that."

"Well, I'm thankful to Ethan for his interference. As for Brody, I figured he was over there lecturing you. So Evi, I'd like an answer."

I looked at him, then looked out at Lake Everclear. I thought about spending the summer in Ponderosa and I thought about waking up at the beach every day. Then, I thought for a moment about how Ethan would feel about me living with Clark. I remembered Ethan saying he would keep his promises and he trusted me to keep mine. Finally, I remembered telling Ethan when he left me, that if he walked out the door, I *would* find someone else.

"I'd love to move to Oceanside with you Clark."

He kissed me.

I added, "I can't wait to do this in our new home. For now though, I know a place where we can be alone for a little while."

His eyes lit up. He smiled. He kissed me harder.

We left Clark's rental car parked in town and I drove us just a few miles away to a dirt road that follows a small river. Summer time made finding an uninhabited location a bit more difficult, but since it was a weekday, I was able to find a small sandy spot by a creek. We took a blanket from my trunk and made ourselves comfortable in the shade. Clark and I removed our shoes and stretched out on the blanket. The depth and sincerity of his love for me was undeniable. We remained in each other's arms for a couple of hours. Of course, once I got hungry, it was time to go.

Clark and I went to my house. My mom had dinner ready, and I was overjoyed to introduce him to my parents. During dinner, we explained calmly, together, that I would be moving back to South Carolina with him. I assured my parents that they did not need to worry about this decision. They could trust me and they could trust Clark. He was very reassuring as well when explaining that we were certainly going to have separate rooms and we would be roommates for six weeks. Clark was very successful at winning them over. He was such a gentleman and so very genuine.

The truth, I don't think they were too thrilled. After all, there was no mistaking nor hiding our feelings for one another. However, they told me they trusted me and gave us their consent.

After rearranging my end of summer travel plans, I flew to Florida to pick up my car and I drove to South Carolina. I couldn't believe I was living with a boyfriend.

❊ ❊ ❊

Settling into Clark's condo was a bit awkward. I immediately regretted my decision, but there was no turning back. I had to push through the next five weeks and make the best of it. A nearby restaurant hired me to hostess and the tips were actually quite good. When I wasn't working, Clark and I swam in the pool, played in the ocean, or walked on the beach. Overall, once the awkwardness of the situation subsided, it was a perfect way to spend the summer.

Clark worked very hard to get me to relax and feel at home, and it worked. I started to realize again that I was in love with him.

One day, after swimming, Clark and I were in the kitchen making lunch. I had a feeling he wanted to tell me something, so I was just staying busy until he was ready to say whatever was on his mind.

"Evi," he said very seriously.

"Yes," I stopped what I was doing and gave him my attention.

Standing behind me, he stepped close to me so as much of him as possible was pressed against me. He put his hands gently on my hips. He whispered in my ear, "I know I said this to you when we dated over a year ago, but I want you to know that I do love you."

I sort of knew this was coming. I looked at my hands resting on the counter. I remembered all of the times Clark had held me, comforted me, listened to me, forgave me, accepted me, and I remembered the times he kissed me. He never gave up on me. Then, I tried to remember things I had done for him that could possibly mean anything of importance. It had been such a one sided relationship.

"Clark, why do you love me?" I asked, still not facing him.

"I love you because I fell in love with you the very first instant that I saw you. I will do anything for you. You being near me makes me happy. You're my home. You're kind and you know me, deep down, you know me. And Evi, I trust you."

I paused. What was wrong with me? Why did I think about someone who didn't want me? Then feeling his hands on me and thinking about his words, I replied, "I'm still in love with you too Clark. I'm glad you asked me to come here with you."

I had been living there with Clark for two weeks and that was the first time my heart pounded for him. That was the first time since he had gone to get me in Ponderosa that my heart was his. I turned around and looked at him. I didn't even need to say anything. He leaned towards me and placed his hand in the center of my chest. I said in a flirtatious tone, "Do you feel it? My heart is beating for you."

He responded softly, "Forever."

He wrapped both arms around me and we kissed.

As our embrace began getting more and more heated, I stopped him and said, "This is dangerous Clark."

He held onto me, looked into my eyes and said, "No, it's not Evi because we will never do anything that either of us will regret. I love you and I want all of you, but I'm willing to wait until you're ready or until we're married if that's what you want. When I went to Idaho to get you, it was because I truly need you with me. I didn't bring you here to lure you into doing something you'll regret. I can think more clearly when you are near me. I can breathe when you are with me."

I couldn't believe he said he can breathe when I am with him, because that was exactly how I always feel with him. I could relax and I could breathe.

I took his hand and walked him to the couch. I pushed him down, then crawled on top of him. I pressed my bare stomach against his, then I gently touched his lips with mine. Without kissing him I whispered, "I love you Clark."

He put his hands on the outside of my thighs just below my hips and pulled me to him. I smiled in approval.

"I love you Evi."

Those words from him filled me.

We spent the afternoon in each other's arms. We ate lunch, napped, played games, and watched TV. I had a perfect glimpse of what my life could be like with him forever, and I really loved it. Clark was not going to let go of my heart.

The next three weeks passed smoothly and quickly and before we knew it, it was time to move back to Charleston. Clark and I packed up what little we had and left to begin our junior year of college.

Chapter 21

"Um, Miss Jordan? Hello? Excuse me? I think we lost you."

Confused, I blinked.

"Miss Jordan, the last thing you said was that Ethan had graduated and had been deployed to the middle-east."

"Oh! Mr. Moore, I am so sorry. I guess I got distracted. I was thinking about spending a few weeks in Charleston, then deciding to return to Ponderosa for the summer after my sophomore year. I got lost. I apologize."

"It's quite alright. Can you pick up where you left off? You and Ethan separated, he graduated, next…"

"So, yes, after an unsuccessful job search in Charleston at the conclusion of my sophomore year, I came home. I spent some time that summer with Brody and Kieron. I worked and soon enough, it was time to move back to Charleston."

I skipped entirely over my mental detour that included all of my experiences with Clark and told the interviewer, "It was time to start my junior year of college and I still had not heard from Ethan since he had broken up with me in April. Piper and I moved into an apartment near campus. Life progressed. School was uneventful."

I thought for a moment, refocused and offered, "I think I'm back on track now Mr. Moore. I'll move ahead for you though."

My story continues…

At the *end* of my junior year, I rented a studio apartment in a historic house in downtown Charleston. I had already planned to work full time and would be starting my student teaching rotation as a senior in college. Instead of returning to Atlanta, Clark was going back to Oceanside and asked me to join him. Since he was only going to be an hour away, I told him I would visit him, which I did a couple of times.

My feelings had faded for Clark, and since I was living alone, I was starting to think about Ethan again. I began to wonder if I was ever going to really get over him. The thought haunted me day and night. Then, one afternoon, early into my move, I was unpacking. An old purse in a box caught my attention so I opened it to see what I had left inside from its last use. Receipts, pens, a lip gloss, a few pieces of dusty, stale gum covered the bottom. I unzipped the inside pocket and gasped. Our ring bag was there. My hands started shaking. I took it out, opened it, and poured the rings onto my palm. Without hesitation, I put my ring on my finger, then I held Ethan's ring between my fingers and pressed it to my lips. I remembered Ethan giving me my ring, and I remembered the Bible.

A box was nearby that I thought had our Bible in it, so I crawled hastily to it and ripped the tape from the top. Our Bible with our names written on the Family Marriages page was there. I picked it up, hugged it to my chest, and I cried hard for the first time in a long time over missing Ethan. Our two year wedding anniversary was a couple of weeks away. I wondered where he was and what he was doing in that exact moment. I wanted to scream at him for leaving me: just scream, no words, no insults, no questions, just a loud scream.

My decision to break up with Clark for good was much easier for me once I began thinking more about Ethan. I called Clark and broke up with him offering the same reasoning as before. I told him that I loved him, but I felt that he kept my attention diverted. I told him it was time for me to work on myself.

Clark gave our relationship one last effort by sharing some information about Ethan that he thought would win me back over to him, but I didn't have any emotions left at that moment for either of them. I decided I would be happier alone. All I wanted was to focus on school, work, and my upcoming student teaching. Clark left me alone. I think he was worn out from fighting someone who didn't even exist in our world anymore. Besides that, he and I both knew he deserved someone who loved only him.

Having settled my relationship with Clark, I called Ethan's mom for the first time in a year. I asked her to keep my call a secret, and she said she would. She then explained that Ethan had been assigned a second twelve month deployment in the middle-east. That news hurt. I told her I missed her and her family and I asked her to tell Brody hello for me. She said she missed me too and that she would give everyone my best.

With past doors closed, locked, and sealed, I sucked up my emotions. I worked, completed my senior year and my student teaching, and I graduated with a degree in education. Being truly alone that year became comfortable and it was nice to have my independence and focus only on myself. I had spent three of my college years dating or pining over Ethan or Clark. The fourth year I chose me! Alone felt good.

Right after graduation, in May of 2015, I moved back to Ponderosa to live with my parents. It was comforting to be going back to Lake Everclear. I went home confident, secure, and stronger than I had been since I was fifteen years old!

After returning to Ponderosa, I learned that Ethan was on a twelve month assignment in Korea. I tried not to think too much about it. Deep down, I had complete faith that he was on the path that God had for him, and I just needed to find my own path. Life progressed.

At some point in time, Ethan had a little cabin built next door to his parents so he'd have a place to stay when he was on leave. I never visited. They live off the beaten path so there was never a reason for me to drive over to his side of the lake. Brody and I were still best friends, but we would hang out at my house or meet on the mountain. I was pleasantly surprised at myself for not going over there just to catch a glimpse of Ethan's new home. I stayed focused on me.

In February of 2016, I was substitute teaching since it was my first year out of school. With Ponderosa being such a small town, there weren't many teaching jobs available. I didn't want to move to the city yet, so I stayed home and worked part time.

One quiet evening, I was sitting alone in my room watching TV when my phone buzzed. Expecting Brody to call, I strained to pull my attention from the show to glance at the screen.

It was Ethan.

My mind quickly processed what was happening. I took a breath.

"Hello," I answered emotionless yet soft.

"Hey Ev. It's me."

"Hmm... you huh?"

He made a puff sound, "Yeah, me."

I closed my eyes and squeezed the phone, "Hi Ethan."

"Evi, I'm home. I'm on a company leave. I'll be here in Ponderosa for a couple of weeks."

I'm not sure why, but I wasn't really surprised to hear from him. I guess I knew he obviously still came home to visit. I assumed he was calling to just say hello and catch up like he used to do. I was mad, then happy, then very guarded.

"I'm glad you sound well Ethan. It's a relief to hear your voice." I took another deep breath and decided to cut to the chase. I coldly asked, "So, why are you calling me?"

"I'd like for you to have dinner with me."

"Is that an invitation for *someday*, or do you have a specific date in mind?"

"Evi, will you join me for dinner at my house… now?"

I got sick! I couldn't speak. I figured he knew I needed a minute because he didn't call my name or ask if I heard him or anything. The phone was silent.

When I got air back into my lungs so I could respond, I wanted to yell, but I literally gritted my teeth and just asked, "Now Ethan? Why now?"

"Evi, it's been a long time since I've seen you. I'd like to say hello face to face. I'd like to show you my house. I'd like to… have dinner with you."

I paused again before responding. Then, with no enthusiasm, I said, "Okay Ethan, I'll be there in a little while."

Like I said, I hadn't seen his cabin and quite frankly, I didn't have anything else to do, so I made myself presentable for a dinner date and I headed to Ethan's.

Driving to his house, I decided to go into the situation wisely knowing he had probably been seeing other women. I vowed not to rekindle old feelings. There was so much he didn't know about my past three years. I had had to shut down how I felt about him and try to block out my memories of our one quick year together. I knew I had to be cautious, very cautious.

That night was very snowy. The falling flakes were huge and sticking to everything on contact. The driving conditions were slow because the streets had not been cleared, and the reflection of the headlights on the blowing snow made visibility difficult. When I arrived at his house in my little SUV, the garage door was up and Ethan was standing just outside on the driveway. I knew he wanted me to park in the garage so I wouldn't have to scrape my car later when I left.

I pulled into the garage and got out of my car. Ethan had his hands in his jeans' pockets, and he wasn't wearing a coat.

"Hey Evi. You cut your hair?" he asked, making eye contact for only a quick moment. He began stealing glances to study me.

I watched him trying not to look at me. I finally replied, "Hey Ethan, yes I did. I cut it two years ago and have kept it at my shoulders since. Having hair to my waist became quite a nuisance."

I closed my car door.

"I like it," he softly said.

Ethan walked towards me and turned sideways to pass by me between our cars. I kept my eyes on him as I leaned against my car door to give him room to get by me. He looked right at me for a quick moment, and it was like we were in high school again. It felt like he drew the air out of my lungs as he slowly went by. He seemed so nervous, and suddenly so was I.

Instead of following him though, it is part of my nature to go outside, so I stepped out into the falling snow. I held my arms out with my hands facing up. I turned my face to the sky and let the snow fall on me.

"Isn't it beautiful?" I said with my eyes closed.

"Yes." I almost couldn't hear his reply.

I knelt down, picked up some of the freshly fallen snow and let it cascade through my fingers. Ethan didn't say anything. I knew he would expect that of me. I live for the outdoors and the snow.

I turned to him and said, "I didn't realize how much I missed this until now. I love the ocean, but I now know this is where I belong."

"Yes, this is home," he softly replied.

"Idahome!" I smiled big as I said it.

Ethan smiled too and motioned for me to go into the house.

"Wait one second please Ethan."

He turned and looked at me. Before stepping into the garage, I shook the snow from my hair and brushed the snow off of my gloves. He smiled at me again and looked down at the ground, then he walked to the door leading into the house. I stayed a few steps behind him.

Ethan pushed a button and as the garage door closed, I followed him in the back door. He held the door open for me and repositioned himself to let me walk in front of him. As I stepped inside, he held his hand out as if escorting me into the next room.

We slipped our shoes off and I hung my coat on a nearby hook. Without speaking, I walked into the kitchen. I looked up and stopped completely frozen. Oh my, the windows. The entire back wall of his living room was glass! The view overlooked the lake. It was frozen over and covered in snow. It was so magical. I walked directly to a window with Ethan following. I felt as if I wanted to climb through and fly over the lake.

"Can I touch the glass Ethan?"

"Of course you can."

"I'll clean the hand prints, I promise," I said while staring in awe of the view before me. I pressed my hands on the window and wished I could hold that scene in my palms and take it with me.

When it snows in Ponderosa, it's actually not dark. Sometimes it's as bright as the sky after sunset, even in middle of the night. I could see so far. I stood staring out the window with a lump in my throat. I could have stayed there forever. Ethan stood very still and very quiet behind me.

"I built steps to the lake Evi."

What was I supposed to say to him? I was quiet, still absorbing the view, and beginning to worry about getting hooked again.

Then, I noticed not the view outside, but the view inside. I realized I could see Ethan staring at me in the reflection. He wouldn't take his eyes off of me. He didn't see me looking at him in the reflection, so I didn't draw attention to my notice of him. I just wanted to watch him without him knowing it.

"Did you bring our rings Evi?" His expression turned hopeful.

Still not knowing I could see his face, I thought about lying to him so I wouldn't seem weak. Suddenly, I felt cold. I crossed my arms in front of me grabbing my elbows. I was trying to protect my heart.

I replied, "Yes Ethan. I put them away for a while, but... but I started carrying them again a year ago. I *never* leave them behind. They've been my only comfort, my only hope that you'd keep your promise to me, that I could trust you to come back to me."

Suddenly, unable to control myself, three years of tears fell while I still faced away from him. "You left me. You left me! Oh God, it hurt, it still hurts."

I wanted to scream. While crying, I noticed his tears too when he stepped close to me. He didn't turn me around. I don't think he wanted me to see his face yet.

He barely whispered, "I'm so sorry. Will you let me prove to you that I want you to forgive me?"

I continued crying.

Then, beginning to hold back tears so I could speak I said, "You left me Ethan. Then you didn't call me or even try to contact me for almost three years! You promised me you'd stay with me. Then, you broke up with me as soon as you thought I was getting in your way. You don't get to be forgiven so easily."

"Evi, I needed to focus on my job, and I needed a plan for bringing you home to me. I realized we got too close too soon. I had nothing to offer you. You were still so young and..."

I interrupted, "I think I deserved a part in the decision. And also, you used that same excuse that I was 'too young' when you got back together with Hannah before you left for school over six years ago! Your job is important. I'm too young. Your ex-girlfriend loves you and she was good to you. Do you have any more excuses you'd like to share as to why you left?"

"Evi, we both were young then. I needed to build a life for us so we could be together. I knew the risk of losing you, but all I could do was pray that you would trust me to keep my promises. I needed you to trust that I meant it when I said I was married to you. I just couldn't give you the attention you would have needed or that you deserved these past few years."

I was still so in love with him. I didn't know what to do next. I placed my hands on the window again, and I looked out across Lake Everclear. I had to let my mind go back to thinking about the beauty outside for a moment.

"Ethan, did you even think about me for the past three years? Did you ever, at any time, pick up your phone to call me? Did you ever think about what you did to me?"

"I kept a picture of us on me all the time. And of course I thought about calling you, every day, but I wanted you to finish school and focus on living your life. My mom kept me as up to date as she could on you from talking to your mom. I knew when you were back here in Ponderosa. I almost took a leave last summer, but I knew I'd get more time with you if I waited for an official company leave. That's why I'm here now. I came here to get you and bring you home to me. I'm here to ask you to please forgive me, to try to understand why I left, and to come back to me."

He continued, "As for what I did to you," he paused as he thought of what to say next, "Evi I chose you! I may not have done things perfectly these past years, but I chose *you*. I chose you when I was seventeen. Every day I want you to know that I have always loved you and I will always love you. I want you with me, now."

I was silent. He was silent.

I had to make a decision and face the results whatever they were going to be.

I whispered so low, I wasn't sure he heard me, "Okay. No more looking back,"

We stood silent for a few more moments. I knew I was going to forgive him. I knew I still wanted him. I knew I had never stopped loving him. I didn't have anything else to say. I had no more arguments, and my anger had just simply subsided.

He placed his hands on my shoulders and gently slid them down my arms. He asked, "Am I still your only one Evi?"

I paused to take a breath and said, "Of course you are. Always Ethan."

"Good, because you're still mine."

He completely stole my heart back.

I finally turned around and looked up into his amazing eyes. He looked so sorry and so sincere. He pulled me and with each soft gentle kiss he whispered over and over, "I'm sorry, I love you."

I put my hands on his waist and closed my eyes, but he said, "Evi, keep your eyes on mine." He slowly lifted me up to him. My legs went around him and locked. Slightly squeezing me, he slid his hands down my rib cage, to my waist, to my hips, and under me. We pulled each other as close as we possibly could, and he carried me to his room.

Our lips never separated. That kiss was not like our first kiss at all. It was a connection between two married people who had been apart for far too long. We belonged to each other. We didn't let go of each other even for a moment. We held each other so tightly, I'm still not sure how we went from standing beside his bed fully clothed to being wrapped in his blankets with absolutely nothing between us.

Ethan attended to my every need while we were together. I felt like he had been reading my mind for the past three years. He must have rehearsed exactly how to touch me, how to kiss me and how to be truly one person with me. All of my senses were awakened. Neither of us had any inhibitions. I focused on his hands, his breathing, the smell of his neck, the words he said, and the sounds he made... oh the sounds and the words. Every single wonderful thing that can come out of making love with someone existed that night. There was so much love and passion between us, I couldn't imagine how anything could ever be any better than that for as long as I lived.

Not sure if I wanted to rest or try to begin again, with Ethan resting on me, his warm breath on my neck, still winded, I remembered. I couldn't stop the thoughts and the emotions of my memories from consuming my brain. He had left me. He left me!

I released a harsh, grinding cry. I pulled the pillow from beside me over my face and I screamed, "I hate you! I hate you Ethan!" and I cried more. I violently pushed him off of me, and I turned over onto my stomach, burying my face and pounding my fist into the pillow.

Ethan was stunned. He didn't move a muscle at first. Then, he very cautiously placed a hand on my shoulder and rested his head on my back.

"I hate you Ethan. I hate you." I said it again but with less power.

"I know you do. It's okay Evi. I know you do. I'm sorry." He let me cry this time, unlike our first time together. He knew I did truly hate him, but only because I loved him so much.

I think we fell asleep, or at least I did. When I awoke, his hand was still on my shoulder and his head was still on my back. His body heat was keeping me warm.

"Ethan," I spoke in a raspy, sore voice.

"Yeah Ev."

"My arm is cold."

"'kay."

As he pulled the blanket up and covered my arm, I turned back over to face him. I cried softly. I was so sad that he had taken away three years of my life with him. I said, "What you did wasn't fair Ethan. It wasn't fair. I deserved to have you, to have this. I didn't do anything to deserve what you did to me. You didn't love me enough. That hurts."

"No babe. No Evi. I loved you too much. I swear, I loved you too much. Please, please try to understand that you deserved so much more than I could give you at the time. You deserve more than I may ever be able to give you. I love you Evi. I'm here for you. I want you. I want you to forgive me. I am sorry. I will say anything you need to hear from me to prove that you are and always have been *everything* to me. Everclear, you are everything to me."

I let him pull me onto his chest and cover me with the sheet and blankets. Then he slid my leg over his thigh. I was letting him work me into the position he wanted me in.

Once he finally settled, he said, "I love you. I always have, I always will. I needed to be apart from you to give you everything you deserve. But Evi, right now, right... now... you tell me if you want me. Do you want to give me your life again? Do you trust me? You are my only one. I never even thought about loving or being with anyone but you, but do you still love me and want me?"

I had released my anger. I had let him know how much he hurt me. My actions spoke volumes above what any more words could achieve.

225

I looked into his eyes and I didn't even hesitate. I smiled, "Am I going to be getting dinner out of this or not?"

Ethan laughed out loud, "Yes, you will get dinner."

"Okay then. Yes, I do want you, but I want you, again, right now!"

Intensity and volume were lowered, love and affection were the same… hope and desire… significantly increased.

Mmmm, so romantic. I was so in love.

Later, that evening, we bundled up and headed out into the snowy night to have dinner at a local burger place. While we were eating and talking, I realized something special about our relationship. Sometimes when God takes something away from us, He does this so *He* can use it, mold it, then give it back to us a thousand times better.

I think God spoke to Ethan's heart, "Trust *Me*. Trust *My* timing. It's okay to leave her. I will take care of her. Focus on your job, build a life for you both, *then* go back for her!" So he did. Ethan listened to God, not me.

❄ ❄ ❄

I spent the entire week with Ethan. He took me home and I packed a bag. "I'm going to Ethan's mom! I love you!" I yelled like we had a play date or were going bike riding.

"I figured! I love you too Everclear!"

Ethan and I played, ate, and stayed in bed late every morning.

The second week together, Ethan's home was beginning to feel like my home. I was ready to venture around and explore. He was messing around somewhere, so I decided to try out the steps he had built to the lake. I got half way down before I realized I had made a big mistake. Ethan built the steps, but he had not shoveled them lately.

"ETHAAAANNN!" I screamed.

He came running, and as he reached the top of the stairs, I slipped, and thank God, I landed on my butt. I slid the all the way down to the bottom on my rear end.

"Agh!" I screamed the whole way down.

My momentum propelled me onto my hands and knees when I got to the bottom. I rolled onto my back landing in at least a foot and a half of snow. I laughed so hard!

From the top of the steps he yelled, "SH** Evi! What the hell are you doing out here?! You're gonna kill yourself!"

I'd never heard Ethan cuss before so of course I laughed even harder.

As he walked down the stairs he yelled again, "Geez! How am I supposed to get you back up there? I'm going to have to throw you over my shoulder and carry you up!" He was seriously mad, and it was hilarious!

"I built these steps so you'd STOP falling down the mountainside Evi. God, you are so clumsy."

For a second I heard what he said. He built the steps for *me*. I didn't let it sink in right away though.

"Just go get my skis Ethan. I'll get down here without falling… backwards… with my eyes closed!" I yelled bragging while continuing my uncontrollable laughter at him.

"You ski backwards?"

"Uh! Yes! How do you not know that? Gold medal expert Park, Big Mountain, and Skier Cross baby, among other accolades. Nationally ranked all the way through high school."

"Seriously?" he said looking shocked and impressed.

"Oh... I'm goooood!" I boasted.

"Oh... yes, I know! Of course that does make me wonder what else I *don't* know about you though," he replied in a flirty voice. "Let's go babe and stay off the steps. I'll come shovel and de-ice them later."

Ethan helped me up and we slowly ascended the staircase one step at a time. He never let me go.

Chapter 22

Our rings remained with me and safely tucked away during our few weeks together. I had a feeling Ethan was thinking about them, but was afraid to ask. Maybe he thought I'd say no to wearing them. After all, we'd only spent those two weeks together in two years and ten months. Yes, I was counting. The rings were constantly on my mind, but I was waiting for him to ask for them.

At the end of our three weeks together, Ethan returned to Korea. We talked on the phone and often chatted through video. Keeping in touch wasn't too difficult. We began making plans for me to go see him so he wouldn't have to use his leave time. He only had a few months left in Korea, then he had two years until he had to decide if he was going to re-enlist or transition to civilian life. Since I was still living with my parents and substitute teaching, I had all the flexibility in the world.

Close to the end of March, I called Ethan from my bedroom for a video chat. He answered cheerfully of course. We greeted with our usual "I love you" and "I miss you" before I got right to my reason for calling. Without wasting any time on casual conversation, I said, "Ethan, I have an emergency, I'm really scared and I don't know what to do."

"Oh boy, this ought to be good. What is it this time?" He smirked.

"I held something up in front of me."

"Well, what is that, a highlighter?" he asked.

I didn't say anything. I held it closer to the camera so he could see it. The plus sign! And *there* was the expression I was looking for the first time: mouth dropped open, processing, silence, more processing, and finally, shock!

"Are you there alone?!" he yelled as if agitated.

I was stunned. I got sad. I thought he was going to break up with me again. Every bad emotion possible starting boiling up inside of me.

I replied, "No, I asked our moms to be here. Why?"

"Mom! Mrs. Jordan!" Ethan yelled again. Surprisingly they actually heard him. I was dumbfounded when they ran into the room.

"What Ethan?" they both said at the same time.

"Move her into my house now. Please! Pack her stuff and move her in as fast as you can. No, pack her things and have Brody move her in as fast as *he* can. He's probably just off skiing or doing something useless anyway. Oh, that reminds me, Mrs. Jordan, do not bring her skis, and Mom, do not let her go down to the lake until I get home. Do you both understand me? She is not to go down to the lake. She is not to ski!"

"We got it Ethan. We love you honey. Oh and *congratulations*, we think?"

I had my head down. I had been so afraid of what he was going to say, that my heart was panicked. I'm sure I was hormonal! Before they closed the door to my room, "Mom!" *I* yelled that time. "Help meeee!"

Poor Ethan was terrified, and I know he felt so helpless. This was probably my first *real* crisis and he was thousands of miles away.

"Mom… I feel… " Without missing a beat, my mom put a trashcan under me and I heaved over and over and over again. I was so done with that call. I had my head on the desk. Ethan kept saying, "You're okay Evi. I love you babe. You're okay."

"Please! Mrs. Jordan, get her to our house and put her in our bed. Please get her anything she needs and please don't leave her alone. I can't bear her being alone."

My mom responded warmly, "Okay Ethan. I'll take her over there as soon as she's ready. I promise. It'll probably be tomorrow though."

He was so sad. I told him I was okay, but that I really needed to go lie down. I got in my bed but I kept him with me holding the phone tight in my hand. Snuggled under my covers with my head on my pillow, I mumbled, "Thank you Ethan for saying 'our bed' and 'our house'. I feel like our baby and I have a home now."

"You've *always* had a home with me Evi. Now we get to share it with someone we both love together. I'm so excited! I'm so happy." He yelled, "I can't believe I'm going to be a dad!"

After his moment of elation subsided, I looked at him in the phone crying. He looked confused and worried, "Evi, what's wrong? It's okay. This is great news. I love you. God, I love you so much!"

I sniffed and wiped my tears, "Ethan our baby's going to know that we got pregnant before we got married."

"No Evi, we got married four years ago. I never stopped being married to you. I will never stop being married to you. I promised you forever on our wedding night, and it has *not* been forever yet! Where are our rings?"

"Mine is right here." I held it up for him to see.

"Put it on now and don't you ever take it off again." He was so in charge, so commanding.

"Where's my ring Ev?"

"It's with you babe. I hid it in your backpack just before you left in case you wanted it. It's safely pinned to an inside pocket."

He smiled at me and said, "Are you serious? I love you forever. I'll be home soon. I'll call you back later after you rest. I'm going to get to work on planning *another* trip home."

Rest didn't do me a bit of good. I was down and out for months! I quit working all together. Using Ethan's bank account, his parents paid all of our bills and our moms did all of the grocery shopping and housekeeping. Brody came over at least once a day to check on me. Someone else did everything for me. I never left the house except to sit outside on our back deck, because I couldn't go more than an hour without getting sick.

The bright side was, we were finally *truly* married. There was no more hiding the fact that we had "gotten married" when I was only nineteen.

Chapter 23

As far as I knew Ethan had not worked out getting home to me yet. He was overseas and that was, obviously, too far for weekend visits. I had no doubts that he was doing everything in his power to get to me though. There was no energy to spare within me for worry. I trusted him. He was a planner, an organizer, a leader. He was going to work it out.

One morning in early June, I awoke around ten. My eyes opened, I waited for that dreaded feeling. Conditioned for it to creep up within my first few deep breaths, I decided to get those over with. I breathed. I sensed. I realized, "I don't feel like throwing up," I said to myself.

There was no way I was not going to take full advantage of my first morning of not vomiting. Carefully, remaining fully aware of how I was feeling, I slipped out from under the covers. First, I let only my legs drape over the side of our bed. Next, I pushed my body upright to join my legs. Finally, I scooted my bum from the edge of the bed and planted my feet on the warm fuzzy rug my mom had bought for me.

Slowly, anticipating the possible need to run at any moment, I walked into the bathroom. Standing before the mirror I repeated, "I will not puke. I will not puke. Evi, you will survive this day. You've got this." My next statement to myself was, "How the human population is not extinct is beyond me. Why would anyone ever have more than one child if they have to feel like this hour after hour, day after day?" My head dropped. I did not smile. I was not joking.

Taking full advantage of feeling okay-ish, I showered, brushed my teeth (without gagging), combed my hair for perhaps the first time in a week, and I put on a tank top and the smallest pair of boy-shorts I had that I could still fit into. My belly was shaped like half of a soccer ball was inside of me. Although I was aware of how good my damp hair felt on my back and shoulders, not getting sick yet was a miraculous feeling. I shuffled out to our living room, I looked out at Lake Everclear and the mountain I grew up skiing on, and I thought, *home*.

My body was going to need to be fed very soon, so I slid the doors open, then turned away from the view, took a few steps, and plopped onto our couch to build strength. It was so soft and comfy. I put my feet up on the coffee table. I widened my legs placing them a bit more than shoulder width apart, I laid my head back, closed my eyes, and I threw my arms out by my sides. I WAS HOT!

The front door opened behind me, but I didn't turn around.

"Mom?"

"No, it's me Evi."

"Hi Sonja."

"I brought you groceries Evi. How are you today? Have you been sick this morning?"

In my whiniest voice I said, "No, I haven't been sick but I still feel like if I move too fast I'll throw up at any second. But Sonja, I'm soooo hot I can't stand it."

I heard bags rustling by the door.

"Probably hot flashes. Pregnancy hormones you know," she said as I heard more rustling.

"It's horrible though! What do I do?"

"Well, is the ceiling fan on?"

"Yes, it's on high."

"Is the air conditioner on?"

"No, it's cooler outside, and the fresh air makes me feel less sick so I have all the back doors open instead."

"Well, why don't you go sit outside then Evi?"

"Ugh!" still whining, "because the *couch* isn't outside!"

"Do you want me to go get Brody so he can move the couch to the back deck for you?"

Bags were still rustling.

"No Sonja. Don't be silly! Brody will just smash it through a window, then Ethan will kill him and it'll be a huge Cain and Abel family tragedy. This baby doesn't need that kind of pressure before it's even born!" I was being infantile and fussy.

I heard a snicker from her.

"You're laughing at me aren't you Sonja?"

"No Evi, I'm not laughing at you."

"Yes you are. I hear you. Uh, I'm hot!" I pulled my hair off of my neck and plopped my arms back out to my sides.

"No Evi, *I'm* not laughing. You're just so dramatic today. You must be feeling better."

"Sonja, why on earth do you have so many grocery bags? You know I can't eat that much food. Brody will just come over and eat it all. You might as well carry all of that food to your house."

"You need food in your house Evi. Once you're feeling better, you will need food around. And, besides that, I won't let Brody come eat it all."

"I know you're a great mom, but I'm not sure you can stop him. He's always here you know?"

"Evi, I will not let Brody eat all of your food."

Mumbling, I offered a different perspective, "Well, he might as well. It's not like I can keep it down." Then I asked with more energy, "Hey, is at least *one* of those bags filled with chocolate?"

"Nooooo Evi."

"Well did you bring me a pot of coffee?"

"No Evi. You know the doctor says you can't have chocolate or coffee. You ask me every time I come here for chocolate and coffee."

"That's because I waaaaannt it! That dumb doctor doesn't know what he's talking about anyway!"

The rustling finally stopped and I heard the door click closed.

Then… "You should listen to your doctor Evi."

It was Ethan! He was home! He was standing there behind me the whole time. He was watching me, listening to me, laughing at me! The five thousand bags of groceries made sense.

You would have thought that if ever there was a moment I would run and jump into his arms, that would have been it, but I didn't. I did quite the opposite.

I fell onto the floor face down and curled in a ball between the sofa and the coffee table. Then I screamed, "Don't look at me!"

Ethan laughed and then barked an order at me. "I have already been looking at you for the past five minutes! Get up!"

"Yeah, but I didn't know you were looking at me then! I don't want you to see how big I'm getting Ethan."

I never thought I would be a girl who'd be so vain about being pregnant and about how much my body was changing. The problem was that I'd been too sick to care and since I was feeling slightly better, I noticed.

I got up, ran to the window and hid behind a curtain. With only my face out, I said to him, "You can come kiss me over here, but then you'll have to turn around so I can go get dressed and do my hair and makeup. *Then* you can see all of me Ethan."

Still laughing at how different I had become in such a short amount of time, Ethan put his hands on his hips and said, "Let me ask you this Evi, do both of my parents come over here?"

"Yes."

"Do both of your parents come over here?"

"Of course."

"And, does *Brody* come over here? Has he seen how you look every day?"

Uh oh, he had me on that one. "Um, yes," I replied very sheepishly.

"Then get your A** out from behind that curtain, NOW!"

He was demanding. First, I knew he was very accustomed to commanding people and second, I knew he was certainly *not* used to being told 'no' by anyone he was commanding.

I thought. I conceded, "Okay, I'll come out, but only if you'll close all of the curtains in the room first and make sure the front door is locked."

He politely obliged.

Satisfied, I stepped from behind the curtain so he could see me just the way I was. No, so he could see me and our baby just the way *we* were. We belonged to him. We were his.

Later that evening…

"Wait! No romantic interlude story to share?" The interviewer interjected for the second time. "That's a bit of a let-down for the viewers."

"Mr. Moore, have you not listened to any of my stories? I figured you were tired of hearing about the 'interludes' by now." My tone contained quite a bit of sarcasm.

"Ma'am, we're here to film a romantic documentary on military couples to air for Valentine's Day next year. We *want* to hear everything about you and your soldier. We need as much information about your love story as you are willing to give. You just be as open and honest as you are comfortable, and let *us* do the editing please."

I reversed to Ehtan's homecoming morning for Mr. Moore. I said, "Fine. Hmm… Let's see, I can probably summarize the encounter pretty quickly."

"Okay," was his simple reply with pen and paper ready once more.

I continued with my story.

Ethan and I never even made it out of our living room. I stepped from behind the curtain. He was standing about six feet from me with his hand extended to me. I walked to him and took it. Then, I asked him, "Will you make love to me Ethan, pleeeease?"

A deja vu occurred when he instantly dropped to his knees in front of me, lifted my shirt, and kissed my stomach. Looking up at me he replied, "Oh, I plan on it babe. And by the way, that's still a very good word."

I put my hands behind his head and scratched my fingers through his short hair. I bent down, kissed him, and took complete control of everything we did. From there, you can let your imagination run wild! Really wild!"

Next, I'm sure my expression spoke volumes. I smiled as I looked at the floor in a sly way feeling Ethan's hands, his lips and his body all over me. I remembered lifting my arms as he pulled my tank over my head. I slid his shirt from his shoulders and down his arms. The feeling of his warm skin on mine still made me tingle.

I then turned my head to the right and rested my chin on my shoulder as I dreamed about his eyes, his breath, and his moans. I remembered how each time Ethan and I reunite, it's like our first time and our hundredth time. Making love with him is always new, yet he knows me. He knows me so well.

I cut just my eyes back to Mr. Moore and said, "You'd be amazed at how fun this room is. Every surface you see is a playground when you love someone. Do I really need to give anymore details?"

The interviewer looked at me, gave me a half smile and looked back down at his list of questions.

"Oh Evi!" One of our moms' voices rang out behind me like I was fifteen and had just disappointed her.

I wasn't sure which one of them said it so I just responded with, "Seriously mom! You have sat here for two hours listening to me tell the world about my sex life with Ethan and *that* is what shocked you?"

Then one of the film crew from a back room let out a burst of laughter.

I'm almost done Mr. Moore, stay with me.

As I was saying...

Later that evening, Ethan and I were resting here on the couch watching TV. He was lying across it with his upper body and head propped on the arm, and I was lying on my back between his legs with my head resting on his chest.

"What was that?!" Ethan asked with extreme concern.

"What Ethan?"

"I think something just ran across the floor from under the chair over there."

Casually I said, "Oh, probably so."

I made kissing noises and a tiny, tiny brown fur ball pounced cautiously onto the couch at my feet.

"Come, come," I said sweetly in a high squeaky voice. She walked slowly, shaking, with her eyes squinting like she wanted to be held. She climbed up my body and curled into a ball on my chest just below my chin. She looked at Ethan trying to figure out if she could trust him. Keeping her big brown eyes on Ethan, she cautiously lay her chin on her paws, while she rested on my chest.

"Seriously Evi! What the hell is that?" he yelled.

Her tiny head popped up. I put my hand on her bottom to secure her. I said, "She's a Poo-huahua. Isn't she beautiful? Her name is Piper. Hey baby, she's mommy's girl…"

"Evi? You got a freaking dog?! And you named it Piper?"

"Yup!" I smiled at her, then still using my squeaky baby voice I added, "I lived with Piper for three years, why would I want my roommate to have any other name?"

"Oh my …. Ugh… Evi… Noooo…"

"Oh settle down. She's sweet, and besides she spends most of her time at your mom's house with Brody."

"Geeez! Are you kidding me? So basically you and Brody have joint custody of a dog?" he asked rolling his eyes.

"Huh? I guess you could put it that way." I laughed.

"Great."

That subject was dropped.

Then Ethan asked, "Hey, you only lived with Piper for three years? Who'd you live with your senior year of college?"

I responded with basic facts, "I got an apartment downtown and lived alone. I focused on school, my job and my student teaching. I sat home each night working, planning, resting. Nothing special. I didn't even go out my senior year. I was my old independent self again."

"Oh," he replied.

I assumed he had more questions, but I knew we'd get to everything we'd both been through over the past three years as time progressed.

We sat there, all four of us, on the couch, together: Ethan, me, our baby, and Piper.

"Ethan,"

"Yes babe."

"I'm *still* sooooo hot."

"Well, tell her to get off of you."

"I can't she's inside of me."

He tried to jerk up from under me. Piper jumped down to the floor.

"Don't move so fast Ethan, I'll throw up."

"Evi, are you telling me our baby is a girl?"

"Yes Ethan, she's a girl."

"Who else knows this?"

"Just you babe. I have been saving this secret for just you. We have another secret together. This one, however, will be out in about five months."

Ethan kissed me and with a smile that could not be erased, he said, "We're naming her Brighton, because she already brightens my life." He hugged me, hugged us.

"Ethan! Let me go!" I jumped out of his arms and ran down the hall. He followed me. I grabbed my hair before I even got to the bathroom. Within seconds, I was bent over the toilet.

Ethan followed. He curled around me and sat me on his lap. He held my hair for me and rubbed my back. I had a sneaky suspicion he was happy about this. I, of course was beyond miserable, but gosh it sure was a comfortable way to be throwing up!

"I missed you Ethan," I whined and coughed.

"I'm here now. We're together now. I've got you."

For a moment, Ethan scooted me to the side so he could get me water and a washcloth. He came back to me, sat with his back against the wall, placed me between his legs, and held me like I was the baby. The cool cloth he rubbed on my face was soothing. He whispered, "I'm here Evi. I'll take care of you." A few moments later he asked, "Evi, why is there a blanket sitting here? I thought you were hot."

"You'll see."

I turned and threw up a few more times. Each time he held me. In between my episodes, I took a moment and said, "By the way, absolutely *no one* is allowed to use this toilet! This is where my face has been for three months! That *is* an order!"

"Noted," he agreed laughing.

"I mean it Ethan. I'll know. I can smell everything! It's horrible."

"Okay babe. I promise."

I rested in his arms and like clockwork, my adrenaline kicked in. I started shivering like I was terribly ill.

"Blanket Ethan."

He covered me, kissed me, warmed me.

I never remembered feeling so sick yet so comfortable and loved in my entire life. I was all his.

Ethan put his hand on my belly and I put mine on top of his. I played with the ring on his left hand and we stayed there, next to the toilet, in each other's arms.

Chapter 24

Ethan waited a while to tell me that he never bothered to ask for another leave. He didn't want to hurt my feelings by telling me that the army didn't care that he basically *knocked up* his girlfriend, nor do they grant leave for morning sickness. My condition was irrelevant. You see, even though Ethan and I felt married, and our families accepted us as married, we still were not legally married. He was a single man, a soldier, with no children. I meant nothing to the army. To say he is far more legally bound to them than me, would not be an understatement. Years ago, on one of my trips to New York to visit Ethan, someone told me, "Be careful dear. It sounds like he's young and strong and smart. If the Army wanted him to have a wife, they would have issued him one." I laughed at the time, but it was true. Until our marriage was legally documented, Ethan was essentially married to them not me, not our baby. I've always known that.

All that mattered was that he was finally there with me, so I was okay with him not asking. In our home in Ponderosa, I was safe and had several people taking care of me. Although neither of us liked being apart, we both knew I was okay.

Overall, the timing of his leave ended up being perfect. Ethan informed me that his deployment in Korea was done. I was beyond excited. That visit was his break between base transfers. He had been assigned to the United States. I could move to wherever he was going to be, if I wanted. We were getting closer and closer to a life together.

Ethan received his PCS orders and found out he was moving to Fort Jackson in South Carolina. That base is where a lot of new soldiers are sent for their combat basic training. Ethan's a strong leader and has combat experience, so his skills would be very useful there. We'd both be teachers!

I was so excited not only to know that he was going to be in the US, but also to hear that he was going to South Carolina. If I was going to move anywhere with him, I hoped it was going to be somewhere I actually wanted to be for a while. We could spend weekends and holidays in Charleston or at the beach. I was very excited.

A few days after Ethan got home, since I was feeling better, I decided to go shopping with my mom in town. We had a light lunch, walked along the waterfront, and visited a few stores. It was the first time I'd been out of the house in a couple of months.

Ethan stayed home working on the lawn and around the house. Brody took care of most everything for him when he was gone, so he was excited to get out and do some work himself with no distractions for a while.

The fresh air and the exercise felt good but after a few hours, I was getting tired, so mom and I ended our outing. She drove me home, dropped me in front of our house, and she left.

When I walked inside through the door between the garage and the kitchen, I saw Ethan standing in the dining room leaning against the table.

"Hey Ethan. Did you get a lot done today?" I asked.

"What's this Evi?" he asked furiously.

"Where'd you find that?" was my only response.

"It doesn't matter Evi! It's in my house!"

"Did you read that?" I asked as my voice cracked and I started shaking.

"Yes! It has my name on the front!" Ethan had *never* raised his voice to me like that in all the years I'd known him.

"Well it's not yours so you should have never read it! How could you do that?"

My heart was sick. Ethan had found my journal that I had written in during the first year that he left me. That was also the timeframe when I was seeing Clark again. This journal ended up in our house because Brody had moved my things there after I told Ethan I was pregnant. My mom pulled the crate of my high school yearbooks, some notebooks and my Bibles out, and Brody just brought it with my other things. The crate was in a closet in the spare room. I didn't even realize it was there, and I had completely forgotten the journal even still existed.

"What is this Evi?" Ethan was shaking the journal at me.

I had never seen him like that. I wasn't afraid of him, though I was confused about why he was so angry. However, I believe that because I was on the verge of becoming a mother, I was ready to fight to protect myself and my baby.

"What does it say on the first page Ethan? Read it!" I yelled back at him.

He stared at me for a moment.

On the first page I had written:

I have to write down every emotion I have about Ethan or I am going to go crazy. He has left me and I don't think he's coming back for me, ever. I don't trust him and I don't trust his promises because he promised me forever. He has hurt me more deeply than I knew was possible, but I will get better. When this book is complete, I will burn it and I will move on with my life. I will stop constantly thinking about him. I will stop letting him hurt me. I WILL forget him.

Then, for a year I recorded every emotion I had for Ethan. I wrote about how often I cried. I wrote about how often I was angry. I wrote about times I didn't think about him at all. Finally, I wrote about Clark. I wrote a lot of intimate details about dating Clark. Looking back, there were three things about this journal that I believe drove Ethan to that furious state.

First, I believe he was just realizing how much he had hurt me and he couldn't bear the pain. He put me in a place of needing someone else. Every situation in that journal was his fault. He could not go back and undo any of it, nor could he fix it, nor erase the images from his mind.

Second, Ethan was having to face the fact that I had spent over a year of our separation with Clark. Ethan and I had not spent much time together. I hadn't told him about Clark because it didn't matter to me anymore. That relationship was almost completely forgotten. Ethan was being driven into an outrage, not because of his knowledge that Clark and I had seen each other again, but because he never knew how close we had gotten. Ethan did not know that I almost gave in to my feelings for Clark. I considered marrying him.

The third reason Ethan was so angry was because he was finally aware that Clark had told me about him leaving me *twice* that day he broke up with me. I'd known all along that Clark tried to get Ethan to go back to me that night, and Ethan turned away. I had had to live with that knowledge for the three years we had been apart.

"Why do you still have this Evi? Tell me!" he demanded.

"I didn't realize it was here Ethan. Besides that, I never burned it because it was my only reminder of my time with you! That journal, our rings and our Bible were the only things I had to hold on to that gave me hope that you would keep your promise and come back to me. I couldn't destroy it. I needed it for a long time so I could remember that you existed in my life. Then, as I got stronger, I packed it away and forgot about it while I moved a little each day towards a life without you. For eight years I have loved you. I've only spent one year with you. Do you have any idea how that feels for *me*? I have nothing but dreams of you! You'll have to forgive me for holding on to one more thing that reminded me you actually exist, that you did actually love me. I just forgot about the journal after a while. I'm sorry it is upsetting you like this."

"No Evi! This is not about me. This is about you and Clark! This is about him touching you. This is about your life with him! This is about you loving him! And you lived with him?! You moved in with him Evi, just three months after we broke up?! I trusted you!"

"You trusted me? What? You… left… me! I shouldn't have to defend myself here, but just so you know, I only lived with him for a few weeks during a summer Ethan, and we had separate bedrooms. Nothing ever happened between us. I promise I have not lied to you about that. However, I'm not sure it's any of your business anyway!"

"Well something did happened between you two! I never touched another woman Evi! I never even thought about another woman. I am married to you! I have been married to you for four years! This book doesn't show that you felt the same way. When I left that night, I believed in you, you were mine! I told you our separation was only temporary! I trusted you to believe in me and wait for me! It took you thirty seconds to call another guy after I left!"

"No Ethan. You don't get to lecture me. That book *is* about my feelings for you even though I was with Clark. And Ethan, again, you left me! Remember? I didn't call any other guys. You left me!" I was now feeling dizzy and exhausted. I looked down at the floor.

Calmly I said, "Ethan, just give it here, I'll get rid of it. Please stop. This is pointless. Arguing like this isn't going to solve anything. It's hurting me."

Ethan wasn't letting it go though. He was still so angry. He kept yelling at me while I begged him to give me the book. I continued trying to reassure him that the only reason I kept it was because I love him and only him. I was starting to weaken physically and emotionally. I didn't know how much strength I had left in me. Yet, he seemed to be getting angrier.

A moment of silence came and as we stood still, I became completely aware that he was looking for a fight. He was mad at me. He really was. However, he was hurting and was more furious with himself, so furious that he couldn't stand it. Ethan couldn't fight himself, so he was going to fight me.

I deeply hoped his moment of silence had calmed him down. I was starting to ache and starting to feel sick again. I needed to rest.

Suddenly, he threw the book across the room and said the most hurtful thing I hope I ever hear come from him. "How'd you even get pregnant Evi? How do I even know this baby is mine?"

"Oh my God! What? What did you just say?" I said breathlessly as I looked at him in desperation.

He might as well have punched me. All of my air was sucked out of my body and I almost fainted. I grabbed a chair to steady myself, then I thought, boy did he just mess up!

I attacked him with every bit of remaining strength I had left in me. I screamed and beat on his chest and cried and pushed him.

"Don't you ever talk about my daughter like that again Ethan! Don't you ever try to hurt her or cheapen her again! She's mine! If you want to leave us, then go! Go! But you will never hurt her! I'm used to you leaving me and hurting me, but you will never hurt her! We will be fine without you! Go find some other woman to play your stupid games with Ethan. You will not hurt us anymore!" I screamed at him until my throat hurt.

He grabbed me, put me in some sort of a hold and lowered me carefully to the floor so my forehead was pressed against the cool, hardwood. I knew he would never hurt me, and he was trying to protect me from harming our baby.

"I'm sorry. I'm so sorry. God, I'm so sorry Evi." He kept whispering it over and over almost like he was saying it to himself and to me.

He held me to the ground. I was trying to feel his hands so I knew my baby was okay and not being hurt. I relaxed a bit. I was hot again. I was so hot and sick. I was trying not to throw up. I needed air so I strained a hoarse gasp. Then, I relaxed more so he would release me. I mustered up the energy to speak.

"You're a good soldier Ethan. You've been trained and you've done your job very well. You weakened me. You fought me, and you broke me. You have won. But you need to know, right now, that if you ever speak of my daughter like that again, I will kill you. She is mine, and I will *die* for her. Do you understand me?"

Ethan didn't say anything. His head was resting on my back, and I felt him nod yes. I know he was trying to insult me. He was trying to hurt me. He never thought of his comment as an insult to our baby. He was playing a mind game with his comment, but I won that portion of the fight.

Exhausted, I crawled on my elbows out from under him. He let me go. When I got a few feet from him, I rested on the hard floor. As I was lying there, all I could think was, *What just happened to my marriage?*

Ethan was beside me sitting on the backs of his heels, watching me with his hands on his thighs. He was looking down at me there with my cheek resting on the cool floor. I knew he was afraid to speak. He offered me his hand. Before I took it, I said to him, "You're supposed to take care of us. You can't use our baby as one of your weapons. She is not a weapon. You are a good dad. You don't have to protect yourself against me. I have always loved you."

He nodded at me with tears in his eyes. I don't think he even understood what he was feeling that afternoon.

With his help, I slowly raised to my feet. I stood in front of him hoping he would hold me, kiss me and walk me to our bed so I could rest for a while. Not sure I could hold myself up any longer, I gripped his shirt into my fists and looked up into his eyes wanting his help. His attention was across the room on the journal. He was still angry. I couldn't believe it, and I didn't think I could take any more.

Ethan separated from me, walked over to the journal, grabbed it, and took something out of a drawer in the kitchen. He then walked back over to me.

"Ethan please, please let me rest," I begged.

"One more thing Evi. Just one more, I promise. I'm sorry. I love you, but this ends right now. Just one more thing."

He stroked my hair and held my chin with his hand. He kissed me so sweetly for a few seconds. Then, he gently rubbed my stomach and said, "I love you so much."

He held onto my hand so I couldn't pull away and he led me out our back door.

I insisted, "Ethan, I need to rest." I twisted my wrist from his grip and jerked back from him. "I can't walk Ethan!"

He turned, picked me up, and carried me down our steps and over to his parents' fire pit. He placed me on the ground and said, "One more minute Evi." I was too weak, so I had to sit on the lawn as he knelt down and lit the book on fire.

"Someday, we are going to talk about this Evi."

"Fine Ethan. I have nothing to hide. I really forgot this book even existed."

The sulfur of the lit match and the smoke plumes instantly made me nauseous. I knew I wanted and needed to sleep, but the lake was calling me. I hadn't been down to the beach in such a long time. My hope was that the cool sand and breeze would ease my sickness. I got up and walked away from him. If that book burning was so interesting to him, he could watch it as long as he wanted, *by himself*. I was done. I wanted my feet in the water. Lake Everclear always revived me, healed me, comforted me.

I walked back to our yard to the steps so I could go to the water. After going down a few steps, I couldn't hold it in any longer. I bent down on my hands and knees to throw up to the side of the staircase. I was curled up on the boards crying and throwing up again and again. In my mind, I knew I needed to call Ethan to help me get to bed, but I couldn't stop heaving. I felt my adrenaline rush coming, and I got light headed.

The last thing I remember of that day is my left hand slipping off of the board on which I was kneeling.

I screamed Ethan's name as loud as I could.

Chapter 25

A hospital, I awoke in a hospital room and I didn't see anyone around me. I looked at the ceiling and the machines beside me, and I tried to remember what had happened. As my memory returned, I felt my abdomen reaching for my baby. I placed both hands over my face and cried a harsh and exhausting cry. I wasn't pregnant anymore. I wanted my daughter more than I had ever wanted anyone. I became her mother the moment I found out I was having a baby. I felt lost. I didn't want family. I didn't want Ethan. I wanted Brighton.

I was glad to be there alone.

I closed my eyes and tried to stop crying. I tried to just go back to sleep. My head hurt My body hurt. My heart hurt. I wanted to undo everything that had happened to bring me to that moment, and I wanted to undo ever knowing Ethan even existed in my life.

I was certain someone would be coming into my room soon. It wasn't possible that a nurse, or my mother, or Ethan wasn't nearby. I tried so hard to go back to sleep so I wouldn't have talk to anyone, but I just couldn't.

There was no clock that I could see, not that I cared about the time anyway, but without one, I wasn't sure how long I had been awake before Ethan did return. He walked into the room quietly. As he entered and looked at me, I was staring blankly at him. I was trying to decide if I was angry with him, still madly in love with him, or if I had lost all emotion in our relationship. If I would have opened my mouth, I would have cried.

Ethan rushed to my side and sat on the edge of my bed. He stroked my hair. He kissed me again and again, then he lay across me and cried.

I had spent eight years wanting him, loving him, forgiving him, waiting for him. Those years were flashing through my mind. What was I going to do? Did I want a marriage that only existed in our private world? Were we really just pretending? Should I walk away?

"I asked your mom and dad to sign your care over to me. I wanted to be the only one with you when you woke up. You've been unconscious for two days. I heard you scream and I ran to you, but you had already fallen down the stairs. I carried you and held you the whole way to the hospital. You never opened your eyes. I begged your mom to please release you to me. You're mine. You always have been. I hope you always will be Evi."

"Where's my baby Ethan? When did I lose Brighton?"

"Evi, we lost her almost right away. You were too far along for her to be protected in the fall. Your family was here, that was when I insisted that you are my family and I should have the rights to your care."

"When can I go home?"

"I'm sure the doctor will want you to stay at least another couple of days. You have a severe concussion, and a lot of scrapes and bruises, but no broken bones."

Lying there, I processed everything he had said. When I asked him about going home, I actually wasn't sure which home I wanted to return to.

He said, "You're going to be okay. You're going to recover."

"You're wrong. I'm not going to be okay. And even though I may recover, my daughter has died Ethan."

He was speechless. There was no way to comfort me.

"Will you call my family and update them? I still don't want to talk to anyone or see anyone. I want to go back to sleep. Will you be staying with me?" The thought that crossed my mind when I asked that question was will you be staying with me forever, not just for the day or night. I was still afraid deep down that he was going to be leaving me again.

"I'm not leaving without you Evi, not today, not ever. As soon as you're well enough, you're going with me."

"I need to sleep." I turned over and tears fell.

When I awoke later that evening, I was ready to eat and more ready to talk. I felt like I needed to explain some things to Ethan that he didn't know about and things he seemed to misunderstand. I also wanted to tell him these things, because I was hoping I would have a clearer understanding of how I was feeling about him now.

"Will you please get me something to eat?" I asked.

"Of course," he replied anxiously.

I added coldly, "Then, I think we should actually discuss what has happened and what's going to happen with us."

"Evi, we don't need to talk about anything right now. Everything can wait until we get home, or we can just work through this together day by day. We have forever, I hope."

"No, I want to work this out now. You've shut me down before when I wanted to explain myself to you and you're not going to ignore me this time. Maybe we wouldn't even be here right now if you would just let me be honest with you. Instead you turn away and get so angry over nothing! You will sit here, and you will listen to me. Now!"

"Okay babe. I'm here. Tell me everything you want to tell me. I'm ready."

I began.

"You know Clark and I started dating again after you left me, but we didn't start dating until July when I moved back to South Carolina and in with him. Yes, I moved in with him. It was a difficult decision to make but you left me! You married me, and within a year, you left me."

"The journal you found was mine and you should have never read it. It was not meant for you and I think you know that. It was my private way of remembering you. I needed it. I loved you for almost four years while you were with someone else. Then you came for me. You made love to me. You married me. You gave up on me. You have no idea how deeply you hurt me Ethan."

I wiped my tears and took a breath before continuing.

"At first, I wrote about missing you. In July when Clark came to Ponderosa, all I could think was that he never gives up on me. He never leaves me. He comes for me over and over. So, I went with him. We got back together. Then, I wrote about my time with Clark.

"You have to know though, I never got over you Ethan. Everything you read about Clark, every moment I wrote about, I was with him, but thinking about you. But Clark knew that.

"Then, one day before we broke up, in an attempt to keep me and hopefully make me get over you for good, Clark told me his side of the story about the night you left.

"You remember quite well, that you took me to our favorite hotel room, you sat me down, you refused to look at me, and you very coldly broke up with me. Then you just left me there alone. Perhaps in your mind, you were coming back, but you should have never broken up with me. You should have married me right after graduation. I would have missed you, and prayed for you, and loved you as your wife. Instead I did all those things as the ex-girlfriend you didn't care enough about to even continue *dating* while you were deployed.

"Well, here's the part I didn't know at the time, you didn't leave the hotel. You went and sat in the stairwell because you wanted to make sure I was going to be okay. I wasn't okay though, so I texted my best friend to come stay with me and Clark arrived.

"Clark knocked and rushed in as soon as I opened it. You heard and saw everything. You sat there in the hallway listening to me cry, listening to him comfort me. You heard everything. My worst moment, up until this one, you sat off to the side and let someone else take care of me. I still don't know how you could do that."

Desperate, he interrupted, "Evi, please. Let me try to explain."

"I'm not done Ethan! You don't get to speak yet."

I went on, "After Clark held me and calmed me down, I needed to rest. He took the key from the dresser and went to the stairwell to get ice. You were sitting there. He told you to go back to my room and fix what you had done, but you refused. You refused, and for the second time that night, you left me. You didn't love me enough to go back for me.

"After Clark told me that, I thought back to the way he was acting that evening when I got out of the shower and it all made a lot more sense. I thought he was disappointed in me, and he probably was, but he was more disappointed in you. I had to sit through that night not only in complete pain that you left me, but also in humiliation knowing how much I had hurt him!

"Clark let your words haunt him Ethan. He came here to Ponderosa to get me and take me back to live with him. He couldn't bear to be apart from me. He was never going to let me forget how much he loved me. I believed for a long time that perhaps Clark was the one I was supposed to be with, but I never could stop thinking about you. Clark knew I would always belong to you. I always had and maybe I always will."

"Maybe Evi?"

"There's one more thing you need to know about Ethan."

"Okay. What is it?" he whispered, clearly feeling out of control.

"You have hurt me. At sixteen I had to learn from my brother that the man I planned on marrying went back to his ex-girlfriend. Then that man finally came for me, made love to me, said he was going to marry me, then broke up with me. The man I planned on spending my life with didn't even invite me to his graduation. He moved half way across the world without calling me, ever. Oh, when he did come back to me, he got me pregnant, and is sitting with me while I go through losing my daughter. And through all of this, the only thing you've ever apologized for is leaving me in that hotel room alone three years ago."

"Evi, I've never realized this is how you truly feel." His tears fell. "I can hardly bear all the things you've had to face. How can you still look at me? What have I done to you?"

"Well Ethan, it has been a rough eight years, but I've healed over and over again. I've never stopped loving you. We vowed to God we'd love each other in sickness and health, for richer or poorer, for better or worse. We've had our share of worse, but I wouldn't trade the good for anything."

In desperation he said, "I will spend the rest of my life making things up to you. I don't deserve your constant love and forgiveness, but I am so grateful for it Evi. So grateful."

"Ethan, I love you. I am curious about something though. Do you truly feel we are married? Or has this been a fantasy? Did we create a situation so we wouldn't feel guilty about being together?"

"You're my wife Evi. I want a family with you. I want to fill our home with love and children. You are the only one I want. I am married to you."

"Yes, that sounds great. But, I want my life back. I want the last eight years back. And more than anything Ethan, I want my daughter back." I turned away from him.

"Evi, I'm here. We're going to get through this and we'll get better each day. I want Brighton back too. I love her too! We need to get through this together."

I pushed the button and called for the nurse.

"I want you to go Ethan. I'm an adult. I'll sign myself out of the hospital."

"Evi, I'm not leaving you. You can't make me leave," he said with insecurity in his voice.

"I don't have to make you leave Ethan. I don't want you here. Besides, you'll have to go to work any day now. The Army is going to make you leave."

The nurse came into my room, and I asked her if she could help me call for some food because my boyfriend needed to go to work.

"Ethan, I love you so much, but I have never and will never be your priority. Maybe, when we had Brighton, we would have been your priority together, but I don't believe I alone can hold onto you. I need to be all you want in this world, not the girl you love on weekends and holidays."

"This isn't over Evi." He left. He actually left again.

❀ ❀ ❀

Two days later, I called my parents to get me from the hospital. They had assumed Ethan was with me the whole time. I wanted to recover alone. Sure enough, Ethan was transferred to Fort Jackson and he did leave that week. I don't know if he was planning in his mind to come back for me, or if he agreed with me. Maybe he felt that he had hurt me too many times to face me every day while carrying that guilt. No matter, I was still only twenty-four, and I was ready to start fresh.

Although I knew Ethan was in South Carolina, I decided I wanted to move back to Charleston. I found a small studio apartment downtown for little Piper and I, and I was able to get a teaching job at a private academy on one of the islands. I closed the door on my old life. I asked Ethan's family and my family to promise me that no one outside of us would ever know about the past few months.

Once I was settled into my new life, I contacted Piper to update her on my relationship with Ethan and to let her know I was living in

Charleston again. She was living in Florida and was engaged. She asked me to be a bridesmaid, and I couldn't wait to see her at her wedding.

Thankfully, Piper was getting married in December so I would have plenty of time off to go be with her. I didn't want to go home for Christmas. I did not want to see anyone from Ponderosa just yet.

Piper and her fiancé were having their wedding on a private beach south of Fort Lauderdale. The scene was as beautiful as was the bride. I walked down the aisle to the altar with my hand holding the arm of a groomsman. I kept my focus on the minister as I took my place in line with the other bridesmaids. Then, I turned to watch Piper walk down the aisle with her dad. A tear rolled down my cheek as I watched in awe of her beauty and peace. I actually did not miss Ethan or even think about him. Piper was the only person on my mind.

Throughout the ceremony, my attention remained on the wedding. Then, I started feeling a draw to look at the guests. I hadn't noticed the people in the congregation up to that point. I looked out and slightly to my right... and there he was. Yep, Clark was there, staring at me, smiling at me, pulling me. Suddenly, once again, I could breathe. A weight had been lifted. I dropped my head and fought like crazy to hold back tears. I worked really hard to regain my focus on the minister so I wouldn't miss anything.

At the conclusion of the ceremony, the groomsman escorted me back down the aisle. I smiled at Clark and remembered running into his arms the first night we ever met. I knew he was coming for me. I knew I would be running to him again.

As the guests were released, I stood off to the side waiting for him and he did not delay. He walked right up to me as confident as ever and said, "Hi my name is Clark Ravenel. I'm from Atlanta, Georgia, and I am a graduate of the Citadel. What's your name?"

"Hi Clark. My name is Evi, I mean Everclear Jordan. I used to know a wonderful young man named Clark Ravenel who was a cadet at the Citadel. Do you know him?"

"I do know him Miss Jordan. He's still exactly the same. He fell in love with a beautiful girl from Idaho when he was nineteen, and he has never loved anyone else since the moment he met her."

"Does this mean he may still be interested in that girl?"

"Nope, it means he *still* plans on marrying that girl. He promised her forever, and he meant it. He has never let her down, and he will never let her down."

Clark pulled out an engagement ring and knelt down on one knee. He said so lovingly, "I don't know what has happened in your life since I last saw you two years ago, and I can't wait to listen to you tell me about every moment. I don't want you to leave out a single detail. Your experiences make you who you are. I have always loved you! I will always love you! I will never let you go again. I mean it Evi. I want forever to start right now! I will not take 'No' for an answer. God has brought you back to me for a third time and this one is meant to be. Will you marry me forever, as soon as possible?"

I didn't hesitate, "Clark, I can't wait to marry you! Yes!"

A crowd cheered behind us, and Piper and her husband ran to congratulate us. We sheepishly hugged them, then stepped aside to avoid stealing their glory. We just wanted to be with each other and not the center of attention.

Clark took my hand and kissed it. Then I kissed him so gently and thankfully. Our eyes never lost focus on each other. We walked to the dance floor and held onto each other.

After the wedding we stayed together in his room. We couldn't keep our hands off of each other, but we decided to wait until our wedding night to be together.

Clark had already been invited to Piper's wedding, but she made a point to call him and tell him that I was also going to be there and that I was no longer with Ethan. She also added that she knew for certain I would never be with Ethan again.

Clark wasn't going to miss this opportunity. He flew from Atlanta to Florida and patiently waited to get to me. The timing was perfect... just like God had a hand in it.

Clark was working for his dad, and although he had work to do, he convinced his boss to let him take a few extra days off since it was the Christmas holiday. His family was disappointed that he would be missing Christmas day with them, but they were happy he was with the girl from the pictures that he had been in love with for years.

Since Clark had flown to Florida, he rode back to Charleston to spend Christmas, and of course New Year's Eve, with me. I also couldn't wait to introduce him to my other best friend Piper. They loved each other and the three of us had a wonderful week together.

I told him everything, absolutely everything. He was so sorry about me losing Brighton. He held me, cried with me and promised to be with me.

"Can you forgive me Clark? Can you live with me and love me even though I've been through so much and I've left so many times?" I asked unable to understand his kind of love.

"I didn't know how I was ever going to get you back Evi. I didn't know why I kept waiting and waiting for you. I could not give up hope that you were meant to be with me. I am so sorry for all you've had to go through. I'm so sorry that I couldn't prevent you from being hurt. But I am so grateful that the path you've been on, brought you back to me. There is nothing you've done that needs to be forgiven."

We set a date to get married in Atlanta in June as soon as school was out. I would quit my job at the end of the year and move to Georgia. Clark returned to Atlanta, but we promised to be together every weekend.

My Spring Break was approaching and I was planning on spending it with Clark's family. I was packing my suitcase and packing Piper's food and bed when I heard my door open and close. It scared me so I grabbed Piper and cautiously peeked around the corner to the living room.

"Clark! What the heck are you doing here? You nearly scared me to death!" I rushed over to him still holding Piper. I grabbed the back of his neck, pressed against him and kissed him a lot.

He placed his hands on my shoulders and pushed me away very gently. Then, he looked into my eyes, "I came to tell you I don't want you to come to Atlanta this week Evi."

"Why not? We promised your parents I'd be there this week. We are going to Atlanta."

"Well, I'm not taking you to Atlanta ever again as just my girlfriend."

"So you don't want me going back there until June?!"

"No, we're getting married now. I can't wait any longer Evi. We can have a big reception in June. Our families and friends will all be there, but I've waited six years for you and I'm done waiting. We're getting married today."

"It's not that simple is it?" I asked, then worried, "I don't even have a ring for you."

"We can get a ring for me later. I don't care about that. I've worked out the details. I have a few friends from the Citadel coming to witness for us. The minister from the church we attended here in Charleston will officiate. We're getting married out at Folly in just a little while. No one will know but us, well, just for now at least. I know you have something perfect to wear in that closet. Go get dressed. My friend will drive you to the beach when you're ready. I'll be there waiting for you."

I didn't argue or even question him. Clark was so confident, in charge and sure. He was all I wanted and needed. I happened to have a white, tea length, ball gown that I knew Clark had never seen. I curled my hair quickly, added more makeup, got dressed, and went out to meet his friend.

Sitting on the seat in the car was a beautiful bouquet of flowers with a note that read: *Everclear, I chose this day to marry you because it is the only day in our past that I can't bear to remember. This is the day you left me six years ago. But from now, to forever, it will be the day we love more than any other. Our life, our family, our love story starts anew in a few minutes. I love you Evi. I'll see you at the altar.*

We arrived at Folly Beach, and I was escorted to Clark and the minister.

"Miss Everclear Jordan are you ready to marry Mr. Clark Ravenel?"

"Yes sir. Very ready." I handed my flowers to the girl standing beside me.

The minister continued, "I have prepared vows for you but please feel free to include your own as well."

Clark and I exchanged vows and said "I do" to one another, and when offered the opportunity to speak before we kissed, I asked if I could speak first. He nodded.

I said, "Clark, I'm not sure I deserve you. I'm not sure I will ever deserve you. You have rescued me from myself for six years and never stopped believing in me. You welcome me, you love me, you forgive me, you carry me. You are the only reason I can still breathe. I promise to tell you 'thank you' for loving me every day. I promise to love you every day. I promise to love whatever may come. I promise to have children with you, and to tell them that their daddy is my hero and the best daddy in the world. And finally, I promise to keep my promises. I love you."

Clark didn't speak at first. Instead, he pressed my hands to his face. He looked at me and then at the minister, then back at me again and said, "You've said everything I wanted to say Evi with one exception. That is, I promise to make your heart beat for me forever. You are and always have been my only one."

"You may kiss your bride," the pastor concluded.

This may not have been my first kiss, nor his first kiss, but it was our first kiss as one. We took a little extra time to enjoy it and to love our moment, our beginning.

There was a photographer at our wedding so we had lots of pictures taken. The sky was clear and the temperature warm. The ocean was singing throughout the entire ceremony. We laughed and played knowing we were meant to be together.

On our way back to my, well our apartment, we briefly discussed a honeymoon. Then, we discussed if we wanted to have children right away or wait. I was twenty-five then and he was twenty-six. I suggested we just enjoy our first night as husband and wife and worry about family planning later.

Clark carried me through the door, closed it behind us, carried me to our bedroom, and closed that door behind us. I was all his. He pulled back the sheets on the bed and he made love to me, his *wife*.

Since we got married on Saturday, we woke up Sunday morning and decided we'd go to his family's condo in Oceanside for a few days. We enjoyed more time alone, then early afternoon, we packed everything up, grabbed Piper and headed out. We were excited to go to the beach, and we were excited to tell his parents that we had gotten married. I was afraid they would be upset, but Clark assured me that they were going to love me. He was sure their only concern would be us having to live apart for the three months until school was out.

We arrived at his condo in Oceanside. We went in, and of course I ran straight through to the balcony. After inhaling the air and my surroundings, I went inside. Clark was standing there and had been watching me look at the view. I walked to him, took his hand, led him to the couch, and pushed him down just as I had done a few years earlier. I straddled his lap and whispered "I love you Clark. It's time for our honeymoon to start."

We stayed in Oceanside until Wednesday morning, then drove to Atlanta. Just as Clark had said, his parents were welcoming and happy for us. My family came to Atlanta for our reception and it was so great to see them. I was pregnant by then and Clark and I were beyond happy. He was so proud of me. He was so proud of our babies. Yes, babies. I was having twin boys. I didn't get very sick throughout my pregnancy, and for that I was extremely grateful as well.

Years passed. Our boys Jax and Drake were born and when they were three, Emmi-Kate came along. Since Clark had to work, I had been going to visit my family in Ponderosa alone several times a year. He would join me when he could. He had a great job so we could afford for me to go home every other month or so. It was very important that my parents be a big part of our children's lives.

Winter had arrived, the boys were strong, and I was ready to get them on skis! We arrived in Idaho and I headed off to take all of my babies down the mountain. Clark was going to be joining us later in the week. I promised to send lots of videos and pictures.

I was so excited for our adventure. I loaded all of our gear into our rented SUV and drove up to the mountain. I never really thought through the logistics of keeping the boys up and getting myself down safely with Emmi-Kate in a pack. Confused, I sat in the lodge staring at our piles of gear.

"Everclear Jordan, what do you think you are doing?" Two voices scolded me and laughed.

"Kieron! Brody! I need help," I whined.

"By the way guys, my name is Everclear Ravenel now. This is Jax and this is Drake. We need help. Don't we babies?"

The boys nodded so sweetly. You could tell they felt sorry for me. I thanked God no one was crying.

"Well, first of all, Everclear *Ravenel*, how the heck do you tell them apart?" Kieron asked laughing loudly.

"And second, boys, do you want to go shred some cords?" Brody chimed into the conversation.

Again, my boys just nodded and looked at me to see if these weirdos were safe.

"It's okay boys. This is Brody, and this is Kieron. They are mommy's very best friends. I taught them how to ski many years ago, so now they're going to help me teach you two to ski."

"Oh! Seriously Evi!"

"You big boys should not contradict me," I said still using a baby voice.

They rolled their eyes at me and laughed. Brody grabbed Jax and his gear, Kieron grabbed Drake and his gear, I reminded each of them who they were holding, and I hoisted Emmi-Kate onto my back. I took a few pictures and off we went.

I'm a good skier, but handling now four boys, and a baby, and a camera was almost more than I could take. Once my sons were comfortable with Kieron and Brody, I asked if I could leave them so I could take a few runs alone. The big boys seemed unnerved at my request, so I told them to go inside for a little while. I bought them all a basket of fries and that seemed to keep them distracted.

"Don't feed Emmi-Kate fries. She'll choke. Just give her little crackers until I get back. Here are their juices. No beers!"

"Wait, you're leaving us that one too?" Brody pointed to Emmi-Kate.

"Yes! You'll all be fine," I insisted.

Kieron joked before I walked away, "So we have to keep them all alive for how long?"

"Kieron! Knock it off! I'll be right back. They're humans, not porcelain dolls." I left before they could offer any more arguments.

On my own, I floated down the slopes, hit a few jumps, skied some bumps, and slid backwards for old times' sake. I thought about Brighton, as I had every day since I lost her. I thought about how old she would've been if she were there with me, and how fun it would have been skiing with her and raising her on Lake Everclear. My life with her would have been so different than my life is with my boys and Emmi. After four or five runs, I headed back to the lodge to my family.

Brody and Kieron helped me pack up, and they hugged us all as we said goodbye. I told them Clark was coming in a few days, and we'd be back up so he could watch the boys ski. They told me to call them each time I came up so they could help me and get Jax and Drake really strong on their skis. I also told Brody to come get Piper for a few days. She always loved spending time with him.

"Are you boys ready to go to Mr. Poppy's for ice cream?" I cheered.

"Yes!" Jax and Drake yelled. Emmi-Kate had fallen asleep.

"Bye Brody. Bye Kieron. I love you and miss you both so much. I'll call y'all soon."

When we arrived at Mr. Poppy's, I packed Emmi in her front carrying pack and brought the boys into the restaurant so we could sit. I was tired but still needed to take care of all of them at once. Eating cones in a rental car was not going to happen. I texted my mom to let her know where we were and that I'd be home very soon.

A waitress brought us our ice cream and I started working to keep everyone tidy and snacking. Jax and Drake are so calm and sweet. It's such a blessing not having rowdy boys. Manners and love were our daily lessons.

Emmi was still sleeping, but I needed to adjust her so I could help the boys. I slid out of the booth and a gentleman behind me asked, "Can I help you ma'am?"

I turned, "Ethan! What are you doing here?"

"Brody texted me and told me you'd be here. He thought I should come say hello and just see for myself that you're okay. But, you look like you could use a hand."

"Um… okay… sure. I'm so hot. Can you pull her off of me, so I can sit down? Then I can take her back."

Ethan cradled Emmi so carefully as he stared at her face. When I was ready, he handed her back to me.

"So are you going to introduce me to everyone?" he asked.

"Uh, sure. This is Jax, this is Drake and this is Emerson-Katherine. We call her Emmi-Kate. Boys, this is Mr. Ethan. You know that funny guy named Brody who was helping you ski Jax, this is his big brother. He's a soldier."

"Like daddy?" Drake asked.

"Yes, sweetie. Like your daddy used to be. Except, Mr. Ethan here is still a soldier and daddy works with grandpa."

I informed Ethan that Clark had actually enlisted in the army for four years after he graduated from the Citadel.

"Mommy says daddy's her hero!" Jax said raising his spoon over his head with a mouthful of ice cream. "Yeah baby, I do." I wasn't sure what else to say.

"Gosh Evi. How do you tell them apart?" Ethan laughed a little and then added, "They look exactly like their father."

"They do, don't they? I see a lot of Jarren in them too though. They definitely seem to both have Jarren's laid back disposition." I laughed too. "However, people always ask me how I tell them apart. They just don't look alike to me. They are as different as any other people in this world. They're my life, aren't you boys?"

"Mm, hm…" they both mumbled and nodded while continuing to shovel ice cream into their mouths.

Emmi was waking up and squirming. I shifted her so she could see what was going on and she smiled at Ethan. Then, she immediately reached for the ice cream.

"She looks exactly like you Evi! Holy cow! Exactly like you."

"Well, thank you Ethan, because I think she's beautiful."

"Well, she is. You both are."

I blushed.

I asked Ethan how he was doing and noticed he was wearing a wedding ring. He said that he and Hannah had gotten married and they were stationed in Oregon. They didn't have children yet, but were starting to talk about it. Hannah liked working and hadn't decided how to fit kids into her schedule yet, but they were seriously thinking about starting a family soon.

I told Ethan that I had moved back to Charleston right after we broke up. He was shocked that I was so close to him and he didn't know it. I told him I never saw any point in going backwards. I told him I saw Clark at Piper's wedding, and we were never apart again.

I felt bad for him because I wasn't sure that he was truly happy, but clearly I was. My husband lived for me, did everything for me, our children and I were his life. I love Clark so much and was so glad the way my life was going.

After catching up, the boys finished their treats and were exhausted. I also needed to feed Emmi-Kate something besides ice cream and crackers. Ethan helped me get the boys cleaned up, and he held Emmi for me while I got out my wallet to pay the bill. As I fumbled for cash, he handed the waitress money and she walked away.

"Thank you Ethan. You didn't have to do that."

"I know, I wanted to."

I held the boys' hands in one hand and Emmi in my other hand, and I looked at Ethan and whispered to him very softly, "They'll never know they have big sister in Heaven Ethan. I think about her every day." A few tears fell from my eyes. Since my hands were full, he gently wiped them for me. After all, they were tears for his baby.

He then wiped tears from his own eyes and kissed me on my head, "I do too Evi."

In a cheerful voice Ethan said to my boys, "Hey, it was really nice to meet you guys. My brother Brody told me you two are going to be champion skiers like your mommy someday."

We walked to the door together and Ethan held it open for us.

"Daddy!" Drake yelled and he took off running down the sidewalk. It scared me, but Clark ran faster and grabbed him before he got into the parking lot.

"Hey buddy! Where's your... mommy?" Clark looked up and saw me standing there with Ethan. He walked straight to us and held out his hand to Ethan. "Ethan, it's great to see you again. I hope you've been well. Thank you for your service."

"Thank you Clark. It's good to see you too."

I had a sudden flash of the last time the three of us met on a street. I was with Ethan then. It's strange how life changes. Then, Clark broke my concentration when he leaned to me and took Emmi-Kate. He kissed her on her lips, then kissed me on my lips. "Hey babe, I couldn't wait another minute to be with you and the kids. I flew out here a few days early. I hope you don't mind."

Seeing him made my heart pound and butterflies in my stomach flutter. "Clark, I'm so glad to see you. I missed you so much; of course I don't mind. I love you."

Jax began jumping at Clark's legs because he was holding Emmi and Drake.

"Jax baby, come here," I said. He let me hold him, but he leaned really far to get a kiss from his daddy. He was not going to be left out. Clark kissed him on his forehead and cheek and said so sweetly, "Hey Jax buddy, I missed you."

It was time to move this along so I said in a meaningful tone, "Ethan, it was great to see you. I wish you and Hannah the very best. Maybe we'll be in town at the same time again in the future and we can all get together." I squeezed his arm just above his elbow and gave him a kiss on the cheek.

"Yeah, maybe. Y'all have a good time this week."

"Bye Ethan." My voice cracked and tears formed in my eyes. He noticed, but he quickly walked away.

Clark kissed me so sweetly and said, "You knew this day would come and so did I. Are you okay? I'm not worried. I just want to know that you're okay. You've been through a lot and you're probably really tired right now. I'm here. I love you."

I cried on his shoulder for just a minute with our children staring at me like I was crazy. I laughed at their little faces. I kissed my husband very deeply, and I said, "Wow! I am perfect. We are perfect. Thank you for loving me, thank you for marrying me and thank for giving me these babies. I love you Clark, more every day. Now let's go put these angels down for their naps." I raised my eyebrows at him.

"Mmm… Let's go," he seductively replied.

Chapter 26

I woke up in a hospital with a terrible headache. I didn't look for anyone. As soon as I opened my eyes and realized where I was, I felt my stomach to see if I was still carrying my baby. Thank God I was. I held onto my stomach and cried. I was still not noticing if anyone was even around me. All I cared about was my baby.

"You're okay. Your baby's okay." I heard my mom's voice.

My mom shook Ethan's shoulder, "Ethan, Ethan, wake up dear. Evi's awake."

I'm sure I looked scared. I heard Ethan's voice, "You're okay. Our baby's okay." He looked exhausted and very confused.

They were both there beside me and so was my dad, Jarren, Brody, and Ethan's parents. Someone pressed a button for the nurse to come check on me.

"How long have I been here?" I asked.

"Just two days Evi," Ethan answered. "We're all here. We haven't left you."

"What happened?" I asked, completely unaware of how I ended up there.

Ethan still seeming very confused explained, "You fell down the stairs to the lake. You hit your head and have a pretty bad concussion, but you'll be okay. Our baby is okay. You are early enough in the pregnancy that she was protected from any harm."

"Why have I been out for two days?" My throat was dry.

"The doctors wanted to keep you asleep for a while so the swelling could subside and you wouldn't have to feel the pain."

"How far did I fall?"

"We don't know. I heard you scream and I ran to you. You were unconscious and bleeding. You weren't at the bottom of the staircase but you were close to the bottom. I picked you up and carried you to my parents' house and told them to get the car. I got in the backseat and held you the whole way to the hospital. You were unconscious the entire time. You never woke up. You were bleeding. You scared me. You scared me. I was so scared." Ethan put his head on my chest and started to cry.

"It's okay babe. I'm okay, Brighton's okay," I said to him.

"Evi, do you remember how you fell?" my mom asked.

It was all slowly coming back to me, "Yeah, a little. I was dizzy and sick. While I was bent over on my hands and knees, my hand slipped off of the step. I fell head first, and I screamed for Ethan. That's all I remember."

Ethan seemed to be praying while speaking, "Thank God you were already down on your knees. This would have been so much worse if you were standing. I love you so much Evi. I'm so sorry about fighting with you that day. I'm so sorry."

I guess Ethan had told everyone about our fight, because he sure was open about it then. He's never open about anything.

"It's okay Ethan. It's over right?" I smiled at him. I was in a lot of pain. My body ached, my head ached and I just wanted to be alone with my husband and my baby for a while.

"You all can go home now. I'm fine. You don't need to sit here and watch me sleep. Come back later or tomorrow. I want to rest some more. I love y'all."

I knew there was no way Ethan was leaving, and I also had a suspicion that there was no way Jarren was leaving either. Jarren had taken care of me my entire life. He wasn't going anywhere.

They each kissed me before they left.

"Ethan, please don't go," I whispered.

"You don't even have to say that Everclear. I'm not going anywhere unless it's with you and Brighton."

He kissed me and I fell asleep.

I'm not sure when I woke up, but Jarren was sitting with me.

"Hey," I said to him.

"Hey Ev. You doing okay? Need anything?"

"Just water please."

"Ethan went to get something to eat. He'll be back soon. Then I'll go home for the night and come back tomorrow morning as early as I can."

"Okay."

"Evi, since we're alone, if you feel okay, can you tell me why Ethan was so angry with you the other day?"

"Yeah. I don't care if you know. I have nothing to hide and neither does he."

I was only going to tell Jarren the part of the argument that was relevant to my situation. At the time, I felt that no one else outside of Ethan and I needed to know the full story.

I began telling Jarren, "Our fight started because Ethan found and *read* a journal I had written in about the first year after he broke up with me. The fight escalated because of what he read."

I continued, "You know Clark and I started dating again after Ethan left me. We didn't start dating though until July when I moved back to South Carolina and in with him. April through July, I wrote about missing Ethan, then when Clark and I got back together, I wrote about Clark."

Jarren was listening carefully.

"Well, I never really got over Ethan and Clark could easily sense that. One day before Clark and I broke up, in an attempt to keep me and hopefully make me get over Ethan for good, Clark told me a story about the night Ethan left. Ethan never knew I was aware of the whole story of the night we broke up."

I rested my head back onto my pillow and looked at the ceiling as I told Jarren more.

"Ethan took me to a hotel room and sat me down and very coldly broke up with me. Then, he just left. However, I didn't know at the time, but he didn't leave the hotel. He was sitting in the stairwell, because he wanted to make sure I was going to be okay."

"I texted Piper to come stay with me. She was out with a bunch of our friends and Clark was in that group. She immediately showed Clark the message, and he ran straight to me. He had run up the stairs but didn't see Ethan because Ethan was sitting on the set of stairs leading up to the third floor."

I nervously turned my eyes back to Jarren, "Clark knocked on my door and rushed in as soon as I opened it. Ethan heard and saw everything. He was in the hallway that whole time listening to me cry, listening to Clark comfort me. He heard everything."

I rested for a moment and took a deep breath. Then said, "I asked Clark to get me some ice while I showered because my face was swollen from crying so much. Clark took the key from the dresser and went to the stairwell to get ice. Ethan was sitting there in his uniform looking down at his hands."

Clark said, "Ethan, what are you still doing here? You need to get back in there and fix this!"

"I can't go back to her. I have a job to do. She's strong. She's going to be okay." Ethan was trying to convince himself.

"Telling yourself that doesn't mean it's the truth. You need to go back in there. You can't leave her. How can you do this? Evi loves you! You can't leave her like this!"

"I can't go back either. She's going to be okay."

Clark gave him the perfect opportunity to fix it, "Ethan, here's the card. You can't leave her. If you don't go back in there, you will never get her back. I promise you I will make sure of that! You choose right now, if you're going or if I'm going."

"It sounds like you're already trying to make her forget me Clark."

"Evi is strong and she's not going let me or anyone else near her right now, but that's not the point. She doesn't deserve this. She's not someone you can just throw away Ethan."

"You don't understand. I trust her. You don't know her. You don't know us. She's going to be okay." Ethan responded in a quiet but stern voice.

"No! You don't understand. You choose right now if you love her enough to keep her. If you don't go back in there, I will do everything I can to make sure Evi knows you didn't love her enough to take care of her. You see Ethan, I do love her. That's why I can't stand to watch you do this. I would never treat her this way. I will be here every minute for her."

Silence fell between them for a brief moment before Clark said one more time, "Take the key Ethan. Evi wants you; she needs you. This is the last time I'm going to offer it."

Ethan got up, looked at Clark and said, "Take care of her for now. But know, I'll be back for her and she knows that. I promised her I'd be back. Don't fool yourself Clark. She'll always belong with me."

"And Ethan left me… for the second time that night."

I finished my story to Jarren, "After Clark told me that, I thought back to the way he was acting that evening when I got out of the shower and it all made a lot more sense. When he was sitting on the floor of the hotel room and just kept repeating that he was 'thinking, just thinking' I figured out that he wasn't thinking about me, he was thinking about Ethan. I thought he was disappointed in me, and he probably was, but he was more disappointed in Ethan.

"Clark also let Ethan's words haunt him. He came here to Ponderosa to get me and take me back to live with him for the remainder of the summer before my junior year. He couldn't bear to be apart from me. He was never going to let me forget how much he loved me. I believed for a long time that perhaps Clark was the one I was supposed to be with, but I never could stop thinking about Ethan. Clark knew I would always belong with Ethan. I always had and I always will. So, two days ago when Ethan and I had our first real fight, this is what it was about."

Jarren simply said, "Clark sounds like a really great guy Evi. You were blessed to have someone so close to you to help you through all of that."

"That sums it up nicely Evi. I'm sorry I didn't let you tell me all of that two days ago. It will never happen again babe. I mean it." Ethan's voice softly spoke to me from behind the curtain in the doorway. He had been standing there listening to me tell Jarren a portion of what had happened between us.

"I'm going to go home now Evi. I'll see you tomorrow. I love you." Jarren kissed my hand and left. He patted Ethan on the shoulder as he walked out.

"I never knew that you didn't call him Evi. I thought you called him."

"No Ethan, I called Piper that night. I needed a friend. Clark took care of me though. Being with him a second time only reminded me, again, that I couldn't and wouldn't ever love anyone but you. You were all I could think about. I felt so bad that even though I did love him in a way, he was always a distraction. He kept me from going insane worrying about you. I tried so hard to tell myself every day to trust you. We were married and I could trust you. Finally, I knew I was being unfair to him. I decided I would be happier alone rather than feel the guilt of not loving him the way he deserved. I belonged with you. You are my only one. Do you feel better now?"

"Yes. I'm so sorry I didn't give you the chance to just explain that. I'm so sorry."

"Ethan, I want to tell you one more thing while we are clearing the air."

"Yeah, what is it?"

"I came to your graduation ceremony."

I smiled softly at him when I said it, but I think I hurt him. He may have been better off not knowing. He pulled my hand to his forehead like he was praying again and a tear fell.

"You were there?" he was barely able to speak.

"Nothing in this world was going to keep me from seeing you graduate. In addition to that day being your graduation, it was also our first anniversary. You graduated on May twenty-fifth. I couldn't, I wouldn't have spent that day anywhere but near you." I smiled softly trying to uplift him.

"How'd you get there, and get in?" He knew attending his graduation would not have been simple due to regulations.

"I called your mom and worked out a plan for there to be at least one extra ticket for me, and I made her promise she would never tell you. Then, I booked a room at the hotel we stayed in together a few times and I got on a plane. Your family was in the same hotel, but I only stayed one night. I didn't leave my room until it was time to take a cab to campus. Afterward, I caught a late flight back to Charleston."

"My God Evi, that had to be so hard for you."

"It was probably one of the most difficult moments of my life, well next to being sixteen and having the man I planned on marrying go back to his ex-girlfriend of course." I laughed and rolled my eyes at him still trying to lighten the mood a bit, but he wasn't ready for a lighter mood yet.

Another tear fell, and then more tears as he said, "Evi, how could you bear that alone? How could you not come to me that day? How painful was that for you? I can hardly handle thinking about you sitting alone, then having to leave alone. What have I done to you?" Ethan rested his head on the edge of my bed still holding my hand.

"I'm better now Ethan. It has been a rough three years, but I'm healing."

"I will spend the rest of my life making things up to you. I don't deserve your constant love and forgiveness, but I am so grateful for it Evi. So grateful."

"Ethan, I love you. I am curious about something from that day though. I am surprised that you didn't see me. I really thought for a few moments you looked right at me. I hoped you noticed me. But after the ceremony, you didn't come to me. Did you see me?"

Ethan lifted his head as he spoke, "One of my classmates who was next to me as we stood on the field at attention whispered and said to check out the blonde girl sitting on the far right of the stands. We weren't allowed to move or talk. I cut just my eyes over, and I thought the girl sitting there looked just like you. It hurt my heart to even imagine you at that moment. I stared for a few seconds, then looked straight ahead again. I knew there was no way it could have been you, so I just ignored it. I shut down my feelings."

"Hmm, I thought I saw you look at me."

"Thank you for telling me you were there. It means everything to me that you came to my graduation, and I did notice it was on our first anniversary. I'm sorry. God, I've caused us so much pain." He kissed my hand and pressed it to his cheek.

"Evi, so much of this conversation is strange because I had a dream of your life without me. It scared me, no it terrified me. Promise me that you know our marriage is real. This is not a fantasy or a joke. We are a family. This is our family. I love you and I love our baby. Nothing and no one will ever separate us."

"Thank you Ethan and of course our marriage is real. Now, I'm hungry and I'm ready to go home," I said softly looking at my belly.

"I'll ask the nurse if I can take you to the cafeteria to eat babe."

He leaned down and put one hand on my belly and the other on my head and he kissed me. "Can we brush your teeth first though?" he asked and we both laughed.

Ethan helped me get up and stretch. I brushed my teeth and my hair, and refused to spend time looking in the mirror. It was horrifying. My body and face were cut and bruised from my fall. Noticing my shock, he hugged me carefully rubbing his hands on my lower back. We kissed more. Again, thinking I would lighten the mood and draw attention away from my wounds, I said to him, "Hey at least you're trained for all of this."

He looked so serious and said, "Evi, there is no training that could prepare me for the possibility of losing my wife and my baby."

I felt bad for what he must have been going through while I was unconscious.

Ethan finally called the nurse to see if I could walk around and go get food, but they wouldn't let me walk that far just yet. I still had a headache, and they wanted me off my feet for another day so the bruising could heal. The doctors also wanted to make sure the baby was secure.

Ethan brought me dinner and I felt so much better after eating. I hoped that meant my morning sickness would be gone for good soon.

I was released from the hospital two days later, and Ethan wouldn't leave me. He still had to go to Fort Jackson, but he had another nine days with me. I was more energetic and needed him to know that my fall had nothing to do with him. He hadn't even realized I had gone to the steps. He thought when I walked away, I had gone back into our house. He said he would have never let me go to the lake alone. When he heard me scream, he said he got sick because he immediately knew I had fallen down that hill and it was serious.

Chapter 27

The final week of June, I was completing my fifth month of pregnancy and Ethan was to report to work. We discussed me moving with him right away and having our baby there, but I had to be honest with him. Even after everything we had just been through, I wasn't ready to move away from our house on Lake Everclear, or from our parents and families. He understood. We knew his time was more flexible and we'd be able to see each other more often anyway. I needed to stay in Ponderosa. The nausea wasn't completely gone and there was no way to know how long it was going to last. At our home, I had people to help take care of me every day. Work would keep Ethan busy, but in South Carolina, I would be alone all day. So, we made the decision to separate again.

Before Ethan left, we briefly talked about actually getting married. Again, I was the one who said no. I told him, "We are married Ethan. Just for now, let's hold off on any ceremonies." My main reasoning was that I wasn't feeling much like a bride. I was tired, sore and still a little bruised.

We agreed I'd sign the baby's birth certificate with Parker as my last name and really, no one would ever know the difference. They don't check marriage or driver's licenses when you are signing a birth certificate.

Even though Ethan was so much closer, once the reality of him leaving set in, it still felt like he was going to be a world away. I know I made his leaving very difficult, but when it was time for him to go, I cried until I couldn't breathe.

"You can't do this to yourself Evi. You have to calm down. I love you. We're going to see each other a lot now. I'm just going to work. That's all. I'm just going to work." He wiped my tears, kissed me, held me. He stayed so calm, so reasonable. Ethan is very skilled at turning off his emotions. I don't know if he believed what he was saying so he truly wasn't sad, or if he was dying inside but trying to stay strong.

The following months, Ethan visited a few times, then he was able to get an official family leave for Brighton's birth in November. He got here to Pondersoa the week before she was born so he could set up her room. I wouldn't let anyone else do that for us. That was our job together.

Brighton's birth was, well the usual. I had her naturally. It took about six hours, so there was a lot of screaming and a lot of pain, as you can imagine. Ethan never left my side. He never even had to take a break to get water, or fresh air, or to stretch. As long as I wasn't moving, he wasn't moving. When I wanted to walk, he held me up and walked with me. He never let me go. He was calm and wanted to help. I actually don't think an entire army could have pulled him away from me.

Our daughter was finally born, and they handed her right to me. After a few minutes, they cleaned her up. Ethan cut her cord, and they handed her to me again. My whole world forever revolved around her. I suddenly became hers. I belonged to her, but we belonged to him. He would die for us.

Ethan was able to stay for two more weeks and spend the holidays with us. After he realized how tired I was all the time, he rearranged the nursery so I could have a place to sleep while I nursed Brighton. He had a custom recliner made just for my size! It's the best gift ever. She and I love it and we spend hours in that chair together.

Ethan soaked up every second of being my husband and her daddy. He wouldn't let anyone come to our house during the time he was home with us. Essentially, other than seeing her at the hospital, no one saw her again until she was two weeks old.

Before he left, he always reminded me to stay away from the lake, stay off the steps and stay off my skis. He forbade me from skiing down the mountain with our baby in a pack. Yes! People do that. My parents did that with me and my brother! Of course I would not have taken her down this young, but he didn't know that.

Ethan went back to work. We had video calls every single day, and he visited over a few weekends while I was still getting my strength back.

When the topic of moving to South Carolina came up again, there was no question that I was ready to be with him. *However,* now don't judge me, I was still not ready to take our baby away from our home. He lives in a little apartment, and we live here in this beautiful home that he built for us. We're living on *my* lake. This is still home for now. In addition to that, winter had set in out here and with a new baby, I did not feel like packing until early summer.

I, no we, will be moving very soon though. Ethan's coming for us very soon. He just hasn't told me the exact date yet.

"So there Mr. Moore. I have shared almost my entire love story about my soldier with you. Feel free to edit any parts you wish. There are many more stories that I could fill a book with, but I think these will give your viewers a perfect sense of our nine years, oh my, nine years together?

"I hope you are able to convey to those who will be watching a few important points. I want your viewers to not only know our history, and our love story, but know us. I want them to know who I was when I met Ethan and who I slowly became because of him.

"I believe our love story is unique to us, but also exactly like many others. I began my dating years never doubting that I would wait until I was married to give myself to someone. Then, no matter how hard I tried, as soon as I was faced with the gift of true love, I had to rethink everything I believed. Perhaps I should have waited, but I paid for my decisions every day for almost three years.

"I didn't fall in love with Ethan because he was a soldier, a hero. I loved him long before he made the decision to dedicate his life to serving our country. I didn't give myself completely to a romanticized version of a man. I gave myself to the one man I had wanted since I was fifteen years old.

"I want you to tell our love story as one that is possible. I'm not perfect. Many of my decisions could have cost me this life with my soldier. For Ethan and me, our decisions worked out perfectly, but for too many others it doesn't. I hope the young people out there who will be watching this next Valentine's Day will see our story as a possibility for them.

"This only works out though if they are willing to love only each other, and *trust* God's timing. I'm grateful every minute of every day that Ethan came back for me. It could have ended differently, but I've been blessed. My soldier came home for me. He is my only one and I am his."

"I will try to convey your entire story to our viewers. I do have one more question though regarding how to conclude your story together."

"Okay. What is it?"

"Are you saying at this point in time that you have been in love with this man since you were fifteen years old, which is pretty close to nine years, and in this nine years you have only been together for a total of a little more than two of those years, you have a baby together, and you're still not legally married?" Mr. Moore asked.

"Huh? I guess not sir. You do have to consider though, to Ethan and me, we have been married since May 25th of 2012, which means we've been married for five years now. Oh my, what is today's date?"

"It's May twenty-fifth?" the interviewer replied.

"It's our five year anniversary! Brighton! It's your mommy and daddy's five year anniversary! We need to call daddy! Do you have everything you need now Mr. Moore? I need to feed Brighton, put her down for a nap and call my husband."

"Yes, I believe we do. I appreciate your time. We'll start packing up and taking the lights and screens down. We'll only be here for a little while longer."

Before getting up, I rested my head back on the couch. I held Brighton straight up above me and in my baby voice I said, "Look at you. I made the most beautiful baby girl in the world. You have your daddy's brown hair, and your mommy's blue eyes, and curls. I did make the most beautiful baby girl in the world."

In a split second, someone took her from me and said, "No WE made the most beautiful baby girl in the world."

Ethan was home! My goodness, he's good at surprising me! He was home for our anniversary. This was the first time in five years we were going to get to spend our anniversary together. He looked wonderful. I needed to touch him.

I jumped up. Just as I was about to leap over the couch, he held out his hand for me to stop. Holding Brighton in one hand, with his lips pressed on her cheek, he walked around the couch to where I stood in utter disbelief. He put his hand in his pocket and pulled out a beautiful diamond ring. He knelt down on one knee and said, "This is the *last* time I am *ever* going to ask this question. Everclear Jordan Parker, will you *and* Brighton marry me, right now? Forever?"

I burst into tears and said, "Yes!" and I kissed him like *I* was starving. The three of us held one another.

"So are you ready to get married for real? No more seeing each other on just weekends and holidays Evi! Are you ready for forever to start right now?" Ethan asked me.

"What?! Now? Of course!"

The pastor from our church, a bunch of our friends, his parents, my parents, our brothers, and our family members came in to our house.

Ethan said, "I had everything set up outside in my parents' backyard while you were doing this interview."

I couldn't believe he had prepared all of that for me, for us. He had been working on it for months with the television station and our friends and families.

The cameras continued rolling. Ethan was in his dress uniform, and because I was on camera all afternoon, I was already in a nice dress, ironically, a white one probably because I almost always wear white. We were ready.

"Ethan?"

"Yes?"

"One more thing."

"What is it?" he looked concerned.

"I *have* to go feed Brighton first. I am about to die here. All of this is going to have to wait a few more minutes. This body belongs to her now. Sorry."

We laughed.

Ethan sat with Brighton and me in the nursery. He kissed me, then her. While I fed her, he stroked her hair, then mine. There was no way he was leaving our side.

He said, "I can't believe I'm going to get to come home to my beautiful wife and baby every day from now on."

Everyone went outside and waited patiently for us to join them. We had a beautiful wedding and reception. We took pictures on the beach. Ethan of course carried Brighton in one hand down the stairs and held onto me with his other. He never let me go. I'm still forbidden from carrying her down to the lake, but I *will* be skiing with her in a few months! After the day ended, we put our baby to bed and closed the door to her room very quietly.

I turned to my husband without hesitation, slid my hands up under his shirt and pulled it up over his head. I rubbed my hands down his chest and kissed him. He guided me to our bed with his hands in mine. He moved around behind me, unzipped my dress, slipped it to the floor, and with his hands on my waist, he kissed me all over my back. He turned me to face him, pulled me close, then motioned for me to lie down.

I smiled and settled into our pillows.

Ethan stood beside me and stared at all of me. He then carefully turned me over. I faced away from him as he ran his hand up and down the entire length of my body. Turning me over onto my back again, he slowly placed every part of me exactly where he wanted me. He lowered himself to our bed and sat in the exact same place he had sat with me in our hotel room the night before we made love the first time. His hands slid teasingly from my knees, up my thighs, up my body feeling every inch of me. Then, he placed himself on top of me.

He whispered, "This is real. We made it. Now, close your eyes."

Ethan traced my lips with the tip of his tongue. I wanted him. He kissed me very softly at first, then, very passionately. We celebrated another wonderful moment alone together.

Printed in Great Britain
by Amazon